A Single Petal

A Single Petal

Murder, politics
and passionate love
in ancient China

Oliver Eade

ISBN: 978-1-907203-42-8

Typesetting by Wordzworth Ltd
www.wordzworth.com

Cover design by Titanium Design Ltd
www.titaniumdesign.co.uk

Printed by Lightning Source UK
www.lightningsource.com

Cover images by Oliver Eade and Nigel Peace

Calligraphy © Ken Teh

Published by Local Legend
www.local-legend.co.uk

For Yvonne Weilun

Acknowledgements

I am grateful to my father-in-law Dr Chen Yaosheng, to my half sisters-in-law, Huilian and Ronglian and their husbands, Liuping and Furong, as well as to Yvonne's extended family in China, for opening doors on an amazing culture that extends back over five thousand years. I also thank our Chinese friends, guides and the many hospitable people we've met on our several trips to *Zhongguo*, as China calls herself. Their warmth and generosity, and my desire to know more about the land of Yvonne's ancestors, have encouraged me to write this book.

I am also indebted to Nigel Peace of Local Legend for his helpful editorial advice.

The Author

Oliver Eade is a retired hospital doctor who has travelled extensively in China and studied its culture and history deeply. He has a unique sensitivity and talent for revealing the lessons of history and their relevance to our modern life.

Oliver lives in Roxburghshire with his Chinese wife Yvonne and is among a group of Scottish writers working with a professional drama company to commemorate Scottish history. His own comic fantasy play, The Gap, has been taken on tour.

He has published more than forty short stories and his other works include four mythological novels for young readers:

Moon Rabbit (Delancey Press, 2009)
ISBN: 978-1-907205-12-5
Winner of the Writers' and Artists' Yearbook New Novel Competition, 2007.

Monkey King's Revenge (Delancey Press, 2011)
ISBN: 978-1-907205-16-3

Northwards (Austin & Macauley, 2010)
ISBN 978-1-84963-13-75

The Rainbow Animal (Mauve Square Publishing, 2012)
ISBN 978-1-4717-2065-9

Also:

Changing Faces and Places in China
(Self-published through Blurb.com, 2010)
A photographic journey across China.

www.olivereade.co.uk

Contents

1.

Bamboo Death

To bow three times before the Buddha felt wrong. With his faith destroyed because of what happened, it seemed as if he were trying to seek enlightenment from a lotus flower that has no strength, no *spirit* – a flower whose petals fall apart when opened. Such imperfection could lead nowhere. But a single petal? Surely a single, undamaged petal could achieve perfection.

At the very least, that should have happened, thought Teacher Feng, but it was his only consolation.

Empty of prayer, he turned from the effigy and from the smoke and the sickly smell of incense, whilst his mind lingered over the petals of a flower, travelling back to the day his daughter Feier came running in from the courtyard of their home in a village in what is now called Hunan Province, screaming at the top of her voice:

"*Baba*! Come quickly! Beside the path near the lotus lake. On the way to the Miao village! Hurry!"

Feng felt angered. He was preparing a lesson for the village children in the schoolroom, the only reasonably-sized room in their single-storey house built around an untidy courtyard littered with 'useful' junk.

Although he'd been the obvious choice, he still felt an immense pride at having been given the job of local teacher, albeit poorly-paid, by the Governor's prefectural magistrate. His pride helped him overcome the shame of never having sat the civil service examination, about which all other local scholars were delighted. He simply hadn't appeared for the examination on the day, but there was one thing the other candidates were all agreed upon: that Feng would not only have been successful but would have excelled himself, rapidly rising in rank to become a mandarin or even advisor to the emperor himself in the capital, Chang'an.

The emperor lived in a different world to his forty-odd million subjects. Although trained in matters of war, his true passion was for poetry, painting and calligraphy. He would spend days on end, brush in hand, recreating on yellowed paper a separated life in flowing characters and colourful images, unreceptive to the eunuchs who impatiently rubbed their delicate hands and fussed around in the imperial ante-chambers worrying about the state of the nation. War, he left to his generals, each of whom had his own military agenda. Their rivalry, a trivial annoyance for the emperor, had caused waves of unease to spread throughout China. Her enemies were beginning to cast greedy glances over uncertain boundaries at the growing frailty of a country whose name was synonymous with the centre of the civilised world.

The emperor needed men of Feng's ability at court – men with brains – and the other young scholars knew this, but envy and jealousy are more natural companions to the human spirit than patriotism and humility. Even those who had failed the civil service examinations, or who couldn't afford to bribe the examiners (the majority), rejoiced in consoling Feng with the thought that there could be no greater act of faith in the throne than to pass wisdom down to the emperor's youngest subjects in the remote countryside. With Feng tucked away in a remote little village, his existence would no longer threaten to block their career paths.

Feng had good reason for not appearing before the examination board, one which the officials thankfully accepted, thereby saving him fifty blows with a thick rod. His wife, Meili, had died the day before he was due to leave for Houzicheng. She and Feier, their only child, had been stricken with the flux which spread like Yellow River flood waters across the province. Not he, the local doctor, nor prayers to the Boddhitsava, had been able to save the mother as her sick body, drained of all fluid, rapidly shrank to dried skin and bone. But, Buddha be praised, the girl survived. Now, eight years later, she was strong, healthy and would soon be fifteen and a child no longer. She'd inherited her mother's gentleness together with Feng's wit and desire for learning. In his early years as a teacher he'd practised his skills on little Feier, teaching her a hundred new characters between each passing of the full moon, educating her in the art of calligraphy and in the great Tang poems, explaining the works of the newer, radical poets, like Su Dongpo, of whom he possessed a valuable calligraphic scroll. He also instructed the child in the complexities of the glorious history of China, the central kingdom, and had read to her transcriptions of the enlightened master from Shandong, Kong Fuzi [1].

Ironically, moments before Feier had rushed screaming into the schoolroom, Feng's mind had wandered from the characters on the page in front of him as he sat squatting low before the teacher's table with its curved painted animal legs and scratched, pocked surface. He'd been thinking about the child… about his dread of losing her to the family of an unknown would-be groom. When she reached fifteen he'd have to approach the marriage maker, an old lady who'd always looked askance at his modern ways, his desire to include girls in his classes, his wish to bring knowledge to all the people regardless of sex, religion or status. Her disgust was so apparent she would cross the street to avoid rather than acknowledge him. She hated his eagerness for reform, his love of the villagers… his genius. Without wishing to, he had made her feel unimportant, for before he arrived with his daughter she'd been highly respected in the village, second only to the *sun wu kong* [2] at the temple. Now they often questioned her authority and wisdom and fewer gifts came her way. The idea that this old hag would, out of sheer spite, marry the girl off to a spineless groom with a gorgon of a mother had plagued him for months. There were even women who beat their young daughters-in-law and nothing could have been more painful to Feng than the thought of anyone harming his child.

When Feier had rushed into the schoolroom that day it wasn't with *her* he felt angry. It was with himself. Her sudden presence reminded him that he loved her more than anything else in the world and yet had failed to come up with a solution to his dilemma. The pitifully small dowry he'd be able to offer meant other approaches to find a husband for the girl – sons of important officials, skilled trades-people, even merchants – were out of the question.

---

[1] Confucius

[2] head monk

He'd even discussed it with his good friend, Li Yueloong, in the nearby Miao ethnic minority village. He'd have preferred a Miao son-in-law with a heart of gold and no prospects to a man with money and a mother-in-law from hell, but until recently there'd been more girls than boys in the Miao village. Resilience of girl babies and the endless drain on marriageable young men to the emperor's army throughout the prefecture meant that girls from families with little means, like Feier, would be left with the scrapings from the bottom of the rice pot: either witless young men, little more than puppets of devil mothers, or widowed old men seeking breeding machines to give them sons before their ghosts slipped away to face uncertain approval from ancestors.

If only I could have another few moons, Feng had been thinking when his daughter burst into the room, his calligraphy brush hovering over the paper.

"*Baba* [3]? What's the matter?" asked Feier as her father turned his worry-drawn face towards her.

"Nothing that should concern you, dear child." *Stupid man! Everything concerns Feier! And everything about Feier concerns me.* "But why the interruption? Can't you see I'm preparing for my class?" he added, trying without success to appear stern.

"*Baba*... there's a man on the path. On the way to the Miao village. He's lying there. I think he's..."

The child stopped mid-sentence, and Feng knew why. She didn't *have* to use the word that frightened her so much. Ever since her mother's death eight years back, the very mention of the dead would cause the girl's beautiful deer eyes to darken.

"Where?" she'd once asked her father when he tried to reassure her that her mother, a good woman, would have been reincarnated into a higher existence, maybe as a princess or the daughter of one of the emperor's favourite concubines. "But she'll not know me," the child had cried. "She'll never want to hold me to her again, tell me stories, brush my hair and pin it up when I become of age to marry."

Somehow the thought of seeing her reincarnated mother again and not being recognised by the woman had terrified the young Feier. If death could do that to people, what else might it hold in store? It would take

---

[3]   father

forty-nine days, Feng had told the girl, before her mother's karma finally decided her fate: god, spirit, human or animal? Every seven days they visited the temple, burned incense and prayed to the Buddha. Feier was sure her Mama would walk through the door of their home when the forty-nine days were over, and that life would resume as if nothing had happened. That she felt cheated when this didn't occur was plain for Feng to see, but how else could he have described death to the child when he understood nothing of its mystery? Always, he would avoid the subjects of death and his wife's short life on earth, but hardly ever did he stop thinking about them… until the spectre of Feier's impending marriage loomed above the horizon of his own life and brushed aside all other thoughts.

"There's a bamboo pole sticking out from his belly… and he smells like a pig's bottom!" the girl explained.

Alarmed, Feng threw down his calligraphy brush and ran from the schoolroom, grabbing Feier by the hand. Her hand felt so warm and alive in his grasp. Soon, with the girl gone, he'd have nothing left to remind him of the warmth of life; only his scrolls of dead poets' playful words about some other life, and fading memories of his dead wife's beautiful face.

Thanks to the Jade Emperor the child had acquired her looks from Meili, for his own fox eyes and panda jaws in a girl would have given the mean old marriage maker's malice unimaginable opportunities for cruel revenge. Once she'd been asked to find a groom for the daughter of a local carpenter, and there was not a single redeeming feature in the young girl's face. Everything about it was wrong; either too big or too small. The marriage maker suggested she find a pig in the next village, the Miao village, for she felt sure their pigs were uglier than the Han peoples' pigs and might even find the girl attractive. At least, that was the story that went around whilst the girl hid herself away for weeks before being carted off in a covered rickshaw, dressed in red, to Houzicheng, the town on the other side of Three Monkey Mountain.

Feng stopped to catch his breath outside the village. He was less fit than his agile daughter. Too much sitting around in the schoolroom had put layers on his belly that would have horrified Meili, but he no longer cared about his appearance. Feier played the doting daughter whatever he looked like. Stopping there, holding on to a post, panting and gasping whilst Feier stood quietly beside him as if she'd run no distance at all, he was again reminded of Meili. Like their daughter, she was quick and lithe in her movements, never tired and, for a woman, seemed so strong. Why, oh *why* had she died? And, thinking back, why hadn't he forced himself to sit the examination the following day? Had he done that, had he sprung straight back up like a blade of trampled grass, his mind wouldn't now be filled with the pain of losing Feier to some hard-edged peasant, for without a doubt if he had been given employ in Chang'an she would soon be wedded to a caring and educated court official.

"Sticking straight out of his belly? Like the branch of a tree?" Feng asked on recovering his breath.

"Yes, *baba*. And that smell! I had to cover my nose!"

What a pretty, sweet nose this was! But it was the girl's eyes he'd miss most of all. As with the eyes of her late mother, they shone like jewels. Never could he feel truly unhappy whilst still able to look into those eyes; soon, unable to see them, apart from on special visits, and then to see them filled with the pain of an unhappy coupling, he knew he could never again feel joy.

"No voice, no movement?"

"No, *baba*!"

A man killed by a bamboo stake so close to their village? It dawned on Feng that it could have been little Feier impaled by the bamboo, for doubtless the dead man would be a villager who'd surprised a roving villain. Perhaps he'd been visiting the lake for the very same reason as his daughter: to pick lotus flowers to bring his family harmony on the seventh day of the seventh moon.

"The man's face, Feier? Did you recognise it?"

"Half of it was gone, *baba*. He only had half a face!"

"Half a face? What do you mean?"

"Maybe an animal... perhaps a tiger or a bear... has taken it. What'll happen to him with only half a face after forty-nine days are over, *baba*? Will he come back as half a goat... half a person?"

"Face or half a face, he must have a name, Feier. *And* a spirit."

Feng took his daughter's hand again and they ran on, past the path that climbed to the temple on the hill, past the sumptuous residence of Chen Jiabiao, the mysterious nobleman who often travelled to the imperial city and the source of whose wealth was forever a fall-back topic for local gossip whenever items of news grew sparse. When they came to within sight of the lake, Feier pulled her hand free from Feng's and held back. The man saw why. From a distance, it looked like a mound of brown earth on the grass beside the path with a pole sticking out from it.

"Stay here, my child," he said, for he saw raw fear in his daughter's eyes.

After hastily surveying the scene for reassurance the perpetrator of the ugly crime wasn't lurking in the undergrowth, about to snatch Feier from him, he approached the body. He needn't have worried. The smell alone would have kept even the most hardened murderer away.

From where Feier still stood, frozen in fear, they could hear the monotonous hum of flies. Closer, the noise bore into his skull and the stench of rotting flesh was overpowering. Feng cupped a hand to his nose and mouth as he leaned over the corpse. His presence angered the flies whose hum rose in pitch and volume whilst he lowered his own face to within a few hand-breadths of what remained of the face of the murdered man. When he saw the exposed flesh alive with flies and maggots, a dead eye dangling from its socket on dried tissue stands, he turned and retched. With a mix of horror and relief, he saw Feier now standing only a few feet away. She'd followed him. Rushing forwards, she hugged her father.

"*Baba*... I..." she began, as if wishing to say something but unable to do so.

"Don't look!" warned Feng.

"It's *him*, isn't it?"

Feng nodded. The brown tunic, the shoes and a belly that outstripped even Feng's bulge, as well as the white tiger tattoo on the back of his right hand tightly gripped around the thick bamboo pole... they didn't need a complete face to be sure it was Merchant Chang. And Feng felt sick not only at the gruesome sight and the stink emanating from the corpse, he felt sickened for having confided in his old friend; for having told him about the disappearing Miao girls.

2.

Disappearing Girls

It was from Li Yueloong that Feng had first heard about the disappearing Miao girls just days before his daughter found the body.

He'd got to know Yueloong after he began weekly visits to the Miao village where he'd set up a small school. The emperor had recently decreed that all ethnic peoples have at least basic instruction in Mandarin, the language of the ruling Han people. Although hitherto there'd been little exchange between the Miao folk and the Han of his own village, this was due more to convenience rather than any antagonism between the separate communities. Each had a world of its own, although the beautiful embroidery of the Miao women was much admired by Feng's fellow villagers. And they not only understood Feng's reasoning, but also praised the teacher's altruism for spending his day off teaching Miao children. Feier would always accompany him, and her speed and skill with the calligraphy brush, for one so young, became an example for all to follow and later, for the more competitive Miao children, a challenge. After their day of toil in the schoolroom, Yueloong would feed Feng and his daughter before the twelve *li* [4] hike back over the hill and past the lake to their own village.

Yueloong and Feng had two things in common. Each had lost a wife and each had a daughter. Xiaopeng, the Miao girl's Han name, was almost

---

[4] One *li* equals a third of a British mile.

two years younger than Feier. A wary child and lacking Feier's sharpness of wit, she was also delightfully pretty. She had the softly-rounded cheeks, the small nose and the wide rabbit eyes of the Miao women, and she'd fix Feier with those timidly attentive eyes as the older child prattled on with Han tales of Nu Wa the creator goddess, the Jade Emperor and Chang-e the Moon Goddess, and as she expounded on the way of the all-encompassing Dao and talked non-stop about the goings-on in her own village. Xiaopeng would barely utter a word, but it was clear she adored the older girl. When it came to weaving, embroidery, and the culinary arts, Xiaopeng won hands down. Feier marvelled at the child's dexterity and the way she kept house for her father, putting to shame her own feeble efforts to maintain a tidy home, although many a time Feng would reassure his daughter that in modern China it was the mind and the calligraphy brush that mattered, not the loom and kitchen utensils. "Why," he would tell her, "there are women at court in Chang'an who can recite poetry and paint birds and bamboo groves with brush strokes as bold as any man's!"

When Feng first heard that young wives and girls, even those of Xiao-peng's age, had gone missing, he racked his brains for a solution to the mystery, for through Yueloong and Xiaopeng he'd grown to love the Miao villagers as he loved his own people. He was most distressed, the week before Feier found Merchant Chang's body, when three of his brightest Miao girl pupils disappeared. From man-eating tigers to *gui*, the restless ghosts, from secret pacts and peer pressure to seek wider horizons to Tibetan bride thieves, Feng and his friend had discussed all possibilities. But they could come up with no sensible explanation.

"Other than the fact that they're all Miao girls!" suggested Feng.

"And pretty *because* of that," added Yueloong as if Feng needed to be aware of the fact. True, but in Feng's opinion no Miao woman came even close to the other wordly beauty of Han women from Hangzhou [5]. This was why he had always felt certain Meili's ancestors must have lived in Hangzhou.

Yueloong, a busy farmer, couldn't watch over Xiaopeng every second of the day. There was no-one else to keep house for him or prepare his meals when he was out in the fields with his solitary water buffalo, and

---

[5]   It is often said the most beautiful women in China are found in Hangzhou.

Feng could see how worried the man was about his beloved daughter as they puzzled over the missing girls.

"I should tell the *sun wu kong* at the monastery and talk to Chen Jiabiao... even seek audience with the prefectural magistrate," he told his friend. "Someone *must* have some idea... *must* have seen or noticed something. A girl can't just vanish like the morning mist," he said.

His flights into poetic metaphor were always lost on the dour farmer.

"Bloody tearing us all apart in the village!" replied Yueloong. "And it's not only here that it's been happening. Many of our younger sisters in the Miao village on the road to Chang'an have also gone. But because we're Miao folk our Han rulers don't seem to care. Some of the men here, they say..."

Yueloong looked away, uncertain how to put this to his friend from the other side of the lake.

"...well, they blame the Han people. *And* last year's drought. Our women would be highly prized by the Tibetans and the Mongols. The cloth they weave, their embroidery - we fetch a good price for these things, get good money to help us through hard times. Some are saying you Han people have stolen our girls to sell on into slavery. Of course I'm not saying *I* believe in such stories..."

"I think I'd have noticed, my friend," interrupted Feng with a chuckle. "We pretty much live each others' lives in my village. You could hardly hide a chicken away without everyone knowing. And there'd be talk if someone suddenly went around with strings of coins slung across his shoulder. No, Yueloong, there has to be another reason. Besides, how could an unhappy girl taken into slavery make beautiful cloth? She'd be of no value to her new masters. She'd be like a beautiful waterfall whose course has been altered by a landslide and has run dry."

"No poetry, please, friend Feng! I'm not in the mood. Of course I don't believe in those ridiculous rumours. Nothing could be further from the truth. Our men are just seeking scapegoats."

"Look, I'll do those things I said. Talk to these people. Then we'll put our heads together. We'll put a stop to this. Before Xiao..."

He checked himself. He knew nothing could be more painful for Yueloong than the thought of Xiaopeng being taken from him. The girl's mother had died in childbirth and the welfare of his quiet, loving daughter was his sole purpose in life. Feng couldn't imagine how his friend would be able to continue without her, and unlike Feier and himself, the child's marriage would not separate father from daughter for the Miao people lived in a very close-knit community. In all probability, she'd remain in the same small village, with no mean-minded marriage maker to send her far away.

When Feng and Feier had arrived back in their village that evening, the teacher had been delighted to find Merchant Chang waiting on his doorstep, his long-suffering black donkey tied to the plum tree with one weary hoof raised off the ground. The inn was full and Chang had called round to see if Feng could spare him a room for the night - as he *always* did when he came to their village.

"My friend, my humble house is yours whenever you need it!" welcomed Feng. "*Nǐ chīle ma*? [6] And your worthy companion… has *she* been fed?" He nodded at the donkey.

"Mimi? Fed and watered," replied the tubby merchant. "At least they did that at the inn. As for me, well, you know how I admire your daughter's cooking."

"Your baskets, Merchant Chang? May I help you in with them?" asked the girl, knowing full well it wasn't her cooking the merchant admired. She must have been the worst cook in the prefecture.

"You may indeed, my pretty one. My back's killing me these days. I need a wife to massage it twice a day, don't you think?"

Feier blushed. She went over to pat the donkey.

"Such a beautiful daughter you have, Feng. And her hair? When will it be pinned up [7]? Soon, I expect, judging from that figure of hers."

Chang had been looking at Feier as she stroked the animal and whispered softly in its ear. Feng felt ashamed to think it took another man to remind him the girl had acquired the curves and breasts of a woman. He'd only ever thought of her as his little girl with the beautiful eyes of his poor late wife.

"That's another thing!" he said, an image of the awful old marriage maker hovering at the back of his mind. "But first make yourself comfortable, friend. Treat my house as your own. Feier and I'll take care of your

---

[6] Chinese greeting. Literally, "Have you had food?"

[7] In Tang Dynasty China, marriageable girls pinned up their hair at the age of fifteen.

precious goods. Then whilst she's preparing something for you we must talk. I have so much to tell you since we last met... and you, doubtless, will repay me with your usual witty tales!"

Merchant Chang had gone on into the house whilst Feng approached his daughter.

"Feier! How can you be so rude? You turn your back on my friend without saying a word! He was paying you a compliment. You could have at least thanked him... and answered his question."

Feier flushed and continued to stroke the donkey's nose. She said nothing. Feng hated chiding the girl but, after Yueloong, Chang was his best friend.

"I... I had to pat Mimi," she said at last. "She... she looks so sad, the way she's holding her hoof up."

"Feier?"

"*Baba*, you won't force me to marry him, will you? Please say you won't."

She had looked up at her father. Her moist eyes melted the frost in his heart.

"Oh, my little child, that would be the very last thing on my mind! You and Merchant Chang? What on earth has got into that pretty head of yours?"

"The way he looks at me. And I heard what he said to you."

"Feier, you *are* a woman now. Not to me, but to other men you are. He was paying you a compliment and that's all."

"Well, I don't like it! And why doesn't he have a wife himself? At his age!"

"Shhh! He might hear you, child. Funny thing, now you mention it, but we've never spoken about that. S'pose I never thought it important. Anyway, as the wife of a merchant she'd hardly ever see her husband. Be more like a widow, ay? Now let's stop all this nonsense talk and relieve this poor dutiful beast of her burden. Then, my dear daughter, show our guest the respect he deserves. For my sake?"

"Yes, *baba*," the girl replied meekly, and together they set about un-strapping the laden bamboo baskets from the back of the donkey.

"Enough valuable stuff there to fill a prowler's chest with coins!" joked Merchant Chang as Feier staggered in from the courtyard with a basket of goods.

"We don't have…" began the child, but she was interrupted by her father standing behind her with the other basket.

"Feier's right," he said. "Until today I'd have said we never have prowlers. Not like the streets of Chang'an. Nothing ever goes missing. But I have the most extraordinary story to tell you. Leave the basket there, Feier. Go and prepare food whilst I tell our guest all about the Miao girls."

Feier had set the basket down and scurried off in the direction of the kitchen.

"The Miao girls?" Merchant Chang appeared intrigued.

"The Miao girls. From the village beyond the lake. Please, sit down, friend Chang. We'll talk about it over a glass of wine. Feier!"

The girl reappeared in the kitchen doorway.

"Warm up some plum wine for Merchant Chang… with the food."

"Yes, *baba*."

Feng and Chang sat at a round stone table in the cluttered courtyard.

"You've been to that village?"

"Of course. Best Miao cloth in the whole province! And I should know. But what's this nonsense about the Miao girls?"

"Before today I'd have said 'leave everything outside… nothing ever goes missing in these parts for we're not in Chang'an'. But now? And all because of the vanishing Miao girls."

He called out to his daughter.

"Feier! Hurry! Our guest is thirsty and hungry!"

Feier returned a short while later with bowls of vegetables, rice and soup. She hesitated as she tried to work out how to place the food on the table without having to brush against the merchant, for the man's size presented quite an obstacle. Detouring round to the opposite side, from beside the safety of her father, she reached across and placed the bowls in front of the merchant.

"Such pretty hands, friend Feng!" the man said, his eyes fixed on the girl's blossoming young breasts. "Not the hands of a working girl. You're right to be teaching her calligraphy and opening her mind to our great poets."

Feier quickly pulled her hands away, hiding them in her sleeves. She hurried off to fetch a jug of warm plum wine which she put on the table between the two men, together with their best glazed cups. After giving

Merchant Chang a respectful bow, she requested permission from her father to leave.

"Be sure you can show me three more characters on your scroll for Merchant Chang to enjoy when he's finished his meal!"

Feng chuckled and winked at Chang as Feier took a few steps backwards before turning and heading for the schoolroom.

"A delightful girl, Feng. You must be so proud of her. Soon she'll make some lucky man very happy!"

"Oh friend Chang, if only I could be certain of finding a man who *will* make her happy. There are many who would resent an educated woman who can recite the sayings of Kong Fuzi. Have I been wrong to include girls in my classes? I know that would be the Emperor's wish. He's an enlightened man. But there are some who'd as soon put an end to his modern ways. Prefer to see women as the kow-towing servants of men."

"Have you approached the marriage maker yet?"

"She wears her hair long, as you observed. I still call her my child."

"A child with the body of a woman? Can't go on much longer. Look, let me know before you approach the marriage maker. I may not have contacts at the court in Chang'an, but I'm widely travelled and know more people than you could count on your abacus. I'll keep my ears open. Do what I can for an old friend, ay?"

"You're very kind, but you've enough to concern you. Besides, I couldn't bear it if my little Feier ended up in some distant prefecture. I'm a selfish man, Chang, a *very* selfish man. But my problems are as nothing compared to those of my Miao friends?"

"You teach in that Miao village on your day off and you call yourself selfish?"

"I enjoy it! That's surely the epitome of selfishness... to do things you enjoy and wallow in the praise you get!"

Merchant Chang erupted into a hearty chuckle which caused him to choke on a mouthful of rice.

"Don't do yourself down, Teacher Feng," he said when the coughing had subsided. "So tell me, why should I feel so sorry for your Miao friends?"

"Their girls are disappearing!"

"It's that diet of theirs. Not enough rice, too many vegetables. Look at me!" He patted his overflowing belly. "It would take a pretty bad famine to make *me* disappear!"

"This is serious, Chang. Their girls have simply vanished. Why, my three best Miao pupils, *all* girls, didn't turn up last week. Their classmates shrugged their shoulders when I asked where they were. Disappeared like the others, they said."

"Gone to seek their fortunes together, perhaps?"

"Miao girls of thirteen, fourteen? No way! Something's up, Chang."

"What about your friend the farmer?"

"Li Yueloong?"

"Is that his name? I believe you once said *he* had a daughter."

"That's what really brought this home to me. He dotes on Xiaopeng, and what worries me is she's such a pretty child. Just thirteen years, but already has well-formed young breasts... and he told me it's only the pretty ones that are vanishing."

"Most Miao girls *are* pretty. I'll say that for them, despite their meagre helpings of rice."

"Li is terrified of losing the girl. Like me, he's a single parent. She means everything to him. If Xiaopeng disappeared I don't know how he would keep going."

"He'll lose her to a husband one day. Has he thought about that?"

"They're different from us, the Miao people. Very close. He'd never lose her in his own village. And for them looks count far more than wealth. He'll not be faced with the problems I have."

"How many?"

"What?"

"How many of these girls are gone?"

"I don't know. A lot, Farmer Li says. And the magistate's doing nothing."

"And the other Miao villages... like the one on the road to Chang'an?"

"That's just it. They, too, are suffering. Yet here, less than half a day's walk away, not a single Han girl has been taken."

"Taken?"

"It has to be, Chang. Someone is stealing these Miao girls."

"For?"

"That's the thing. Pretty girls. All with breasts... old enough to bear children. Young wives, too. The ones still with fine features, smooth skin and sleek, glossy hair. Why, there are many children now without mothers as well as parents who have lost daughters."

"And your friend and the other Miao people… they have no suspicions about who's responsible? Maybe someone in their village angered a high-up government official. Could be his retribution?"

"It's us Han people some of them are suspecting. Not my friend Li, of course. But he warned me, and I fear rivalry between our communities. We're both peace-loving peoples, but this business..."

"Which is why you're telling me!"

"You'd have heard in time, anyway. But as you say, all those people you meet. Someone must've noticed something, heard whisperings… or seen a Miao girl where one shouldn't be seen?"

"So the prefectural magistrate knows? And who else?"

"Oh, the Miao folk prefer to keep themselves to themselves."

"The *sun wu kong* at your monastery? Has *he* been told?"

"I haven't... I don't… you know… since Meili died…"

"I'm seeing him tomorrow! Next port of call!"

"I would've myself, but you know how it is with Feier... the temple... the things they say there. She never could forgive them for not reincarnating Meili as herself again in our village."

"Children! They're a total mystery to me, my friend. But I understand. You steer clear of the temple. Say your prayers in private, ay? Let the Buddha find his own money."

"Praying's nothing to do with money. That's what's so nice about people like Yueloong. They're far closer to ways of the Buddha than most of those overfed monks."

Merchant Chang peered wistfully at his belly then roared with laughter.

"So you think I'd make a good monk?"

"Yes... but not because of your belly."

"I'd be delighted to ask the *sun wu kong*. Make enquiries. Of Chen Jiabiao, too. I have some spices for him from the west. Something from the land of the Buddha that can burn holes in the roof of your mouth, they say. Can't think why anyone would want to ruin food with that stuff, but Chen goes into a state of ecstasy just thinking about it! Perhaps the real pleasure comes when the fire finally goes out!"

"At least Chen could put pressure on the local magistrate, maybe the Governor. About time that man showed a bit of responsibility."

The merchant's grin vanished.

"Be careful what you say, Teacher Feng. He's a man with a memory as long as a leopard's tail... and a bite to go with it."

"Only between friends, Chang. But he really must know. So many Miao girls in this prefecture have vanished. Maybe more elsewhere."

"He'll not care a damn so long as he gets his taxes. Funny how he and Chen never seem to get on. But you're right. He's got to know. Why, if those girls continue to disappear..."

"That would destroy the Miao people. *And* us if they raid our village in search of evidence."

"I'll report back to you after tomorrow, friend. It's the least I can do. And now let's enjoy your daughter's wine whilst I tell you about the rest of the world. You live like a silkworm in a cocoon here, Teacher Feng. That poor beautiful daughter of yours, she'll know nothing of the latest fashions for the women of Chang'an, ay?"

When they finally snuffed out their lamps and dragged themselves off to their beds, with Chang in the guest room made up by Feier, both men were so disconnected from their surroundings by virtue of three jugs of wine they even questioned how many beds they were looking at and wondered whether their legs were still attached to their bodies. Feier hated it when her father got drunk, and it only happened when Merchant Chang stayed the night. Once, she'd diluted the wine in an attempt to keep her father sober. The merchant sussed out her plan immediately and, because of his fury, she'd been beaten. The following day when Chang was gone, Feng crumpled. Tears streamed his cheeks as he hugged his daughter and begged her forgiveness.

Feier had many reasons to dislike Chang, but she said nothing to her father for she knew he held the merchant in high regard, and perhaps the man *could* help solve the mystery of the disappearing Miao girls. Those three pupils of her father's were all good friends, and what if Xiaopeng were to be taken? Xiaopeng was everyone's darling.

3.

White Tiger

"That tiger on his hand, *baba*... why did he have it?"

Feier was peering at the body from behind her father. Feng focused on the tiger tattooed onto the back of the merchant's right hand, the one that was still gripped around the bamboo pole emerging from his bloated belly. The beast, partly obscured by dried blood, was an exquisite work of art. He'd seen it before but never thought to ask his friend why it was there. It had white and black stripes – the guardian White Tiger of the West – fearsome jaws open in a snarl, a sinuous body curved into a semi-crouch, hind legs raised, and forelegs with extended claws reaching out to the base of the dead merchant's stiff thumb. The flicked-up tail curled round the side of the man's broad hand, giving it perfect balance in preparation for that lethal, never-to-be spring. The darkly vacant eyes stared at the bamboo wedged between the corpse's thumb and forefinger. Had they seen the man who'd killed Feng's friend? Had those eyes of terror failed to alert the beast whose spirit should have leapt from Chang's hand and sunk dagger teeth into the attacker's throat? Suddenly art seemed a useless thing to Feng, powerless to save a good man who'd only been trying to help the hapless Miao villagers... trying to prevent an otherwise inevitable conflict between two peace-loving communities.

"*Baba*? That tiger? It always frightened me."

"To guard and protect him. Huh! Fat lot of good it was! Oh, what *have* I done?"

"You, *baba*?"

"Don't you see? I asked him to help me solve the mystery of the disappearing Miao girls, and now this! Feier, I feel awful! I've caused his death."

Feier appeared strangely uncomfortable. Feng dismissed this as simply due to his reference to death. What fear the word still engendered in the child!

"No, *baba*! Remember how you said that with Mama it was her destiny she had to die. Why should it be different for Merchant Chang?"

The teacher felt his daughter's small, comforting hand touch his shoulder. He gently stroked it, silently thanking Buddha she was there with him at a time like this. He couldn't imagine an existence without the girl.

"It's not always that simple, Feier," he replied. "This is my doing! I must now bear the responsibility... but it adds urgency to solving the mystery of the Miao girls. These things have to be connected. It'll be something big if they had to silence a respected man like Chang. He must've been onto them! Oh, why didn't he come back to me straightaway?"

Feier glanced at the dead merchant, her scorn barely concealed.

"What about the body, *baba*? Shall I get help?"

Feng hadn't thought beyond his guilt.

"The temple," he said quietly. With the prefectural magistrate living on the other side of Three Monkey Mountain and Chen Jiabiao closeted in his large house on the hill, unapproachable to a lowly teacher, the monks seemed the obvious solution.

"Do I *have* to?"

The teacher looked up at her. One day the girl would have to overcome her phobia about the temple and what it stood for.

"You can't go on blaming the Buddha forever, Feier. Go quickly. Tell the monks. They'll take Merchant Chang to the temple. And get them to send a messenger to the magistrate at Houzicheng. I'll wait here... just in case."

The girl, clearly terrified, stayed put.

"Why? He's very dead, *baba*."

"They say with crimes like this that those responsible may return to the scene. Maybe the murderer will want to remove the body? No, don't look at me like that. I'll be fine. Just be quick."

Feier turned and began to run back in the direction of the temple when a sudden thought opened a yawning chasm of doubt in her father's mind.

"Feier!" he shouted. Thank the Buddha, she heard him and stopped. "Come back! At once!" The child's relief was obvious. "Perhaps you're right about the temple. He'd have told them!" explained Feng. "Who else apart from Chen Jiabiao could have known? Someone there might be afraid he was getting too close to the truth. A conspiracy, perhaps? When Chang came to them with his questions, his frankness, they'd have considered him better off dead. How stupid of me!"

"Where now, then?"

"Li Yueloong!" he replied. "We must go at once. Their village men can see to the body. But I don't know what the poor farmer's going to say or do! I persuaded him to put all his faith in my friend's ability to solve the mystery. Some friend I'm turning out to be!"

"*Baba*, don't belittle yourself! Remember how you used to tell me to try my best? Well, you tried your best."

"But to end like this?"

"Come, *baba*!" Feier tugged at her father's sleeve.

"Just a moment!"

Holding his nose with one hand and reaching forward with the other, Feng grabbed the bamboo pole.

"What *are* you doing?"

"This pole's our only link with Chang's killer. I'll take it. And it'll help me protect you if we meet the monster." The bamboo was so firmly embedded in the merchant it was impossible to dislodge with one hand. Releasing his nose, Feng grasped the pole with both hands, pushing it backwards and forwards before lifting it free from the corpse. He failed to notice the look on his daughter's face. "See how reluctant the murderer is to leave his victim! He'll be back, for sure. Better make haste to the Miao village!"

The teacher wiped the gore sticking to the sharpened tip of the bamboo pole onto the merchant's garment, sending the flies into a buzz of frenzied fury. Fashioned by a single diagonal blow with a sharp axe, the tip was as pointed as a knife. Opposite the tip, where the axe would have first struck the bamboo, was a short thumb-nail shaped projection.

"Odd!" observed Feng. "Anyway, it's formidable weapon. I'll hang on to it ' til I've found friend Chang's killer. Come!"

Feng and his daughter continued along the path past the lotus lake, strangely still and peaceful, the lotus flowers half-closed in the sinking sunlight, and on beyond the grove of almond trees to the rice fields. Here the path was raised up on a long narrow bank above the flooded rectangular paddy fields striped green with rows of rice plants stretching to the hazed distance. Silhouetted against the rising sun were the bent figures of women hard at work, up to their knees in water, heads hidden under wide-brimmed conical straw hats. It angered Feng to think that some of these women must have passed by the body of Chang without bothering to think how or why the man had met his end. Wayside bodies of skeletal strangers were not uncommon, but the merchant was widely known in all local communities; the teacher prayed to the Buddha that Feier would never finish up like one of those toadstool women, slave to Sheng Nong the god of farmers. Nonetheless, he never failed to marvel at the precision of their planting, every bit as skilful as the calligraphy Feier perfected with her pointed brushes.

By the time they'd reached the far end of the rice fields, the sun hovered above the horizon and the sky to the east had turned a pastiche of yellow, gold and pink. They had at least another hour's journey along the path that cut through the woods and Feng now held the bamboo pole horizontally, like a spear, expecting every shadow to transform into a brigand that would leap at them brandishing a sword. A moving black shape ahead, barely discernible in the gloom, caused Feng to halt and grab Feier by the arm.

"It's Mimi!" exclaimed the girl, laughing. "Poor Mimi!"

She ran to the donkey. Mimi stood swishing flies with her straggly tail, one hoof characteristically raised. Feier hugged the large head, patting the bewildered animal's rubbery pink nose.

"The baskets are still full of his goods. Proves my point," said Feng on catching up with his daughter. "This was no common thief. The evil man's intent was purely to silence Chang. I'm determined to find out what he'd discovered. I owe him that. Yueloong too."

Feier began to stroke the donkey.

"Why is Mimi so far from her master?" she asked.

"She'll have walked off to get help."

"All this way? Across the rice fields, into these woods, instead of to our village? If she'd got to us sooner we might have found him before that beast took away half his face."

"Don't, my child… but you're right. Why would she have strayed so far? Makes no sense."

"Neither does the blood there."

The girl pointed to dark brown stains of congealed blood streaking the donkey's flank.

"Oh, my clever daughter! I'd not have spotted that myself. Can only mean one thing. Poor Mimi would never have borne the weight of Chang's body, so the murderer must have ridden her as far as here, with Chang's blood on him. Perhaps she'd got the better of him, and kicked him off, or… rather more likely, I think… he did this as a distraction. To make us think Chang was killed by the Miao people and that those disappearances are a hoax. Well, I'll not fall for that! But it raises another possibility. A plot by a rival to our Governor? To cause unrest? By helping to spread rumours? Enough to get the lazy good-for-nothing deposed? But to sacrifice my friend for such a cause…"

"You were blaming the monks a moment ago, *baba*."

"Them? Maybe. I know they're not too happy with the new taxes levied on the monastery lands."

"I don't understand taxes, *baba*."

"Costs a lot of money to keep an emperor, his court, his concubines, the army… not to mention the thousands of officials and small fry. But enough of speculation. I'll lift you up onto Mimi's back. We'll take her with us."

Feier let go of the donkey's head and stood back. She had no greater wish to touch the dead merchant's blood with her leg than to brush against his arm when he was alive.

"I'll walk, *baba*."

Feng, his daughter and his dead friend's donkey journeyed the remaining ten *li*, passing over the familiar two small hills before descending into the valley of the Miao. Li Yueloong's single-roomed, stone house was the first building at the edge of the village, standing proud beside his neatly trimmed patchwork of rice fields. His trusty old water buffalo was secured to a stake driven into the ground at the edge of the fields. Feng always felt the sadness of Yueloong's life had become imprinted upon the water-buffalo's face for it portrayed abject misery. With her legs folded beneath her as she chewed on nothing, she cocked her head sideways at the visitors, fixing them with doleful eyes as if to say 'Oh, I've seen you lot before and a fat lot you did for me then!' before looking away and ruminating on private thoughts about a destiny of perpetual servitude.

"Xiaopeng! It's me, Feier! We've come to tell you something awful!" shouted the teacher's daughter.

The little farmhouse was ominously quiet, except for discontented grunts from the pigs foraging at the side of the house where Yueloong grew vegetables sheltered from the wind by a semi-circular bamboo grove. The girl ran on towards the farmhouse, shouting 'Xiaopeng, Xiaopeng!' before she halted, aghast. Yueloong had appeared alone in the doorway, his head bowed.

"Xiaopeng?" Feier repeated quietly, her fear evident in the tone of her voice.

Feng tied Mimi to the water-buffalo's stake - neither animal objected to the proximity of the other - and approached his friend.

"Yueloong? Where's Xiaopeng?"

No reply. The other man remained in the doorway, silent. Feng came closer.

"Friend Yueloong, please tell me Xiaopeng's all right. Why doesn't she come to greet her friend?"

Nothing. Feng reached out and gently placed his hand on Yueloong's shoulder.

"Yueloong?"

The farmer looked up, and Feng knew. He knew from the pain in the other man's eyes. A pain he recalled every night alone in bed, thinking about how cruelly Meili was snatched from him eight summers back.

Xiaopeng had been taken.

4.

Separation

Yueloong retreated into the house. Feier hovered in the doorway, uncertain what to do.

"He needs us," Feng whispered, "now more than ever."

He led his daughter into the single dingy room where the two fathers would sit and talk for hours whilst the girls laughed and played, but which now seemed like a place of death entombing the farmer's sorrow. They shared a single thought: would little Xiaopeng's cheerful face ever again brighten that room?

Yueloong sank to his knees on the dusty floor, banged on the stone ground until his fist bled, and wept. Feng couldn't imagine how, if it were Feier who had been taken and *he* down there on the floor grieving, he'd ever again eat, drink, breathe or live. The vision of his friend in such tormented loss played with the personal terror of losing his daughter until guilt for considering he had woes of his own took over. He knelt beside the other man and rested a comforting arm across his shoulders.

"Feier, make Farmer Li some tea," he said, looking back at the tearful girl.

"No, no!" protested Yueloong through sobs.

"Go anyway," insisted Feng.

He helped his friend to the stone bed covered with sack-cloth and straw. At the opposite end of the room was another bed half-covered with a neatly-folded patterned rug. Xiaopeng's. Her red-clothed bridal doll and beloved carved dragon head lay on top of the rug.

"Yueloong, I just don't know how to share your grief," Feng said when they were seated together. "Somehow I feel it's my fault."

Feier stood heating water in a pot on the glowing embers of the wood fire, preparing tea. She'd done this so often with Xiaopeng when she and the younger girl switched roles and she became student of the domestic arts that she knew exactly where everything was kept, but it felt wrong. Like her mother not returning, being reincarnated somewhere else, as someone or something different, was wrong.

"*Your* fault?" Yueloong looked puzzled.

"Merchant Chang… I was so sure he'd solve the mystery that's befall-en your village… so certain Xiaopeng would be…"

He checked himself. How could he know Xiaopeng was *not* all right? Taken, yes, but that didn't mean they should all give in to despair and fear the worst. Yueloong said nothing.

"I don't know how to say this about Chang, but…" Yueloong looked blankly up at him. "He's dead. Feier found him near the lotus lake. Impaled on a bamboo stake. The one I've left outside. We found his donkey, Mimi, in the woods and… well, there was blood on Mimi. We hurried here in case…"

"In case of what?"

Feng paused. He didn't really know why they'd hurried. One man, if it had only been *one* man, would hardly pose a threat to the whole Miao village. And he hadn't even considered the unthinkable at the time, that Xiaopeng might be stolen.

"Look, I owe it to you - to both of you - to get to the bottom of this whole affair."

"Why?"

The farmer's monosyllabic answers unnerved Feng. Feier looked at him anxiously, obviously upset by the way the conversation was going. The teacher sighed.

"If I hadn't tried to enlist Chang's help, the poor man wouldn't be dead."

There was a pause.

"So you think his killer took Xiaopeng, huh?"

The farmer's voice was flat, without emotion, as if he no longer cared who it was who'd done the deed. He might as well have been referring to the governor's new rice tax or the current shortage of calligraphy ink, but Feng knew his friend's mind was allowing nothing to displace the wretchedness of losing Xiaopeng.

"A man is dead because of my stupid interference," he insisted. "I owe it to his spirit to finish the task of finding your girls."

"Do what you bleeding like. But I'm warning you and your villagers - our men are talking about revenge."

"Revenge? You too?" Yueloong said nothing but Feng, who for the first time sensed his vulnerability in the Miao village, knew his friend well enough to read the expression on his face. "Surely you can't believe we've had anything to do with this terrible business?"

The farmer, ignoring his question, began to rock to-and-fro. He was beginning to irritate the teacher. He'd always accepted Yueloong's uncouth behaviour as the inverse charm of an illiterate peasant. He knew the man would suffer his loss badly, but Feng was merely trying his best to make amends for the living lost and for the dead.

"Look, the man was a Han. One of our own! Why would someone in *our* village want him dead? It's got to be one of the monks… or maybe a bitter official targeting the governor. No-one else I know could be involved. Merchant Chang was a brave man. Too brave, it seems."

Feier brought a steaming cup of tea over to Yueloong and put it carefully down on the floor beside him.

"You also, *baba*?" she asked, turning to her father. He nodded.

"Wait!" Yueloong said, holding up his hand. "Feier, Xiaopeng always speaks so highly of you. No Miao girl could equal the praise she showers on your name." Uncertainty shadowed Feier's face when she glanced at her father. It seemed both knew what the farmer was about to suggest. "Would you, Feier, in return for her praise, do everything within your power to get Xiaopeng back?"

"Yes, Uncle Yueloong. Of course I would."

'Uncle' was a term of respect often used for the friend of a parent, although the girl had never addressed Chang in such a way.

"Wait a minute, Yueloong. I think we should leave my own daughter out of this. Just because…"

The farmer raised his hand for the other man to first hear him out.

"You wonder whether I too blame your villagers. I don't. But I'm a lone voice here. For fighting to break out between our villages would only add misery to sorrow. You've a score to settle with Fate who took *your* friend. Feier wants *her* friend back. I need help here with the rice harvest. If Feier stays behind with me whilst you track down those taking our girls, our men may believe me. We might avoid a conflict that could destroy us all."

Dumbfounded, Feng gaped open-mouthed at Yueloong.

"*Baba?*"

Feier's expression of delight took him by surprise.

"You're threatening to take my daughter hostage?"

Feng felt cornered. Why was Feier smiling?

"Nothing of the kind, Teacher Feng. You and your beautiful child are free to go home whenever you wish. I merely wanted to relieve you of the burden of yet more guilt. Should our men carry out their threat, set fire to your village, and should you and your daughter survive, then further guilt would weigh even more heavily on your shoulders... that you, and perhaps *only* you, could have prevented such a waste of life."

"*Baba*, please! I'd do anything for Xiaopeng. I may not be of much use in the fields but I could keep house for my friend's father, and..." She paused.

It was the 'and' that troubled Feng. He thought back to Chang's description of his daughter's womanly attributes. He and Yueloong had always thought as one, and his friend must have seen the concern in his eyes.

"She's but a child, Feng. Still wears her hair long. Anyone who so much as thinks of touching her in that way would face pain of death - *after* first feeling the force of my anger!"

Feng, outnumbered and taken aback by Feier's response, had little choice left.

"Where will she sleep?" he asked uneasily, taking in the intimacy of the farmer's single room.

"Well, it's *me* who'll sleep with the pigs, if that's what you're wondering. Unless the girl would prefer it the other way round!"

"But the school?"

In his struggle to find an excuse not to leave Feier behind he'd hit upon the one reason for her to stay.

"Precisely!" replied the farmer. "No-one else in either of our villages knows as many characters as your daughter. Why, you've packed so much knowledge into that brain of hers she could even teach the Emperor's children."

"Uncle Yueloong's right. I *could* do it! For Xiaopeng's sake," agreed Feier.

"The children in our village as well?"

"Why not? I could walk with the Miao children to our village every day and bring them back in the evening. If the children become friends the adults are hardly likely to want to fight, are they? You said someone might have been stealing the Miao girls to cause unrest between us. Well, it would be like the exact opposite if we come together. Then they might bring Xiaopeng and the other girls back!"

Feng smiled at his daughter's childish logic, realising she could be right about the separate communities coming together through the children. Besides, there was no real alternative; it would be far too dangerous to take the child with him to Chang'an and they had no relatives in the Han village to look after her. To leave her at the mercy of the marriage maker was unthinkable.

"But Merchant Chang... his body impaled by the bamboo pole... picked over by wild animals... How will you protect...?" he began, still trawling his mind for a reason to hold on to his daughter.

"We've got men here so angered at losing their wives every devil in hell would fear them! They'll accompany Feier and the children. No harm will come to them."

"But your harvest? You said you needed my daughter's help with the harvest!"

"The children will return when the sun's still high. A strong girl like Feier can do twice as much work as little Xiaopeng."

Defeated, Feng sat beside Yueloong, shaking his head. He began to move his tea cup in curious circles on the dusty floor. Feier came over and hugged him.

"*Baba*, I *will* be all right. Don't worry about me. I know how important this is to you. Go tomorrow! Without me to hold you back. See the prefectural magistrate... the Governor himself if you have to. I believe in you, *baba*. You can't bring Merchant Chang back to life but you *will* return little Xiaopeng to her father!"

Feng knew how headstrong the girl was and for this he could only blame himself. Her force of spirit came from him; how ironical that his determination to treat girls and boys as equals should rebound on him like this. He'd have to leave her behind for she allowed him no other option and he would worry about her every minute of every day. That would become his penance for causing the other friend's death; but could it also be a driving force, his reward for finding Xiaopeng, to see his beautiful daughter again?

Who knows, he thought to himself, *perhaps in my travels I might meet a young man worthy of her?*

Only Feier knew the true reason for her wish to stay behind in the Miao village.

~

The path to Houzicheng left the valley of rice fields, a carpet of patchwork greens that spread out from the perimeter of the Miao village to the blue distant mountains, and ascended a steep escarpment. After climbing the first of three hills separating the valley from the plain of Houzicheng, the teacher stopped to rest on a half-moon bridge spanning the steep-banked, fast-flowing Five Crane Stream. He brought Mimi to a halt and, with the bamboo pole that had impaled the merchant serving as a staff, clambered down to a narrow waterfall to fill his flasks.

How his daughter adored Mimi. It had been the donkey who'd made the merchant's visits tolerable for the child, but it was Feier who insisted her father take Mimi with him to Houzicheng where he would demand to meet with the prefectural magistrate.

"*Baba,* you *must* take her! I insist! You can't possibly go alone!" the child had told him. "Besides, she'll keep you company, carry your baggage... and remind you."

Remind me?

Feng knew what she meant. Like the bamboo pole, the donkey *should* have reminded him of Merchant Chang and his purpose. But Mimi made him think only of Feier. She loved the beast, and in Mimi's baskets were bundles of clothes, blankets and neat packages of food the child had made to last him several days. He promised Farmer Li he'd be back with Xiaopeng before the passing of three moons. An empty promise, for he'd sworn he'd only return with Xiaopeng; both knew they might never see each other again.

'*I insist!*' the girl had said when they'd argued over who should keep Mimi.

Just like Meili. *She* was always insisting upon things. Feng couldn't remember ever having refused her, but a mere child like Feier insisting so?

Child no longer! Woman, and a part of Meili, her virtue entrusted to Yueloong?

That was surely the greatest esteem he could have granted his Miao friend; or had guilt left him dangerously weakened?

As for Feier, Feng was proud she'd shown not a flicker of disrespect for his deceased friend since coming across the gruesome scene near the lotus lake. She had hated the man as much as Feng had admired him, but she overcame that hatred out of regard for the dead. She'd promised to burn incense for his spirit every seven days, although not at the temple. Feng had instructed her not to go anywhere near the place until he'd got to the root of the sordid business. Yueloong, a Buddhist convert, had a small image of the Buddha on a shelf above Xiaopeng's bed where Feier would be sleeping. She'd be able to burn incense in front of that image, small though it was.

A woman indeed and already a teacher! In a strange way, Feng welcomed his escape from the daily grind of teaching. It gave him time to think more about his own particular worries about Feier, and would perhaps give him a chance to grow strong for his daughter for without Meili he now needed every sinew of strength he could muster to secure her happiness.

He packed cool water flasks into one of the bamboo baskets before urging Mimi along the stepped path on the other side of the bridge. Not once did she falter or show any of the obstinacy usually expected of her species. Somehow the donkey seemed to connect him with Feier, for Feng was sure the love between child and beast was mutual. It must have been for Feier that Mimi kept on going, her head nodding in time with the obedient clop of her hooves on the stony ground.

The only person he met after he and Mimi had climbed two more hills was an old woman bearing a stack of brushwood on her back, so large she resembled a dead bush walking on bent little legs. She acknowledged him with a token nod of the head. Anything requiring greater exertion might have finished her off, thought Feng, although there was something endearingly tough about her time-worn, shrivelled old body. That she'd ever been young and beautiful like Feier was inconceivable, but she gave the impression she clung to life like a vine to a tree. Behind a rough, contour-lined face that gave little away there seemed to be a determination as fierce as any warrior's, and after she'd passed him by Feng resolved to draw inspiration from the old woman. Like her, he'd never give up. Friend Chang *would* be avenged, Xiaopeng *would* be freed and returned to her father and *he* would be reunited with Feier.

On the other side of the third and steepest hill, steps led down to the outskirts of Houzicheng. Feng had given little thought to the absence of other travellers over the hills, but the emptiness of the narrow streets of the town puzzled him; mid-morning and they should have been bustling with traders, merchants, wives, mothers and playing children. Perhaps his memory was playing tricks, but that was how he'd always perceived Houzicheng: a teeming sprawl of streets wedged between the rammed-earth walls of houses, winding alleys alive with the shouts of men and women and the laughter and noise of their little charges. But he'd not visited the provincial town since before Meili had died. Maybe it was Meili's very presence then that had, in his mind, made the place seem so bright, so cheerful, so energised.

He led the faithful Mimi though a cut that stank of urine and stale food to the market place in front of the temple. It was here that the whole population of Houzicheng and the surrounding district appeared to have gathered. Many market stalls had been abandoned, their wares trustingly protected only by frayed, torn covers.

"What's up?" Feng asked a fruit seller.

"What indeed?" echoed the man. "The new magistrate has gone to pray. For even *more* riches, no doubt! *And* he has the governor with him. Word soon got around, seems like half the world wants to take a look at the fellow. See if he's as ugly as the last one. Me, I couldn't care a damn. They're all the same, anyway. Corrupt as a monkey's backside!"

"*New* magistrate? And the old one? What's happened to him? Called to higher office in Chang'an?"

"Well, there's stories and stories, and stories within stories. No-one really knows."

"Stories?"

Feng wondered about the missing Miao girls. Did *they*, the officials, know? Had his job already been done for him? Would he now be able to collect Xiaopeng and return to Yueloong and Feier?

"Is it about...?" he began.

"Can't say! No-one dares speak it... only that it's to do with what's happening out in the west."

Feng knew about the grumbling troubles with western Turks and Tibetans, but *everyone* knew. There was no secret about their irritating incursions into Chinese territory since the government had grown soft under Tang rule. He shrugged his shoulders, disappointed. He led Mimi to the animal drinking trough beside the well, and from there followed the track along the river bank to the inn where he and Meili would always stay when he'd been studying for the civil service examinations. He tied Mimi to a post at the entrance and called out. A portly man with untidy, greying hair emerged from the shadows and stared at Feng awhile before his fat face lit up with a smile of genuine recognition.

"Student Feng! My old friend! And where's your beautiful wife? Mei... er?"

"Wong Yungchin! I'm so pleased you're still here. I feared... well everything seems so very different."

"Me still here? It'd take more than a hundred drunken soldiers to get rid of me! No, make that a thousand! So you've brought a donkey instead of your wife, friend Feng!" the inn-keeper chuckled.

Feng looked down at the ground. He'd always felt a pang of shame at being the one who'd survived the epidemic, as if it was his fault that Feier was motherless.

"Feng? Did I say the wrong thing? Mei... um... your wife... she's all right, ay? You were the envy of the town to have a woman so beautiful, you know!"

The teacher slowly shook his head.

"She's not well? Just a passing affliction, for sure!"

Feng glanced up at the innkeeper and the other man saw it in his eyes, as he had with Yueloong.

"Oh, I'm sorry, so very sorry. When? How?"

"The flux. Remember? That great epidemic? When half our village got wiped out. Happened just before I was due to attend for the civil service examination. I couldn't… could *not* go through with it. I…"

"You? The brightest student in the whole province? What…?"

"They were very understanding. No blows of the rod. Gave me a humble job as village teacher instead. They thought that was punishment enough, I suppose, but in truth…" Feng found the strength to grin. "I have a daughter. Remember? The girl got her looks from her mother and her learning from me. She helps me in the school now. We go together to the Miao village where…"

Feng stopped short. He knew Wong to be a trustworthy man, but the wall? Could he trust the walls in a town that now seemed so foreign. Did they have ears?

"Just a room for myself, friend Wong. For as long as it takes."

"As long as it takes? You always were a hard man to fathom, friend Feng. But you can have your old room. Where you and Mei… er…"

"Meili."

"… you and Meili always slept."

Oh, to sleep again with the ghost of Meili!

If only the spirit of dreams could have given him that one last comfort, a night of bliss again with his young wife. Nevertheless, it *was* the best room in the shabby old inn and such kindness showed the regard Wong had for him. He decided to tell the man the truth at the right time and when he was certain the walls had no ears.

Innkeeper Wong helped him in with his bags, took Mimi across the courtyard and fed her whilst Feng stretched out on the bed in his room, resting his weary head on the ceramic pillow of a pig. The last time he'd lain there with Meili the pillow was of a chubby little boy resting on his tummy with his feet in the air. When Meili had mentioned this in the morning a younger, slimmer, fitter-looking Wong had joked that the pillow would help her bring a healthy young male child into the world as a companion for their daughter. But as Feng lay there, his eyes following the patterns made by ceiling cracks, the very same that Meili would have seen, he thought back over his life with Feier and came to the conclusion no other child, male or female, could have given him as much happiness as his daughter had.

Or as much worry!

He dozed off thinking about Feier and awoke, still thinking about her, to a background of noisy chatter in the tavern downstairs. The rice noodles at Wong's inn were legendary in that part of the prefecture thanks to Yungchin's wife, Wenling, and it sounded as if the crowd thronging the temple grounds had shifted to the tavern. Doubtless each man would have something to say about the new magistrate and Feng felt it would be wise to listen in on the gossip before seeking audience with the man the following day. Perhaps to find out what had happened to his predecessor would be a good starting point. Also, the smell of Wenling's cooking was exerting a powerful pull on his nostrils.

Wong Yungchin spotted Feng standing reticently in the doorway of the crowded downstairs tavern. There wasn't a single empty seat. No-one else seemed aware of his presence as customers jabbered through mouthfuls of noodles and hot plum wine. The innkeeper beckoned to Feng and made a space for him beside a wiry man with a fox face who was sounding forth on rumours of compulsory conscription to military service for those unable to pay the increasing burden of taxation.

"Something's afoot, I'm telling you," the fox-faced man complained to an older man with a droopy moustache sitting opposite them. He glanced sideways at Feng. "What do you think, friend?" he asked.

"I'm only a teacher," Feng replied. "I have no opinions on such matters."

"A head full off calligraphy characters and poems about clouds and pretty flowers, eh? Well, teacher, things are happening outside that head of yours, and it's not good, I can tell you."

Feng felt a tap on his shoulder. He turned and saw a youth not much older than Feier. The boy's eyes sparkled mischievously, and his mouth was curved into a grin that was difficult to decipher. Was the boy grinning at or with him? Or was he grinning at all? Was it just a curve of the lips? But one thing was certain. There was eagerness and vitality about the youth that Feng hadn't seen in anyone other than Feier.

"You're new here, aren't you?" the boy asked.

"Not exactly! Let's say you'd have been playing with your toys the last time I set foot in Wong's inn."

"Because?"

"Inquisitive indeed! Because I live on the other side of Three Monkey

Mountain and I'm a teacher. Do you need a teacher here in Houzicheng?"

The wiry man slapped his thigh in amusement.

"Jinjin need a teacher? That's a good one. I like it!"

"Well, I only asked because I don't know what he takes in his noodles!" The boy sounded offended, but the 'smile' was still there, so Feng assumed it to be just a curious curve of the lips.

"I'm sorry! Pork, cabbage... and whatever else Wenling puts in to make her noodles so delicious."

The boy left.

"Don't mind Jinjin," the wiry man said. "He's okay - when you get used to him."

"Wong never had any helpers before. Business must be looking up in Houzicheng."

"Oh, that's Jinjin, not business. Things couldn't be worse for all of us here. The new taxes are punitive. It's the only way they can raise an army nowadays. No more beatings or prison for those unable to pay. Just a helmet, sword and spear and you get dragged off to the west never to be seen again. But Jinjin? He works here for free, you know. Slaves away for Yungchin and Wenling and won't take a copper for all his toil. They feed him, mind you, and a kind passing merchant gave the lad some clothes, for he stank something awful when he first appeared, but where he sleeps at night I have no idea."

"I keep telling you, he sleeps with the pigs!" chipped in the man with the moustache. "There's no-one else would listen to his prattling when the rest of the town's gone to bed. Recites poetry to them, no doubt."

Feng pricked up his ears.

"Poetry?"

"No wonder his father kicked him out. A farmer near the edge of town, he is. Used to beat Jinjin black and blue for talking instead of working in the fields. And when he did put his hand to the plough things invariably went wrong. Why, if the boy tried to grow rice it'd retreat back into the ground! Ha ha! And all we'd have to eat would be bowls full of rice arses!"

"Och, you're hard on Jinjin, Yaosheng! He wasn't made for the fields, that one. And anyway, it was *he* who left home. Couldn't face another beating for being caught practising his characters in the dirt with a stick."

"He can read and write?" asked Feng.

"Not exactly. Would like to think he can. Watch out now he knows you're a teacher. He'll stick to you like dried cow-shit. *Never* stops asking questions!"

"Hmmm! Sounds like you need another teacher in this place if a bright lad like that can't read or write properly."

But Feng felt this wasn't the right sort of company in which to extol his views on the education of children.

Jinjin returned with a steaming bowl of rice noodles and a pair of chopsticks. He wiped the chopsticks on his sleeve and handed them to Feng. Yaosheng and the wiry man looked at each other. The latter raised his eyebrows and stood up.

"Think I'll be going, Yaosheng. Nice meeting you, teacher. By the way, I never asked what you're doing in Houzicheng!"

Yaosheng also got up.

"Let him eat his noodles. You'll be able to get his life history from Jinjin tomorrow."

Both men left. Jinjin's eyes lit up on seeing two empty places at the table.

"May I?" he asked Feng, pointing at the place opposite the teacher.

"Doesn't belong to me!" replied the teacher.

The boy sat down, folded his arms on the table and gazed in admiration at Feng. There was something penetrating about those sparkling eyes, as if the boy was already reading his mind, using his eyes to uncover hidden secrets.

"A teacher, huh? So you know all about Kong Fuzi?"

"Who can know but a fraction of what is to be known about that man?"

"True, true. So tell me about life as a teacher in a small village. Without a wife. Must be awful to be without a wife!"

The cheek of the urchin! How on earth does he know I'm widowed?

Feng poked at food in the bowl with his chopsticks.

"Yungchin told me!" the urchin answered, anticipating the unasked question.

Yungchin? What right did the man have to let the boy in on his saddest of secrets? At least he now knew not to tell the innkeeper about the disappearing Miao girls and the murder of Merchant Chang.

"You see," continued Jinjin, "I said to Innkeeper Wong... a teacher with sadness in his face, on his own, from the other valley, at times like this?

37

He'll be looking for a bride, without a doubt, I said. And Wong, he said 'What business is that of yours?' so I replied, but sadness is always my business, master. Yes, I call him master, for one day I plan to own an inn myself, you know. I think of myself as an apprentice, see, and I... I can think of no better teacher than Wong. But you... a *real* teacher? Wow! How long will you stay here... er... Teacher... um..."

"Feng," offered the teacher, reluctantly.

"Teacher Feng!" the boy repeated proudly.

Why should I be giving my name to a guttersnipe? What's come over me?

Feng picked up his bowl and continued to scoop noodles into his mouth. He'd forgotten how good food could taste! One day he'd bring Feier to Wong's place just to get Wenling to show her how to cook rice noodles properly, to learn culinary skills that must have been passed down through generations.

But for whom would she learn such skills?

A pang of pain dampened the pleasure of Wenling's noodles as the spectre of losing Feier to a cruel old widower or the gormless son of a sharp-tongued witch filled his consciousness.

"You have a daughter, too?"

Feng glanced sideways at the boy. What didn't he know? Those men were right. He was becoming an irritant.

"Seems there's little more I can tell you. You know too much about me already!"

"Teacher Feng, *please* don't take offence. I only mean well. I hate to see people sad. Look, Wong made me promise, and I never break a promise. I promised my father if he beat me again I'd leave home. *He* did... so *I* did! Kept my promise, and here I am. Learning how to run a business from Innkeeper Wong."

"And what did you promise my friend Wong?"

"To say nothing to anyone else about the teacher. He believes you must have a very special reason to be here and he thinks it's because of your daughter."

"He said that, did he?"

"Uhuh! And he said she must have taken your late wife's place as the most beautiful woman in the whole province. No... in the whole of China!" Feng couldn't prevent a smile from changing his face. How could he deny his daughter such an accolade? "'The teacher's a man to respect!' He said that too," continued Jinjin.

Feng was beginning to realise this boy was no ordinary urchin. Indeed, there was something quite *extra*ordinary about him, something quite irresistible. Like a pump that can extract water from a deep well, the boy had a knack of making him want to talk.

"It's not about my *own* daughter," he said through a mouthful of pork and noodles.

"Whose, then?"

Feng looked suspiciously behind and on both sides of him. No-one was paying any attention to them, and the background noise of talk and drunken laughter was such that his words would have carried no further than across the table.

"A friend's. A girl of just thirteen years. Gone missing. And she's a good friend of my daughter's. A quiet girl, very different, but..."

"So your daughter's not quiet, then? Beautiful *and* talkative?"

Feng nodded.

"This girl... she's Miao. And..."

The teacher paused. The urchin had already taken him too far.

"And she's vanished. Right?"

Feng almost choked on his noodles. He put down the bowl and the chopsticks and stared at the boy.

"What's the big surprise? Everyone here knows about the missing Miao girls from the village on the road to Chang'an, so it makes sense they're also missing from one on the other side of Three Monkey Mountain. Of course, no-one here seems too bothered, but..." Jinjin turned to check himself that no prying ears were within listening distance before leaning up close to Feng and continuing in a whisper: "I followed one there!"

"Followed what where?"

"Why, one of those White Tiger League devils. To the Miao village. We've had several pass through here ever since the Miao girls began to disappear."

Feng's inner thoughts must have shown as clearly as calligraphy script in the lines of the frown furrowing his forehead.

"Have I said something wrong?" the boy asked.

"What do you mean 'White Tiger League'?"

"You village people! Must be a generation behind us town folk!"

"Stop beating about the bush! What's the White Tiger League?"

"No point asking *me* that. I'm just a brainless peasant boy. I only know what Innkeeper Wong tells me, and that's precious little. But I thought I'd find out a few things myself, didn't I? See, I overheard this big fellow with a white tiger tattooed on the back of his hand..."

"Mouth open... tail out... like it's about to leap on its prey..."

Jinjin looked anxiously at Feng's hands.

"For an awful moment I thought... but no, you don't look like one of them. Yeah, white tigers tattooed onto their hands. Up to no good, Wong says. Anyway, I overheard this man talking. See, that's the advantage of being a homeless urchin. People pay you no bloody attention at all. Why, just the other day..."

"Get on with it, Jinjin!"

"Sorry! I hid under the bridge opposite the inn early that morning after he'd eaten breakfast. The previous night I'd overheard him tell one of the new magistrate's officials... now there's another thing! The old fellow - the last magistrate - he disappeared about the same time the girls began to vanish and these fellows with tattoos started showing up. Coincidence? I don't think so! Anyway... now where was I?"

"You overheard..."

"Oh yes! I overheard them, and they had no idea I was listening to every word. I'd made sure their glasses were always full to the brim with hot plum wine. And the very best, it was. Why, Innkeeper Wong has nothing but the best of everything! That's his little business secret, of course. People are prepared to come from..."

"What did the man with the white tiger tattoo say?"

"'I can get you another one for a hundred coppers.'"

"He could've been talking about anything. A pig? A commission for a government post. A wife even?"

"Correct! So I follow him, don't I? He doesn't recognise me, I'm that unimportant. He takes the short cut across the hills to the Miao village. So do I. Hiding behind trees or bushes when he stops to take a rest or have a piss. Then he comes to the village. It's still quite early but the men are out in the fields. No-one else around apart from him and three soldiers."

"Soldiers?"

"Imperial guards! Can tell from the colour of their tunics. Purple with yellow edges. Mean-faced bastards, they were. Do you think you have to look like that before you get taken on for such a job? I can imagine those guys sitting in front of their wives' mirrors, twisting their faces into knots... making sure they're ugly enough..."

"What happened?"

"At the edge of town. A house. They're too far away for me to hear their words, but you can tell a lot from hand gestures and pointing, you know. And lip reading. I do it all the time when the noise level here builds up to a..."

"Yes, yes! Get on with it!"

"Money! He gives them money. A string of coppers. Then the soldiers crouch down behind a bush and wait. First an old woman comes out of the house to feed the hens. The soldiers don't move. The woman disappears then this girl with hair down to her arse appears. She's carrying a pitcher for water and sets off towards the stream."

"A Miao girl?"

"Well, it *is* a Miao village!"

"Sorry... it's just that... just carry on ... "

In his mind's eye Feng could see the same story unfold in the other village, only it was Xiaopeng, not that nameless girl, carrying a pitcher.

"I'm telling you, it was over in the time it would take a tiger to kill a deer. One of the soldiers grabbed her from behind as another pushed something into her mouth to stop her screaming. The third held a cloth of sorts over her nose. Pretty nose. Pretty girl, come to think of it. You know, they say the Miao girls are..."

"What next?"

"I sneezed. One of them looked at the bush I was hiding behind. I thought he was gonna shoot an arrow straight through me. 'It's only some beggar boy,' his companion says. 'Saw him further back. Let's get this one to the cart before we're spotted.' As if I counted for nothing! But, that's the good thing about being just a beggar boy. Urchin, I should say. I never beg. No excitement in begging."

"So they took the unfortunate girl away in a cart?"

Jinjin shrugged his shoulders.

"With others, no doubt. Other carts, other villages. Didn't hang around to find out. I can tell you, those emperor's soldiers, you could've ground corn with their faces they were that hard."

"So the man with the tattoo was a member of this... er..."

"White Tiger League."

"Doesn't mean there's anything wrong with the White Tigers. Could be a league of respectable merchants. Perhaps it so happens that... well..." Feng felt confused. No way would his friend have been involved in anything so low as stealing girls from their villages, but he somehow didn't believe the boy was lying, merely jumping to the wrong conclusion. "Perhaps some of the traders have been abusing their positions. And that's all. Taking bribes from officials. But the emperor's own soldiers... why? What on earth could the emperor do with a harem of Miao girls?"

"They're pretty. At least this one was. Look, I'm not properly a man yet, so what would I know of what you men get up to. Just have to use my imagination."

"The emperor will already have enough wives, concubines and slave girls to last him eight lifetimes. I can't believe he's sent his own guards to do this dirty business. But..." Feng recalled the way the bamboo pole protruded from his late friend's belly. "But if one of their own number had caught on to some plan hatched by a small group of them... and because he'd been asked to solve the mystery of the disappearances... well, he wouldn't last long, that's for sure."

"You're hiding something from me." The boy's eyes bore into Feng and his enigmatic grin disarmed the teacher.

"My friend, Merchant Chang, had a tattoo of a white tiger on the back of his hand. And then there was the pole," Feng explained to those searching eyes.

"Pole?"

"A bamboo pole in my room. Sticking out of his belly when my daughter found him."

"Dead, of course."

"Dead! With only half a face. Some animal must have devoured the other half."

"Or someone tried to take away his identity."

Feng hadn't thought of that.

"There were still strings of money across his shoulder. What villainous merchant out to become wealthy by selling off village girls would leave behind so much money on the man he'd just killed? Chang was a rich man."

"Rich? In these hard times? Did you never wonder about that?" questioned the boy.

Feng hadn't and he felt angered. What right had this impudent urchin to question the honour of his late friend and bombard him with so many questions?

"Chang was a good man. I had no reason to ask about the source of his wealth. Besides, the fortunes of merchants are like the rains. Unpredictable."

"And the rains come from the clouds breathed out by river dragons, correct?"

"So we are told."

"Suppose, then, a river dragon was to fall foul of the Jade Emperor, tempted by foreign demons only to give up his rain clouds to enemies of Mother China. What would happen?"

Feng felt confused and annoyed by the boy's persistence and agility of mind, although he could not pretend he didn't admire the lad.

"Look, being hypothetical never gets anyone anywhere," he said.

"Except for the great poets. They got famous."

Feng held the bowl to his mouth and scooped up what remained of Wenling's noodles. He wistfully stared at the empty bowl, aware that because of the boy's constant banter he'd barely tasted a thing. Denied the heavenly enjoyment of those legendary noodles, instead of scolding the boy he laughed.

"Tell me, how do you know about poetry? Or dragons or the ways of merchants?"

"It's not how I know that matters, Teacher Feng, it's what I need to know!"

"What more, pray, do you need to know?"

"Why you're still sad after the death of your wife so long ago."

Feng stared at his empty bowl trying hard to recall the taste of the noodles. The boy could not have touched a more tender spot in the man's troubled soul. Trying to remember those years with Meili, remember the taste of happiness, was that why he now had only sadness in his heart?

"And your daughter who has so much of your wife in her will soon marry and leave you, and these disappearing Miao girls remind you of this?"

Feng, still staring at the noodle bowl, nodded.

"I think a beautiful girl must be like the petal of a flower, don't you think? Without petals a flower is nothing. Without beautiful girls, life must be empty and meaningless."

Feng smiled.

"Yaosheng said you're a bit of a poet!"

"Will you *teach* me if I help you find your friend's daughter?"

"I'd do anything to find little Xiaopeng. But I fail to see how..." Feng stopped mid-sentence. For a moment it was like a cloud had lifted and it all became so very clear. "Of course! How stupid I've been. The tree of a thousand petals!"

Jinjin stared dumbfounded at Feng.

5.

Destiny of a Pig

The day her father left on his impossible quest, Feier spent the morning teaching a noisy gaggle of Miao village children in the market place. A young man, Angwan, who'd recently returned to the village because of his father's death to become a shaman-priest in the dead man's place, had gone with three other men to explain the teacher's arrangements to the Han villagers and to fetch the body of Chang. They returned before sunset with a promise of good will from the Han folk and a cart laden with the bloated merchant's corpse. It seemed Feng had been Chang's only real friend in the area for no-one else in either village showed concern over the murder. The vanishing Miao girls, nevertheless, did focus them after being told there might be a link with the dead man. It seemed only a matter of time before attractive young girls from the Han village might also vanish.

Feier was in the fields helping Yueloong with the rice harvest when she spotted the men digging in the distance. On the ground beside a hole a large brown hump was all that remained of her father's late friend. The thought of working in that particular field filled the child with dread; dread that a secret shared only with one living person would some day reach the ears of others.

Out of duty for *baba*, she would burn incense for Chang, but on seeing the body covered with brown sackcloth she knew she could never overcome her revulsion for the dead merchant. Not the partly-eaten, swollen corpse, but the man it had once been, his ugliness, the way he used to look at her as no other village men or boys did, and the lingering touch of his stubby fingers. The revulsion merged with the shame of her relief that he was dead. That would surely count against her when her time came, like Mama, to be thrown to the mercy of events that would decide her fate. Because of what happened, and her disgust, would her samsara dictate she be reincarnated as a pig and be forced to live with the other pigs in Uncle Yueloong's pig-pen? Was hers the destiny of a pig?

The child's father had encouraged her to call his farmer friend 'uncle'. This pleased her, for it made her feel closer to little Xiaopeng, whilst her *baba* had reckoned it would help the Miao villagers more easily to accept her into their fold, although for many years it seemed that would never be an issue for the teacher's exquisitely pretty daughter. But Feier was now mature enough to know nothing is certain. Her father had repeatedly told her so. Friendships like the one between him and Yueloong could prove as fragile as single threads of silk in a storm when faced with strife between communities. Could the teacher's acceptance as spirit brother to the Miao farmer prevent their particular thread from breaking?

When Feier and Yueloong returned from the fields that evening, they found Angwan alone in the farmhouse, his feet up on the table, a cup of tea in one hand and a scroll in the other. Feier held back at the doorway, uncertain about the young man's presence. Had he been saying things to 'uncle'? The young man glanced at her and said something to Yueloong in the Miao [8] tongue. Feier understood only a few words taught to her by Xiaopeng; besides, Angwan spoke too fast.

"Mandarin only, please, in Feier's presence!" interrupted Yueloong.

Relieved to see the man smile, Feier blushed and looked down at the floor. Angwan stood and gave a short bow. Making fun of her? Should she feel angry? Confused by this unnecessary display of deference, she returned a slight nod of the head, an action she hoped Uncle Yueloong would not notice. She knew how Xiaopeng worshipped the young priest, but following recent events everything had been flipped upside down; destinies that seemed certain before were now muddied. The girl had blushed because of a mix of embarrassment and excitement that it was she, not Yueloong's daughter, who'd been thus acknowledged by the young

---

[8] A language similar to Thai Hmong.

Miao priest. But could she be sure he wasn't playing games with her after what had happened?

"*She* should choose," Angwan said. "He was one of her people."

The girl glanced up. Not playing… totally serious. She could tell from his eyes. In fact, no-one other than Chang had stared at her in that way, but the feeling the priest's eyes aroused in the girl was so very different from the revulsion inspired by the dead merchant. Her blush deepened.

"Choose what?" she asked timidly.

"An inscription for the stone on the dead man's tomb. I was looking at these poems here," he held up the scroll, "and I was going to ask Farmer Li since he professes to be a Buddhist, but perhaps the teacher's daughter would have a better idea. Let's face it, Yueloong, you're hardly a man of poetry."

"What poems are there about merchants - men who make money from the hardship of others?" asked the farmer.

Feier's mind went blank. To write an epitaph for a man she thought of as better off dead was one thing, but to expose her ignorance to the young man she and Xiaopeng had so often talked about in those secret, hidden places of young girls was something else.

"The child's tired, Angwan. She's worked hard all day teaching, helping me to keep house and start the harvest of young rice. There'll be plenty of time to think of something for the teacher's friend. But won't you join us for something to eat seeing as you're here?"

Feier's panic magnified. Her culinary skills were hardly up to those of Yueloong's daughter. Things could change so quickly if she were to accidentally poison the young priest.

"No, Yueloong," insisted Angwan to her relief. "My poor mother will be worrying what's happened to me with a murderer on the loose." Feier looked down again. "You know what she's like! But tomorrow I'll call at sunrise to escort Feier and the children to the Han village."

Feier stepped aside from the doorway, although stayed close enough to take in his young man smell as he passed by. It was a smell of strength, mystery and courage, and it made her feel different: a woman, at last. And she was so pleased it was he who would be with her and the children the following day. She tried to persuade herself this was because of his strength and the protection it would give them that made her feel happy, rather than an arousal of the woman within.

"Feier?"

He called back from the path as she stood silhouetted in the doorway staring at him. He was addressing her alone and she held on to the door, as if she might sink to the ground should she let go.

"Yes?"

"A saying from the great master from Shandong, Kong Fuzi, perhaps?"

Feier nodded, smiling; smiling because he'd made no mention of it. No-one else knew, not even her *baba*.

Angwan turned and left, playfully waving the scroll in his hand. He seemed curiously jocular for one who'd just buried a man - and for some-one who shared such a terrible secret. Still smiling, she too felt strangely cheered as she went back inside to prepare noodles and vegetables for uncle and herself.

~

"Thank you, young man!" exclaimed Feng getting up from his drum seat. "One day you'll make a great poet *and* a successful innkeeper. But tomorrow I must hurry on to Chang'an. I'm after an audience with the new magistrate. Don't fancy ending up with a bamboo stake in the belly like my friend!"

"Wait! Tell me, teacher, what's so important about a tree with a thousand petals?"

Feng looked around to reassure himself Jinjin's were the only inquisitive eyes and ears.

"*The* tree with a thousand petals! The one in the Imperial Palace at Chang'an, of course." Jinjin's faced remained blank. "Petals... pretty girls... you've given me the answer, Jinjin."

"The question being?"

"Why steal all these girls? Easy... because of what you just said! For whoever's behind this, it's a justification in the eyes of the Jade Emperor of Heaven to depose the present emperor of Earth. To possess such a thing of beauty as *befits* an emperor on Earth means true power."

"A *thing*?"

"Whatever's happening, I'm sure the man responsible will be trying to collect together *a thousand girls*. They'll represent the petals of a beautiful and very special imperial flower. Think of the *qi* force that will release!

When he has a thousand he can march on Chang'an. And if those soldiers you saw stealing that village girl were really the emperor's guards it seems likely there are already traitors on the inside."

"Can't go just by the colour of their tunics. But what if it's been our emperor all along? Perhaps he wants the girls for an embroidery factory. To make more money to buy off the Turks and the Tibetans?"

"Our emperor? He's too lost in the arts to think like that. No! I must get going by tomorrow. It's a long journey to the capital."

"And get yourself killed? I'll speak with innkeeper Wong first. He'll know someone we can trust. Someone who can get us to the capital quickly on horseback."

Us? Trust?

Feng still found it difficult to believe his friend Chang had anything to do with the disappearing Miao girls, but the seeds of doubt had been sown. And could he trust Wong? He wavered in his deliberation.

"Look, I'm coming with you, teacher," persisted Jinjin. "No argument. I could act as another pair of eyes, right?"

Feng thought for a few moments. The boy was an incurable chatterer but seemed trustworthy. The teacher admired his headstrong eagerness, his youthful naïvity. He'd shut out the incessant jabber if it became over-bearing and Jinjin would at least be a companion he could talk to rather than a mere living creature to pat, scratch and ride, like Mimi. Above all else the boy was bright. Feng prided his ability as a teacher to distinguish half-wits from high-fliers, and this boy was a veritable kite.

"You're right about going by horseback," the teacher agreed. "Time's running out fast. We'll need a couple of horses from the new prefectural magistrate. I'll call at first light. We can leave Mimi with him."

"A donkey for two horses?"

"A donkey and a scroll."

"What can the prefectural magistrate do with a scroll?"

Feng shrugged his shoulders.

"We'll see. It's by the poet Su Dongpo. I always carry it with me. Worth a small fortune. If you really want to risk your life, we leave just before sunrise. But I'll understand perfectly if you don't show up."

"If we succeed - if we get this girl back for her father - would you... er... well, I wondered whether... um...?" Jinjin seemed oddly at a loss for words.

"Not now!" retorted Feng. "I've enough to think about. Ask me tomorrow."

"Your daughter?" blurted Jinjin.

Feng half-turned, his eyes narrowed.

"My daughter?"

"How old? I mean... her hair... does it... you know... still flow free like a mountain waterfall?"

Feng decided he'd had enough of the urchin's impudence for the evening. Without replying, he turned his back on the boy and pushed his way through the noisy crowd to the steps that led to his room on the upper storey. It had a bed, his bamboo baskets and the pole - all that Feng needed. The teacher stretched himself out on the low bed, resting his head on the ceramic pig pillow, and before sinking into a fitful sleep wondered why he'd wasted time with the urchin boy.

$\sim$

Feier was awoken by a tap-tap-tapping on the outside of the wooden wall beside her bed. She leapt up, hurriedly wrapped a blanket around her half-naked body and went to the door, expecting to find an angry Yueloong about to berate her for oversleeping. But it was yet dark, and standing respectfully back from the open doorway was the shadowy form of the young priest.

"We must leave early," he said. "I'll call again just before sunrise with the children."

For a few moments Feier stood still, uncertain what to say, uncertain about those feelings so powerful they threatened to engulf her... feelings that were both wrong and beautiful.

"Thank you," she said quietly. "For not saying."

"I'm sorry. I've come too soon. Perhaps..." began Angwan. He appeared awkward and this made Feier feel protective.

"No. I'll be ready in no time. After making breakfast for uncle."

"Are you sure? You must be weary. But I thought, well, we *could* take another path. Avoid the lotus lake if you prefer. It would take longer."

The girl shook her head.

"Sunrise is fine. The lotus lake too."

She'd stopped short of adding *because with you at my side I'll fear nothing*. She remained at the doorway until the young priest's shadow had been swallowed by the darkness, before turning, still smiling, to dress and prepare breakfast. Only when the farmer appeared, the stiffness in his body after a night with the pigs evident in his curious straight-legged gait, did the girl's smile vanish.

"Pleased to be going back to your own village?" he asked.

"If it helps to bring our villages together, yes, uncle."

"But so many children together? Not even your father has to put up with that."

"Oh, I can be strict. I'll have them working hard. No chance to play up with me!"

"The young man who'll escort you, Angwan… his mother and I have made an arrangement, you know." Feier's face fell like a stone from a cliff. "In two years she'll dance for him at the Lusheng Festival. He'll play the lusheng [9] for her. He's good... *very* good. But... now? What now?"

"Father won't give up, uncle. He won't rest till Xiaopeng's returned to you... and the merchant's death has been avenged."

"Yes, yes, the merchant! I never could see how... oh, it doesn't matter now. He's a good man, your father. No denying it!"

Did she now feel differently about Xiaopeng and her return? Knowing that Angwan and the farmer's daughter were intended for each other sent her mind into a maelstrom of unwelcome emotions. How stupid to hope or think it might have been otherwise. She and Angwan were from separate communities. Apart from that other thing, the only connection between them was through the Miao children's education, and this because of her father and his friendship with the farmer; a friendship founded on peace, not conflict. Besides, Xiaopeng was her friend. How could she wish for the poor girl never to return merely because of those deliciously warm feelings she had for a man she barely knew - and a man destined to marry the younger girl?

But that longing in Angwan's eyes was for her; unquestionably *for her*!

She thrilled at this thought as she and uncle ate in silence. Afterwards, having washed the bowls and chopsticks at the pump outside, Feier fetched her calligraphy box and scrolls then stood waiting at the doorway.

---

[9]   A Miao wind instrument of multiple bamboo pipes.

Had it been so obvious from her body language? Was that why Yue-loong informed her about his daughter and Angwan, to make it all crystal clear? Had Feier's father not easily read her body language about her disgust with the merchant… and would the same body have told Uncle Li a very different story about the young priest and the teacher's daughter?

Without a further word, the farmer left for the rice fields with his water buffalo. The pink glow to the east grew to fill half the sky before a bright rim of sun slipped above the hazy horizon.

~

Feng slept fitfully. Most of the night he was worrying about Feier; whether he'd been foolhardy, even neglectful, to leave her with his Miao friend, and whether he could ever save her from the spite of the vengeful marriage maker. Most of that night, apart from brief interludes of sleep, he lay staring through the darkness at the half-eaten face of Merchant Chang.

The White Tiger League? What nonsense!

As usual, he was up before sunrise. He went downstairs expecting to find Jinjin ready to bombard him with more presumptuous questions but was surprised to discover only Wenling clearing up from the night before. Everything that had escaped the mouths of the inn guests had ended up on the floor.

"I'm so sorry to hear about Meili," the woman said, glancing at him. "Even now some of our customers still talk about her beauty. But you've got a daughter. That's good, for surely her mother's beauty now lives on."

Feng nodded with a sigh. "Yes. I have a daughter. And, yes, she has her mother's beauty." He changed the subject: "That young urchin, Jinjin. Have you seen him this morning?"

Wenling stopped sweeping and lent forwards on her brush.

"Jinjin? I hope he didn't make himself a nuisance last night. Sometimes I fear he chases customers away by prying into their private lives all the time. But Yungchin has a soft spot for him. No children of our own, you see. There was a time when we hoped he might be like a son for us. Take over the inn when we're both past it. But Jinjin? No way! Mind you, he's a hard worker when he *is* here, and quick to learn, but his heart lies elsewhere and, well, you could hardly call him reliable! Pfff! He'd say one thing one moment and decide to do the opposite the next. *And* he keeps disappearing. Always when you need him the most! Vanishes for weeks at a time, then reappears and refuses point blank to say where he's been! Funny thing, that. He could drag the life history out of a man who's had his tongue cut off, but tell you what he gets up to when he disappears? Never!"

"That's just it," agreed Feng. "I was hoping he'd help me out. A friend of mine was killed and one thing's certain. It's linked to the disappearance of all those Miao girls."

"I can't think how Jinjin could help you out. Anyway, I've not seen him this morning. Maybe he'll turn up this evening, maybe not."

"This evening? Oh, never mind! As you say, what could an urchin boy do? I've got to get to Chang'an, you see."

"Chang'an? Whoever heard of such a thing! Has that boy been putting idiotic notions into your head?"

"No, but he might've been some sort of company, however irritating I find him."

"Look, I've a nice soup on the boil. Just sit down. I'll get you something to eat, and you and me, we can get a few things straight. Chang'an, my foot! Why, people are being murdered all the time! The emperor would never be able to get on with his work if the imperial city was swamped by the friends of those who'd had their lives taken unlawfully. As for the missing Miao girls, it's not for us Han folk to interfere!"

Feng sat at a table and Wenling disappeared off into the kitchen. Of course she wouldn't understand and perhaps he'd told her too much already. Pity about Jinjin, though; despite the urchin's cheek enquiring into Feier, there was something endearing about his eagerness to listen and offer solutions. The boy must have taken umbrage at being abruptly cut off the previous night. Feng realised he'd been petty to overreact over Feier. He needed more self-control, but the mere mention of the girl's name clawed at his insides. How else could he have responded?

As he awaited Wenling's return, he wondered what his child would be doing that very moment. Preparing breakfast for Yueloong? Hopefully she'd not disgrace herself with her lack of culinary skills. He regretted he'd not approached one of the village women to teach her the arts of being a good wife, but recalled his fear of losing the girl by handing over that small responsibility. Now it was too late; quite possibly this selfishness had jeopardised her chances of a good match.

Wenling re-emerged from the kitchen with a bowl of soup, some dried pork and rice cake.

"Look, I was hard on you just now," she said. "About Chang'an. It's just that Yungchin and I care. We care about *all* our guests. Chang'an's a dangerous place. Surely one murder's enough! And you have your daughter to think about. Just tell the new prefectural magistrate. That's what he's paid for. Leave it to him. Anyway, he'll know all about the Miao girls like the rest of us. Perhaps he's come up with a solution already. In which case you'd be wasting your time... *and* your life."

"I thought your husband didn't think much of the new guy."

"Oh, that's just Yungchin. Suspicious of all officials. *And* change. Who can blame him with new taxes being imposed each year? Look, leave it all to the magistrate and get back to your daughter. Believe me, as one who's had to endure life without a child nothing could be more precious."

She must have been reading Feng's mind. He'd been wondering how Feier would cope as surrogate daughter to a Miao farmer, for this whole exercise was about reuniting Miao parents with missing Miao daughters.

"You really think the magistrate knows something?"

"More than the emperor would wish him to know, I'd guess."

Feng was reluctant to mention the thousand petals. She'd only accuse him of insanity. She was a good woman, jolly and friendly, but he'd never thought of her as seeing any further than the walls of her own inn. Besides, he knew the risk he'd already taken by suggesting to the urchin the emperor's throne was at stake. With the boy gone, he silently cursed himself. Getting to Chang'an as quickly as possible seemed all the more urgent.

"A horse? Do you know where I can find a horse?"

Wenling folded her arms and looked at him quizzically.

"A horse, huh? Why, I saw a nice pottery horse in the market just yesterday! Some grave robber at work, no doubt, but if you hurry it might still be there."

Noticing him frown, she came up and rested a hand on his shoulder. Her eyes, the eyes of a kind woman but not particularly bright, displayed genuine concern.

"Any other sort of horse and I fear you may never see that daughter of yours again," she added.

Feng finished his breakfast in silence. He settled up with Wenling, for Wong had gone early to market to get in fresh produce for the day. There was no further mention of a horse, of Chang'an or the prefectural magistrate. Feng asked again whether Jinjin had shown up, but the inn-keeper's wife only raised her eyebrows and shrugged her shoulders. She filled his water flasks, gave him rice cake wrapped in leaves and for the last time warned him to return home to his daughter.

Feng led Mimi out into the street and searched the locality for the urchin boy. The sun had already risen above Three Monkey Mountain and he resigned himself to journeying alone without the annoying youth. Perhaps not such a bad thing if Jinjin hadn't already spilt the beans. Also, Feng would have hit the boy were he to make any more remarks about Feier.

He remembered well the old prefectural magistrate's house. Their last meeting was when he went to register his intention to sit the civil service examination and, although the old magistrate had been as ugly as a bad-tempered monkey, Feng respected the man. But this new fellow? And why all that palaver at the temple?

He tied Mimi to a post in the courtyard and made an acceptably short bow to the manservant who'd come to greet him.

"I'm Teacher Feng," he introduced himself. "I knew the old magistrate well and wish to speak with his replacement on a matter of urgency and great secrecy."

"*Nǐ chīle ma?*" the man asked.

Why do we Han always ask whether someone's eaten? As if I'd come to the prefectural magistrate's house only to enjoy a meal!

"Yes. And the magistrate?"

"Indeed! Hold your arms apart."

The long sleeves of his tunic hung limply as Feng held his arms wide whilst the manservant frisked him for knives. Never before had he gone through anything like that.

"This way, Teacher Feng. May I ask if it's about your pay, for these are hard times? We don't want to be wasting the magistrate's time."

"Like I said. Urgent and secret."

Feng always found the minions of minor officials irritating.

"Only warning you! As you'll already know, our last magistrate was a forgiving man. Not so the new fellow. I wouldn't like you to end up with fifty blows of the thin rod for annoying him."

What Feng had to say about the murder and the disappearing Miao girls could hardly be construed as time-wasting, but a request for a horse? He followed the servant into a large room at the far end of the courtyard. How changed it was. He remembered the same room hung with scrolls of poems and paintings, for the ugly old magistrate who'd been so sympathetic after Meili's death had been a patron of the arts. The walls of the reception room were now bare, the Tang figurines gone; only a low, empty table of simple design, a large, sturdy chair, and a bamboo mat on the floor. The room even smelled of cleanliness; a total absence of any discernible scent, pleasant or foul, that spoke of human habitation. There was something unnerving about a building devoid of human smells.

As Feng stood and waited, standing in front of the mat, he practised in his mind the speech he would deliver:

'Magistrate Minsheng, I have a matter of serious concern to report to you... erm...'

But what if the magistrate were to reply: 'And I have a thousand matters each a thousand times more serious awaiting my attention!'?

A more direct approach?

'Esteemed Magistrate Minsheng, I fear for the emperor's safety, for the murder of my friend Merchant Chang on the other side of Three Monkey Mountain must surely be linked to the disappearances of girls from the homes of our Miao brothers, and... erm...'

How was he going to make his theory about the thousand petals sound credible when it was no more than a hunch?

'Most esteemed Magistrate Minsheng, there is something I feel I must discuss with you, for no-one else can be trusted on this matter. There's been a murder. A good friend of mine was killed with a bamboo stake near the lotus lake on the other side of Three Monkey Mountain. I'd enlisted his help to track down evil men who are stealing girls from the Miao villages, and...'

"Teacher Feng! We meet again!"

Feng turned. His jaw dropped when he saw the broad-framed figure of Magistrate Minsheng in the doorway. The man looked so very different in a long elegant purple and green silk gown, embroidered with two white cranes, and the tall, forward-curved black hat of office. So changed from the shaven head and simple yellow and brown monk's gown when he'd last seen the very same man at the monastery near the lotus lake; there were more lines in that inscrutable face, but it was most certainly him.

"Why, I... I... my friend... um... Miao girls..." Feng stuttered, bowing respectfully. His prepared speech fragmented into isolated syllables that emerged from his lips like meaningless bubbles.

"And after such a long time! I now see we didn't pay you enough, for surely otherwise you'd have seen fit to come and offer a little more pittance to us poor monks back then!"

There were three guards outside in the courtyard. Any attempt to make a run for it and the teacher would have been cut down and Feier rendered instantly fatherless as well as motherless. Minsheng stared coldly at him.

"My daughter. Feier. So upset after her mother's death. She... well, it was hard for her. And the Temple always reminded her... about... you see, she thought... she always hoped..."

The ex-monk's broad-cheeked face slowly contorted into an icy grin.

"Teacher Feng, you have no need to make excuses! The good work you're doing is known throughout the province. Indeed, word of it was even sent to the emperor by my predecessor. Educating girls as well as boys? Why did no-one else think of that?"

Uncertain how to react, Feng gave another bow. He'd never before bowed to a monk and, however much finery adorned that huge frame, the other man would in his mind always be a monk.

"But this, I understand, is not about pay, right? My servant has already briefed me."

Magistrate Minsheng went over to the seat on the other side of the table.

"Kneel, Teacher Feng. On the mat. My servant will bring us tea. And my ears, for the time being, belong to you."

Feng knelt on the rough bamboo mat and looked timidly up at the imposing figure looming behind the table. Minsheng seemed a man liable to flip from one mood to another without the least warning. Predictably unpredictable! As for his remark about the monastery... why? All the teacher could do was to tread cautiously.

Minsheng laughed.

"I see you're wondering what a monk is doing here in a government post. I'll put you out of your misery, teacher. I was never truly a monk, you see. Buddhist, yes, but monk... well, let's just say that after the troubles we had under the previous emperor, I was sent to find out what they got up to in our monasteries. Good money ending up in their coffers, land being bought up all over again. Honesty isn't something that resides comfortably with the monks. They could learn from the master of Shandong... *and*, it seems, from our honourable and humble Teacher Feng on the other side of Three Monkey Mountain."

Feng remained bowed forwards on the mat, wondering where this was leading. He recalled Minsheng as the large monk who never said a word, only stood and stared, and that stare seemed to take in everyone and everything at the same time.

"So? Why *have* you come to annoy me?"

The teacher's mentally-prepared speech fragmented into disconnected words and phrases: "Miao girls... Feier's friend, Xiaopeng, disappeared... bamboo pole... half-eaten face... the merchant... his donkey, Mimi ... "

"Ha-ha-ha-ha!" guffawed Minsheng. "Donkey indeed! What a player! They ought to employ you as the emperor's clown. I've no idea what you're talking about but it's all very funny." Suddenly his smile vanished, he leaned forward and fixed Feng with that stare the teacher remembered so well. "Just tell me why I shouldn't detach your head from your body here and now, clown!"

Feng, his head still down, looked at the ground beside his knees. His eyes traced patterns in the stone, and he thought how strangely beautiful they were - and how permanent that beauty seemed for, should Mingsheng choose to remove his head, those patterns would remain. No-one could change them or rub them out. A tiny bug crawled into his field of view and meandered across one of the patterns, so fragile against that permanence, and Feng prayed for the bug; prayed Mingsheng wouldn't stamp on the little creature before slicing through his own neck with a sword, for the ex-monk seemed to be that sort of a man, one who reviled rather than re-spected life. A Buddhist, he'd said? Men like him were no closer to Nirvana than the little bug was to Chang'an. He calmed himself.

"I believe our emperor to be in danger and..." Feng glanced up and into that stare. "And I'm so relieved it's you, honourable Magistrate Minsheng, for I remember how careful, how wise you were at the monastery." Mins-heng's expressionless face told Feng nothing and gave no reassurance. "If it's true... if there *is* a plot to kill the emperor, then China may be thrown into chaos," he continued. "There are hordes of Western Turks and Tibetans waiting to take the lands guarded by the great White Tiger of the west..." Feng looked at the man for a flicker of response and saw nothing. "And to the north, if our armies are weakened in the west, the generals in Dongbei [10] might... well, no-one would be safe!"

Mingsheng turned and left the room, leaving Feng kneeling, trembling. He returned with a wide-bladed sword and the same blankly grim expression, halting in the doorway almost filled by the man's bulk. Feng knew his time was up, his life reduced to the distance between the doorway and his neck. Six Mimi's should have fitted into that distance, nose to tail. He prayed Minsheng would cover the distance slowly, as would Mimi. How Mimi loved Feier. *Everyone* loved Feier. Minsheng had covered half the distance already... three Mimis... level with the table... three Mimis left. A life of three Mimis... oh, forgive me, little Feier...

"Stand up!"

Feng stood, shaking. Why kill me standing - and here? What about the mess?

Minsheng erupted into laughter, prodding Feng's belly with the point of his sword.

"Too much rice, huh? That lovely daughter of yours feeds you too well."

How did Minsheng know he was widowed? Meili died after the man had departed from the monastery. But what did it matter... his head would soon be a bloodied ball rolling on the floor, his body useless like that of Chang. His mind danced with images of Feier finding the merchant's corpse, of her with Yueloong, in the fields, preparing his meals, and teaching. He prayed to Buddha his trust in his friend had not been misguided and that she'd be well looked after, given happiness through marriage to someone strong and wise and gentle. He'd been let down so often he hardly knew what to think as further images floated and danced and teased a mind about to be extinguished like a flickering lamp: the inn, Wenling then Jinjin. Had that boy betrayed his confidence to this monster? If so, why?

---

[10]   The three most north-easterly provinces of China.

But Minsheng did not slice off his head. Instead, he slapped him on the back as if he were a long-lost friend and laughed again.

"Don't look so worried, teacher. You might need this - not that you'll know how to use one."

He took Feng's hand, prised open the clenched fingers and placed the sword hilt into Feng's grasp. The sword hung limp at Feng's side as he stood feet apart, staring at the ground. Strange how he'd positioned himself like that, preparing himself for the cut of the blade as if it mattered that he shouldn't fall until his body was headless.

"*And* a horse!"

Feng looked up.

"With a horse you should make Chang'an within ten settings of the sun - only ten flights of the sun-bird of *Di Jun*, huh?"

And he laughed again.

Feng had never believed in the story of the ten sun-carrying birds being shot down by archer Yi to save the world from being turned into a fireball, leaving behind just one. In fact there were many ancient tales he did not believe were true. He only thought of these as pointers for souls on earth. A moment earlier he was standing legs astride, preparing and wondering; wondering about Heaven. Was there truly a paradise of unearthly beauty where the Jade Emperor ruled supreme, and where he and Meili might again find happiness together? Professing to believe in the Buddhist path to Nirvana through the endless samsara of rebirth and death, he and Meili would probably never meet up again. And little Feier? His heart ached for both Meili and for Feier, but his mind, full of the words of the master of Shandong, was telling him nothing could be that easy. Heaven surely belonged only to those tales. Without further pain and suffering, truth could only mean emptiness of spirit and a space devoid of paths that led to happiness.

"A horse?" Feng queried, his voice hushed.

"Your donkey for a horse! To inform our emperor about the missing Miao girls and the death of your friend... and save China perhaps? Should you return successful, then I shall order new school buildings for both villages. The emperor himself will sanction it, of that I'm sure."

"Emperor? You've met him?"

Minsheng's smile vanished. The wrong damned question! But *he* was now the one with a weapon, and he gripped the sword firmly.

"I know him well enough to warn you that if you put a foot wrong your pretty daughter will end up a slave in the palace. But you won't, will you? I see how you stood feet apart when you thought you were about to lose your head. Most men would have crumpled to the ground, pleaded for mercy, grovelling like a woman. Succeed, and that daughter of yours may even find a place in my bed."

In a flash of anger, Feng took a step forwards, sword raised, but he halted. He saw mirth in Minsheng's eyes. The man was playing with him. Besides, he was no more than a lowly prefectural magistrate. He had no power to take Feier by force. Succeed or not, it would be the emperor himself who would decide the girl's fate.

"Good, good! So... you have a sword, a horse and some provisions, eh?"

"You believe what I say, then?" asked Feng, still uncertain whether or not the large man was playing a cruel game with him.

"Do not try my patience, teacher. Look, why do you think the Governor got rid of the last magistrate?"

Why, indeed? Feng didn't reply. Instead, he stared at Minsheng and studied the writing on his face, for years of teaching had taught him to read people's thoughts from faces, particularly the eyes and the mouth. The magistrate's eyes were set like stones, his mouth straight as an unstrung bow.

"Did you really think I had no idea why the Miao girls are vanishing?"

Still Feng said nothing.

Minsheng erupted again into laughter.

"Oh, what you think is of no importance! It's what you find out to be true that matters. With your daughter's fate in the balance you'll crack this one, I can see. My manservant will get you a horse and provisions. And here, these coins will go some way towards buying the truth from people. Funny how a string of coins can make channels into people's minds, uncover secrets, ay?"

The magistrate slipped three strings of coppers off his shoulder and handed them to Feng. The teacher's eyes widened in astonishment to see a gift of three moons worth of wages!

"But...?" he began.

"Quick! Before I change my mind and exchange this for your head! And that scroll you carry on your donkey. Is it valuable?"

"How did…?" Minsheng's gaze cut off the end of his question. "Sung Po. Priceless."

"Leave it with my manservant."

Feng bowed and backed away, clutching the money in one hand and the sword in the other. At the door he bowed once more, turned and almost bumped into the manservant standing on the deck, holding the reins of a large grey mare, with Mimi's baskets and his bamboo stake already strapped in place behind the saddle.

The teacher felt uneasy. It seemed as if everything had been pre-planned, that the magistrate was using him rather than the other way round, and he read nothing in the manservant's fine-lined face. Mimi stood patiently, one foot raised as always, still tethered to the post at the far end of the courtyard. Feng retrieved the scroll from the basket and handed it to the manservant.

"Merchant Chang told me all about you. And I've been expecting this visit. So remember, Teacher Feng…" Minsheng's deep voice boomed from the doorway behind him. "That daughter of yours – slave to the emperor or the respected wife of a prefectural magistrate with high expectations? The choice is yours."

The slender branch of trust to which he'd so desperately clung snapped when he heard the man's laughter.

6.

Reward of the Flesh

The sun had already risen, reproducing, in long, dark shadows across the stony ground, the Miao farmer's house, his miserable water buffalo and the bamboo grove, when the teacher's daughter first heard the sound of excited children's voices approaching from the village centre. Their noise set off a yapping dog, and for a few moments the animal's barks seemed to keep time with the frantic beating of Feier's heart as she awaited *his* arrival from beyond the screen of pliant bamboo stems. Would that her heart wasn't so pliant in his presence, but there was nothing she could do about it. When he was close, she only wanted him to hold her... and *more*. She bit her lower lip, ashamed of the 'more' as her hand reached up to touch a hidden virgin's breast.

The fact that he'd remained silent had to be significant.

A small group of young boys appeared... then more, and more. They stopped chattering. One had spotted her. He whispered to his friend and pointed, there was a whoop of joy then, quite suddenly, the children rushed forwards yelling "Feier! Feier!" She crouched down to their level, grinning as they ran up to her, jostling each other, pushing and shouting. And she felt *his* presence, saw his strong legs as he came to stand beside her but she remained crouched, explaining to the children how she wanted them all to be on their best behaviour and not to think they could get up to mischief just because their teacher was now a girl.

"Or because she's beautiful!" suggested Angwan with a chuckle.

She stood up, her face burning crimson.

"No girls? Where are the girls?" she asked, without turning to look at the young priest.

"That's for your father to find out."

"I'm sorry. But... so many missing?"

"Even our younger sisters are kept inside now. No-one dares let them out. These boys are going to have to do girls' work in the rice fields too. I tell you, they've given me earfuls ever since I rounded them up. 'Do we *have* to?' 'Can't it wait 'til our girls came back?' 'It's not right, boys doing girls' work!' But their pleadings fell on deaf ears!"

Angwan chuckled, and Feier felt his hand brush lightly against hers as he took the handle of her calligraphy case from her.

"But carrying for a beautiful girl is a man's job," he added. Even if he *was* making fun of her, she enjoyed it. It made her feel warm and strangely whole inside, as if she'd only ever been half a person until that moment. "We can't hang around. We'll have to be back with this troupe of monkeys whilst the sun's still high in the sky if we're to get any work from them in the fields."

When the children closest to her pretended to be monkeys, Feier giggled. Thus encouraged, they leapt around making 'ooh! ooh! ooh!' sounds.

"Fear not, pretty one! I shall protect you from the wild beasts!" whispered Angwan, and he laughed.

Was he teasing her? Feier glanced repeatedly in Angwan's direction, taking care to avoid eye contact, wishing there was only herself and the young priest without the encumbrance of a horde of monkey-children as they walked on to the Han village. She and the priest trailed some distance behind the boys, side by side, and talked. Not only did he speak Mandarin fluently but, like her father, he spoke of things that mattered.

Ever since he'd returned from a period of training with a priest in the Miao village on the road to Chang'an to take over his father's place as family head, her feelings for him had changed ... and long before even then. Prior to his father's untimely death he'd also spent several moons learning the Buddhist ways at the monastery near the lotus pond; essential, he had persuaded his father, to fully understand the Miao teachings of the spirits of nature. Back then, Feier-the-child thought of him as the handsome, bright peasant boy with a twinkle in his eyes; the one she and Xiaopeng would giggle about from behind the safety of young girls' shy hands or half-closed doors. Now a 'woman' herself, freed from paternal scrutiny, she felt only a delicious welling of excitement in his proximity.

Angwan was an intelligent, learned young man. Tutored in Miao folklore and animist beliefs, he could also recite Han poetry and lines from the writings of the great Kong Fuzi. Several times, as they followed the children through the wood, over the hill down towards the lotus lake, his hand would touch hers and she made no attempt to move it away. Instead, she turned her face towards his, taking in the angular lines of his features, his short hair, his strong chin and the movement of that lump in his neck that changed boys into men, and she prayed her father would not be too quick in finding Xiaopeng and returning the girl to her father. It wasn't that she didn't love her little Miao friend; she did, but she loved Angwan more.

~

Feng turned for a last glance at Feier's beloved Mimi as he rode the horse out of the courtyard. His heart sank, for the donkey had been his only link with the girl. He closed his eyes against their moistening.

Beyond the courtyard entrance, the filthy streets were already filled with men, women and children. Street stalls had been set up, and Feng, always a reluctant horseman, steered the grey mare cautiously, careful not to tip Feier's provisions into the mud. Villagers back home took pride in keeping their own little streets free of the filth of human life, but here in Houzicheng it seemed as if residents competed to fill the public area with the most foul excrement and dirtiest rubbish they could find.

Relieved at last to have left the town behind, Feng began his uncertain journey towards Chang'an. The mare, called 'Rou', had already lived up to her name meaning 'gentle'. Untroubled by the harsh, raucous shouts in the town, the scuffles and the smell, she carried him effortlessly out onto the open narrow road where, putting all his trust in the beast, he slouched back in the saddle and tried to think.

So Minsheng had been tipped off! By whom? The innkeeper and his ebullient wife, or that strange, young urchin poet, Jinjin? Had he destroyed Feier's chances of happiness with his pig-headed determination to track down Chang's killer and rescue the wives and daughters of his Miao friends? Would she be forced to become the young wife of that monster of a magistrate? Was being slave to the emperor a lesser fate? At least she would then be in the right place to further herself. Surely someone in the palace would notice that agility of mind behind his daughter's beauty? But he had chosen this path and the destiny that awaited him at the end of it. He would have to play out the interminable game: one life closer to Nirvana or return to Earth... over and over and over again? Of one thing Feng was certain: his path would course through many hells before any destination was reached.

He was already in the worst possible hell: an existence without Feier and without knowing what was happening to the girl.

~

'There is beauty in everything, but a man does not always see it.'

The famous words of Kong Fuzi surfaced in Feier's mind to mock her when she stopped to stare at the spot where the body had been, now stained brown from the dead merchant's blood. A frown darkened her pretty features.

Beauty? Surely not even the master from Qu Fu would have used such a word to describe death. She took in the flattened grass, the random pattern of dried blood, and she recalled the bamboo pole sticking up from the bloated belly, and the partly-destroyed face.

"Was your father a good man?" she asked Angwan. "He let you leave the village when you thought about becoming a priest. Was he also Buddhist like Uncle Li?"

Angwan chuckled.

"*Baba* a Buddhist? No, but they were friends, Xiaopeng's father and mine."

"Xiaopeng never said. My best friend and she never told me!"

"Told you what?" Feier glanced sideways at the young man, but said nothing. "The poor girl! Not very bright, ay?"

In her mind, Feier saw the smiling face of her friend. She so wanted to agree with Angwan and erase the image of the person that separated them, but it remained stubbornly stuck, taunting her for hoping she could take the Miao girl's place. They continued along the path, past the lotus lake; the flowers had opened in the warm sun.

"She kept home for Uncle, did everything a wife would do, worked in the fields, was already gifted at embroidery... When she tried to teach me these things my fingers would tie themselves into knots. And you say she's not very bright?"

Feier's eyes challenged him without accusation. Her question was irrelevant. She only wanted to know why he looked at her in that way. She'd often noticed it before when she was a young girl trailing after her teacher father, and then she'd assumed it was because she was the only Han child there. He was different now, a youth transformed into a proud young man, but the look in his eyes was the same.

"That's just it. Xiaopeng's like all other Miao girls. No freedom of spirit. Why, a girl with a free spirit should fly like a crane. Her mind should travel to places others couldn't even dream of. A girl..."

"Hey!" exclaimed Feier, interrupting, wishing to stop the flow of words that fuelled impossible hope. "We're falling behind. You're supposed to be looking after those children."

She gave Angwan a playful punch in the side and ran on ahead. And she imagined *she* was that crane of whom he'd spoken and she felt strangely happy. The crane left the dead man's final resting place and the blood stain of his life-cut-short, left behind thoughts of missing Miao girls, of Xiaopeng and Uncle Yueloong. No longer did memories of her mother haunt her. She even felt free of the ever-present shadow of her beloved *baba*. Angwan caught up with her when she reached the chattering crocodile tail of young boys. She sensed his happiness without the need to look him in the eye.

"Why did you want to become a Buddhist monk? Xiaopeng told me. Before you trained to be a Miao priest, she said you spent three moons in the monastery," asked Feier, looking the other way. "You people have your own spirits and gods."

"To be close to my crane," was his reply.

"I could never become a crane."

Her mother? Was she now as free and beautiful as a crane?

"You can't *become* what you already are."

They walked on to the Han village in silence. Angwan followed Feier and the boys into the schoolroom. It felt strangely unfamiliar without *baba*. The Han village children were already there, bursting with excitement at seeing the teacher's daughter. They wanted to know all about the body near the lotus lake, for the whole village was alive with gossip of the murder.

"How big was the pole?"

"How much blood was there? Enough to fill a wine jug?"

"How could you be sure it was the merchant if half his face was missing?"

How, how, how?

She looked at Angwan for reassurance. The tiger? Yes, she would tell them about the White Tiger tattooed onto the back of his hand. She'd never forget that tiger she'd grown to hate so much over the years during which the merchant had visited them. Often, she'd wondered whether the man had been a tiger in his previous life.

How she now hated tigers!

~

Feng wished he'd never even met the scoundrel Jinjin. All that nonsense about a White Tiger League! The very idea that an urchin could pretend to know more about his murdered friend than he did was absurd; yet there was something disarmingly open about the boy. A thought occurred to Feng. Had Jinjin also been murdered – like Chang – again because of him? The shifty pair he'd been talking to in Wong's inn, the fox-faced man and the one called Yaosheng with the droopy moustache, they'd seemed only too keen to put the boy down and make fun of him. Were they also in with the White Tiger League?

He now wished for the boy's company, interminable questioning included, if only for reassurance that yet another burden of guilt hadn't been layered on top of the dead merchant and the farmer's missing daughter.

Setting off at an easy trot, Rou bounced Feng up and down whilst the man's mind darted from Feier to the urchin Jinjin, innkeeper Wong, his disturbing encounter with Minsheng, monk-turned-magistrate, and to his bamboo-impaled friend. It seemed the whole world, apart from Feier, knew more than it cared to tell him about the mystery of the Miao girls and the murder he'd vowed to solve. Anger spurred him on.

One good thing: those fretful thoughts of the marriage maker had been swept away by a constant stream of unanswered questions: Merchant Chang's links with the monks and Chen Jiabiao, the White Tiger tattoos,

Minsheng's connections with government or with persons *other* than government, Feier's insistence she remain behind with Yueloong, and now Jinjin's disappearance...

~

Jinjin had been up well before the first cock crowed. He had crept into Wenling's kitchen and filled a cloth with dumplings and rice cakes for the journey with the teacher. He saw no need to ask. After all, he offered his services for free, and if he were to take off with Teacher Feng for a week or two, why, he'd be costing Wong nothing in food! He had wandered out into the yard to look for eggs and that's when he had spotted him again: the man with the white tiger tattoo, the one who'd given money to the emperor's soldiers for taking them to the Miao girl's house.

The merchant was saddling his horse in the yard. Oddly, Jinjin hadn't noticed him eating in the inn the night before. Perhaps he'd been too busy talking with Teacher Feng. Or were Wong and his wife in on this as well? Had this man been kept hidden? Was the teacher in danger? In a harsh and friendless world, Jinjin trusted no-one.

The merchant glanced in his direction but showed no response to his presence; one blessing for an urchin is to be rendered invisible by poverty and shabbiness. Not worth looking at, although in his case this would change given time, thought Jinjin, as he continued his sham hunt for eggs. Men like that would not only look at him, they'd be forced to bow before him! The teacher's daughter, too...

Oh, the teacher's daughter!

Jinjin even searched silly places for eggs, but never took his eyes off the tattooed man for more than a second. The tiger was clearly visible, and the boy wondered how a wise man like Teacher Feng could misjudge the murdered merchant. Everyone knew the White Tiger League was up to no good and, whatever the merchant's involvement, Jinjin saw his chance to earn respect from the teacher and his beautiful daughter Feier. A swallow [11], no less! The boy was fed up with also being invisible to girls, but a swallow? Would that swallow see him for the person he truly was, respect him, bear

---

[11] Feier means 'a swallow' (literally, 'two flights')

him children? If he were to help the girl's father with some crazy mission, then perhaps she would *have* to do all these things.

The promise of the trader leading him to the White Tiger League - and to the girl - gave him an idea. Adjacent to Wenling's kitchen was a room where Wong would sort out his affairs, his bills and his payments. Tucked away on a shelf was a box with ink tablets, brushes, and blank scrolls. Jinjin returned to the inn. Whilst Wenling was busy talking to someone, her back turned, he crept into that room, stole ink, one of the smaller brushes and, on his way back through the kitchen, he found himself a sharp knife. He tied these things into the food bundle and set off after the White Tiger trader. It was early, and he could return and report back in time to join Teacher Feng whose donkey was still tethered in the courtyard, asleep on her hooves.

The trader led his horse towards the market place. He was in no hurry and Jinjin kept a safe distance. It was then that the boy spotted two other figures half-hidden in a doorway, one shaven-headed and wearing a monk's robes. The trader left his horse at the roadside and walked over to them. An empty cart stood between the boy and the three men. Edging his way alongside the wall, Jinjin reached the cart, climbed in unnoticed and waited. The men, thinking they were alone, made no attempt to speak softly and Jinjin caught every word:

"None of the other monks knows a thing!"

"How can you be sure? You've seen who we've got as new prefectural magistrate!"

"Minsheng? Oh, we can buy him off if necessary. Besides, he'll go with the flow of the river, so to speak. I know the man!"

"Hmmm! Pity about Chang! Mind you, we could use his murder to our advantage."

"How come?"

"You'll see! So, Jiabiao, has the time come? Are there enough to satisfy him? One a day for the next three years, ay?"

"One a night, more like!"

Jinjin heard laughter.

"We've three more to pick up on the way back. With those girls, there'll be a thousand of them. A thousand pretty petals, eh? Oh, to be an emperor! Then I'd only have to put up with my wife once every three years, the cantankerous old bitch. In the new court I'll have the pick of the harem.

They'll all be going free because of the new man's thing about Miao girls. Good luck to him, I say! So long as we all get our just rewards."

"Girls? Not interested myself! The cart's ready. Over there. Just shackle it to your horse. The soldiers will be waiting at the edge of the Miao village in case of trouble. You know, this is going to be almost *too* easy. Nearly half the imperial guards have already defected to the new emperor."

Jinjin, in panic, found sacks intended for the Miao girls. He covered himself with one of these on hearing approaching footsteps.

"Can't call him that yet, Jiabiao!" the trader called back from beside the cart. "Could bring bad luck."

A heavy bag landed on Jinjin's back, winding him, but he managed to suppress the urge to cry out. The cart jolted and jerked as the trader hitched it to the horse.

"Hope the girls are as light as those others, Jiabiao! This bit of junk you call a cart weighs as much as a pile of dragon turd! Don't want the old nag dropping dead on us." He chuckled to himself, repeating 'dragon turd' several times. "I like it, I like it!" he added.

The cart swayed forwards. Jinjin's only option for staying alive was to stay as still as a corpse and jump clear at the first opportunity. He remained crouched underneath the sacks, his face bumping against the wooden floor. The sackcloth, used to restrain struggling pretty young women and girls, smelt of body odour. He'd never imagined girls could smell like that. Surely their adorable bodies should bear the fragrances of heavenly blossoms. Perhaps, he wondered, when overcome with panic they might give off a sickly, musty scent. The only females he'd ever got close enough to for his nostrils to take in their smells were his worn-down hag of a mother, silent slave to his sadistic father, and Wong Wenling at the inn, a whirling bundle of noodle-driven energy. Both stank of sweat right enough, but neither could, in Jinjin's mind, be represented by those three beautiful calligraphy strokes for *nu* [12].

But the teacher's daughter, Feier, would be different. *She* would have the fragrance of a flower from heaven.

~

---

[12] woman

Angwan refused to leave the schoolroom even when all the children were seated cross-legged in a semi-circle on the floor, with Feier on a cushion in front of her father's sturdy, squat, teacher's table, the scroll, the ink and calligraphy brushes neatly arranged before her.

"I have strict instructions from Farmer Li to let neither you nor the children out of my sight!" he informed the girl.

"But... " Feier tried to think of something to say that might, within the confines of the schoolroom, hold together two things: her self-respect and Angwan. "But you must be busy now. Have things to do. Return when the sun starts to sink from its highest resting place in the sky. No harm can come to any of us in *this* village," the girl said, secretly willing him to stay.

"Do you know the murderer so well that you can tell?"

The word sent a shiver through her body. She stared open-mouthed at the young priest's smile, for it confused her.

"No, but..."

"No buts! Teach! I can think of no greater pleasure than to watch one particular teacher in action. Observe her every movement. Besides, some of our boys are a bit rusty in the Han language. You may need a translator."

Blushing scarlet, Feier began her lesson. She'd decided to go over char-acters with three brush strokes, starting with 'nu'. Since Angwan was watching, it would need to be the most beautiful calligraphy she'd ever produced. At first, her brush trembled in her small hand, and all eyes, Angwan's included, were trained on her, but as soon as the tip of her brush touched the scroll, everything *baba* had had taught her about technique, about control, took over. Her hand, as steady and certain as a farmer's plough, traced the curved lines of 'nu', recreating the mystery of her gender in ink.

"Bravo!" exclaimed Angwan. "Hold it up so your little charges may see the beauty of their teacher written in her brush strokes!"

Trembling again, Feier obeyed, holding up the scroll for all to see.

"Aaah!" gasped the children, taking their cue from the Miao village priest. And in the dusty ground in front of him, each child carefully scratched the character for 'woman' with a stick.

"Remember, boys, the character you write is the most important you'll ever learn," continued Angwan. "One day that same character will either bear you on dragon clouds to paradise or down, down below the earth to a place of demons."

Feier looked away from Angwan, for his smile had left him.

~

Feng tried to compare Farmer Li's loss, should he fail to find Xiaopeng, with his own: the death of Meili. Although neither man had control over events that caused his loss, with Meili it seemed different. He'd not left her side as her body drained from her in a flux that reeked of death more than shit. Before him, that lovely face turned from a soft, smooth-skinned luscious fruit to a coarsely-wrinkled, salted prune, but her eyes, the eyes of his daughter, stayed beautiful as they pleaded for help. Somehow this magnified the loss when it happened.

"I'm so frightened... please do something," she'd begged before she lost her voice. The doctor gave her dried ginger root, *sheng jiang*, and green tea; a monk from the monastery, for a fee, turned the prayer wheel to send a message of her plight to the Buddha, and little Feier, herself weakened by the flux, could not stop crying. When Meili had become too weak to drink the tea and ginger root, Feng soaked the sleeve of his shirt in the fluid, prized her lips apart and squeezed drops into her mouth, for although she was as dry as a dead animal bone, fluid leaking from her back end still soaked the bed. But the thing that had haunted Feng ever since her death was the thought that he wasn't there for his wife at the very end.

For two days he'd remained awake. Every time Meili's breathing slowed in her sleep, he would shake her back to wakefulness. He felt that if he were to do this until the flux subsided he should be able to keep her alive. The horror of discovering he'd dropped off to sleep, his head resting sideways on his wife's shrivelled breasts, before raising himself to see her vacant, lifeless eyes, was too much to bear. He screamed out as he'd never screamed before or since, and little Feier, who'd been awake all the time, afraid to wake up her *baba*, stared questioningly at him, as if patiently waiting for him to stop screaming and explain it all to her. That he'd not been able to help the child come to terms with the loss of her mother turned Meili's death into a double failure. Now, spending every waking hour trying to make amends for his daughter seemed to focus the guilt and soften the anger. Without Feier, this might have been turned against the world, but as it was the blame faced inwards.

Yueloong's loss was as nothing compared with his own, and this was some consolation as he struggled with a further bout of self-blame. Nevertheless, there was also more guilt and Xiaopeng *had* to be found. Maybe Jinjin was right about the mysterious White Tiger League but wrong about Merchant Chang. More likely, Feng reckoned, it was like this:

A member of a group of merchants, known as the White Tigers because of their trade with the west, had been approached by rebels to assist in some crazy plan to kidnap a thousand Miao girls for a usurper who had a fixation about Miao females renowned for their embroidery skills, and who, on completing his collection of girls, would march on Chang'an to depose the poet emperor. Crazy, but of late China had become a crazy place. Anything was now possible. Merchant Chang had uncovered part of the truth, because of Feng's entreaties, had spoken to the wrong person and forfeited his life. That Minsheng knew more than he was letting on was obvious, and Feng could see the man was using him as a pawn in a game of Chinese chess, giving nothing away so no accusations could be levelled against him whichever way the imperial tide should turn. One or more monks might be involved, or Chen Jiabiao... or both.

What about the old magistrate? The teacher had been given no reason for Minsheng's sudden rise to power. And Wong? How dare that boy implicate the innkeeper and his wife! Meili's spirit would tremble in her new-found life at the very thought of it. She'd adored the jolly innkeeper and his wife.

The road to Chang'an was long and winding, passing over rough mountainous terrain and through towns of little significance. The first night, Feng boarded with a farmer whose small house was packed with six children, four of them sons, and the farmer's aging, rambling mother. The young boys again brought back memories of Meili, who'd always chided herself for not bearing him a son.

"A son? Who on earth would want a son in exchange for our beautiful little daughter?" he would continually reassure his wife, although at the very next opportunity she would say "But how can you ever forgive me for not giving you a son?"

There'd been problems at Feier's birth and the doctor had told them she'd never be able to have another child. He was right about that but not about the dried ginger. It did nothing for a dying Meili.

"So you're a teacher, huh? Give me one good reason why I should send my sons to sit on their backsides all day long so they can learn how to make pretty characters with a brush and ink rather than learn how to feed hungry mouths!" challenged the farmer.

They were seated around a long, low table on which had been placed dishes laden with vegetables, rice and pork. All eyes were glued on Feng as he struggled to think of a sensible reply. Of course there was no reason whatsoever for farmers to become men of learning. In fact, the more he thought about it, the less convinced he felt about his own ambition to have all children in the province educated in the wisdom of sages and poets. He said nothing.

"I guessed so. No answer, ay? But what's a village teacher like you doing going to Chang'an? A hotbed of corrupt officials, prostitutes, money lenders and murderers! No-one in their right mind would go anywhere near the place. Why, they say it's now teeming with foreign devils desperate to seek out the soft underbelly of our motherland, learn where best to strike when the time comes."

"When the time comes?"

"Oh teacher, it does you no good to stare at patterns on scrolls all day long. Open up your eyes to the *real* world!"

"I know more than you think. What do you mean by 'when the time comes'?"

"Time for a change. Pah! It makes no difference to us farmers. Whoever they send to kick our arses, the merchants and stall vendors will always pay as little as they can get away with for our hard-earned produce. The government steals the rest for taxes. More wealth for the powerful rich!"

"You've a very nice house here, farmer," observed Feng, changing the subject. His own humble dwelling could have fitted three times over into the farm house, with room to spare. Farmers had far more money than they owned up to, he thought; they got away with tax evasion on a massive scale; but how to nail them, for they always had ways of rendering assets invisible?

"So! Why Chang'an?"

"Missing Miao girls. Maybe a thousand. From their villages near Three Monkey Mountain and others along the Chang'an road and out to the west. There was a murder. I think it's linked to the missing girls. I have the blessing of our local magistrate to report to the emperor himself. Warn him. And find one girl in particular."

"Why on earth should the emperor be the least bothered about a few missing Miao girls? Or yet another murder? And why should a magistrate send a teacher unless he wanted to get rid of him."

Damn it, I hadn't even thought about that!

"Some more wine, friend!" chuckled the farmer, offering the wine jug. Feng nodded.

"Tell me, have you heard of the White Tiger League?" he asked. "Group of traders with links to the west, I believe."

A frown changed the farmer's jovial, weathered features. He filled Feng's cup and put down the jug. He glanced briefly at his wife who, perhaps from past promptings, stood and ushered the children from the room.

"Tiger tattoo on the back of the right hand? Like it's about to pounce?" the farmer queried. Feng nodded affirmation. "Nothing to do with trade!" the other man added hastily. "But why do you ask?" Suspicion lingered in his frown.

"The murdered man. He was a White Tiger. A merchant too, and a good friend."

"So a teacher of our youth puts two and two together and makes five, huh?"

"You know about them? The White Tigers?"

"Know about them? What farmer doesn't? I'll tell you one thing. They're better dead than alive. Look, I'm not wanting to interfere in your business, but please see common sense. Don't go anywhere near the capital. If you do, just keep quiet about having a friend who was a White Tiger. Besides, there are White Tigers and White Tigers."

"Which means?"

"Which means either way you'll get your throat cut in Chang'an."

"I don't follow."

"A group of brigands that demand money, jade, jewels, gold... anything, from farmers and genuine merchants, even from government officials. Odd thing is, whenever they capture one they make a big thing of his punishment in the capital - usually a public beheading as a lesson to others. But some of us believe the true White Tigers are the emperor's own hit-men.

Out there, pretending to be rebels, turning in anyone they think loyal to the empress's little nephew. The poor unfortunate then gets dragged back to the capital, tattooed with a White Tiger and beheaded with all that ceremony. That's one rumour going around. Mind you, wouldn't make sense *them* getting involved in kidnapping Miao girls, if they *are* the emperor's men. Look, teacher, just forget the whole business."

There was no further mention of White Tigers and Miao girls. Feng and the farmer became steadily merrier as the evening wore on, talking about the iniquity of the new tax laws, the mysteries of the fair sex and the problems of bringing up children.

"A man with a daughter and no wife to guide him? Bad news, Teacher Feng!" announced the farmer on learning the teacher was both widower and proud father of a beautiful daughter. "Sounds like you're in serious need of another woman!"

Another woman?

The idea of removing Meili from his mind and replacing her with another woman, however young and beautiful, was abhorrent. As long as Feier lived, Meili was still with him. His only wish was to do her no more harm by making their daughter unhappy in marriage. Quite how this particular adventure was supposed to bring happiness to the girl had so far eluded him. Perhaps, in his wildest dreams, a reward for saving the emperor's throne from an imposter? This simple farmer had mentioned the empress's nephew. Feng now wished he hadn't, as the man implied, wasted so much of his life bent over scrolls, admiring the calligraphy of the masters, otherwise he'd surely know more about these things.

"No, friend farmer. I don't need another woman. I just need to do the best for the woman I still love even if she's dead. Through my daughter!"

"Her hair is still long although she has the bosom of a woman? Pah! Fourteen, you say?"

"That marriage maker! I tell you, she's evil. I'd rather put Feier at the mercy of the restless *gui* [13] than allow the bitch to condemn the child to a life of misery and servitude."

"Now you're making sense! This trip of yours is all about finding a husband for the girl. What a pity my boys are too young."

---

[13] ghost(s)

Feng chuckled.

"Too young and, well, as you say, what use is a farmer's wife who can only recite our Tang poems and the writings of the master from Qu Fu?"

"Seriously, my learned teacher friend, your daughter would be a lot worse off if you were dead. Then truly she'd be forced to join those women of pleasure in Chang'an to earn enough to fill her belly with food - whilst rich men fill her belly from the other end."

Implying Feier could end up on the streets of Chang'an? Feng's eyes narrowed. He realised the farmer meant well but the man had overstepped the mark.

"I'll turn in, if you don't mind," he announced curtly. "Must leave early tomorrow."

"Hmmm! I see you're still determined to get yourself killed. One less teacher in the world, ay?"

One less teacher? All along, that's how it should have been. One less teacher, not one less mother.

When Feng finally closed his eyes on dangling cobwebs and the dark ceiling, Meili's face remained, her eyes warm and loving.

Another woman? Impossible ... impossible... impossible...

~

Jinjin decided to stay in the cart until they'd reached the Miao village. The road was open and it would be easier to find cover in the village. Besides, he might learn more by listening in to the trader's conversation with the soldiers. If he could find out where they were actually taking the girls then the teacher would be compelled to praise him, take him on as accomplice, teach him more characters, more poetry?

And the ultimate reward?

Jinjin's manly organ stiffened at the thought.

Was the ugly man's daughter *truly* that beautiful? The teacher resembled the backside of a pig, but Wong had gone on and on about the beauty of the man's dead wife. Wong wasn't a man to make up stories. A brush was a brush, a chair a chair and a beautiful girl exactly as spoken. And girls take after their mothers, he'd said. Even though the child's mind would be filled with the poetry and learning of her father, she must be exquisitely beautiful.

The loveliest girl in China?

Jinjin could barely wait to set eyes upon her. He would use every fibre of his body to solve the riddle of the dead merchant and the disappearing Miao girls. The reward of the flesh *would* be his!

7.

Misjudged Enemies, Unlikely Allies

Two White Tiger Leagues? Nonsense, mused Feng, bumping up and down on Rou the mare as she trotted along the Chang'an road. Having left at first light, and paid the farmer handsomely for his hospitality and extra provisions, he ignored the man's advice to turn around and head back to Houzicheng. How ridiculous to suggest the emperor's ministers were creating a White Tiger 'myth' as an excuse to destroy the empress's nephew's power base; though any controversy surrounding the mysterious league of traders made it more likely the emperor would listen to his story about Merchant Chang and the missing Miao girls. But Feng decided he'd had his fill of upstart urchins and ignorant peasant farmers. Even if Chang'an was overflowing with thieves and prostitutes, it remained the emperor's city, a centre of learning where wise men and poets abounded. Should he be refused entry to the palace then he'd scour the poets' quarter for ears that might listen; like those of Jinjin, but without the annoyance of a boy who questioned too freely and gave his opinions however unwelcome. The urchin's encroachment onto the private space of Feier had been the last straw.

Better to keep company with a dumb mare than a runaway peasant boy with a mouth like a flux-smitten arse!

Rou made good speed over the next few days. A fair exchange for Mimi, but why Minsheng had wished to burden him with the heavy-handled sword, he had no idea. The only other life-forms he encountered were over-laden peasants, their care-worn women-folk bearing filthy, snotty infants fixed rigid into bamboo backpacks, and donkey after donkey after donkey. But he hung on to the fearsome weapon thinking it might fetch a reasonable price at a market in Chang'an. After having spent further nights in pitifully humble dwellings along the way, he realised the strings of coins given by Minsheng would be woefully inadequate to fund his return journey. Even after selling the sword he'd be obliged to offer his teaching services for a few weeks before he could return. If only Minsheng hadn't taken the Sung Po scroll, for in Chang'an that might have been worth a small fortune.

Feng made no further mention of the White Tiger League or his true purpose behind travelling to the capital to other farmer hosts. When asked, he said he had secret business that concerned the highest in the land, emphasising that, although a scholar, he was a man of humble means. He should have known better. The ruffians at Wong's inn, Minsheng and the inquisitive farmer that first night, had been right in suggesting he'd wasted his time keeping his nose buried in poetry and the writings of Kong Fuzi. If more street-wise, he'd have known young boys are given unlucky names to ensure evil spirits seeking strong children would be fooled and leave them alone. In China, to reveal the truth in the world outside the schoolroom was an invitation to harbingers of ill-fortune to assume, and act upon, the exact opposite. For them 'poverty' meant limitless wealth. Feng never discovered which farmer sold on the information. So naïve was he that when, a day's ride from Chang'an, a shabbily dressed young man appeared at the edge of the road from nowhere, waving his arms and calling for help, the teacher reined the mare to a halt, slipped down and hurried over to find out what the matter was.

He remembered nothing more - apart from the pain.

~

When Angwan slowed his pace on their return to the Miao village, Feier realised he also wanted to prolong their blissful closeness. Another Miao man accompanying them had gone on ahead to watch over the boys who ran wild amongst clumps of waving bamboo, playing hide-and-seek with invisible *gui*.

Feier's only knowledge of the priest had come from Xiaopeng's girlish talk: a boy able to fight with tigers bare-handed, a master of Chinese chess, who could drink a barrel of rice wine and remain as sober and upright as a monk. As for being a 'priest', Feier knew enough about Miao ways to realise that Angwan officiating at ceremonies in place of his farmer father was not the same as being a Buddhist monk. Not having to worry about his celibacy gave the teacher's daughter a thrill that she tried, but failed, to suppress. She desired to know more - *so* much more - about the man beside her as they sauntered back to the Miao village. She wished for nothing to be left unsaid. His innermost secrets would become hers to treasure and hide, even from *baba*. But how to uncover them, she wondered, glancing shyly at Angwan?

As if reading her mind, the young priest began to open up his past, his future, and his heart. He needed no prompting, and the girl should not have feared disgracing herself with searching questions,

Angwan had been a uniquely bright child. His father, a wealthy farmer, had inherited from the boy's grandfather the right to lead village ceremonies and call on the mountain god to hasten the rains for the rice, and drive away the evil spirits of vermin, pests and prowling beasts. Even as a small child, Angwan would constantly be at his father's side, fetching, carrying, helping in whatever way he could, and the father's pride in his son was evident to all, as clearly as was his disgust with Angwan's elder sister, Little Peach, who was both simple and sickly. But Angwan doted on his sister and a strong bond had developed between them.

It wasn't long before the boy adopted the role of the girl's teacher and protector. From the age of ten he would stand between the twelve-year old girl and her irate father whenever her clumsiness had caused a breakage, or she'd managed to spill his wine, and he would refuse to budge unless the man promised not to beat her. Whether through fear of losing the respect of other villagers, all of whom adored the boy and his adult ways, or of upsetting the ancestors who'd delivered this remarkable child to him, Angwan never found out. With him around, Little Peach was never harmed; because of her younger brother, life was not only bearable, it was enjoyable to the very end.

Eight years before, when the flux swept through every village in the province, Little Peach died. Just fourteen, a good marriage had been planned for her through Angwan. The boy, then twelve, had adopted the role of marriage maker. Everyone knew he would one day take over as village priest. The girl's father would be able to afford a sizeable dowry; although not the prettiest girl in the village, and completely unable to weave or produce any item of clothing anyone would wish to wear let alone buy, Angwan found a good match for her.

She succumbed to the flux four days before the wedding ceremony. Angwan prayed, he wept... he even went to the Buddhist temple near the lotus lake to turn the prayer wheel, for he knew about Buddhist ways from his father's friend, Farmer Li, but nothing could be done. That Little Peach was struck down on the fourth day before her wedding meant the child was doomed, four being the most unlucky of all numbers. Her brother was at her side with their mother, talking to her, telling the stories that she loved, until that very last breath emerged from her thin parched body.

Angwan's anger over his sister's death still showed eight years after the event, but for Feier it filled a cultural gap between them. Her own anger following her mother's death from the same flux had never gone away. Her *baba* always tried to avoid the topic whenever she questioned him, but this young man listened to every word as she set free years of frustration over death, the Buddha and life without a mother. The same illness that had prized each child from the one he or she most loved now seemed to bring them even closer together.

"I have a mother who would love to gain a daughter!" Angwan remarked.

Feier halted and watched as two boys chased one another around the bamboo stems. Why did he say that? And could *she* ever be mother to such lively boys?

"How did you... you know... after your sister died?" she asked, walking on. "Cope?"

The girl nodded.

"Someone appeared in my life," he replied.

Someone?

Feier flashed her distress at him before looking away.

"So different from the others. Clever, with a mind of her own, a smile that melted my insides until they could take whatever shape or pattern *she* might wish for them. And a beauty rarely seen in these parts. Even in Hangzhou she'd be sought after! Although she and I were too young, for she was but a small child then, I knew I could now at last move on, leave my dear sister to her fate and, well, hope that some day… "

"Does Farmer Li know this?" interrupted Feier with bitterness. "You'd surely both be old enough now. Why won't you marry this rare beauty you speak of instead of Xiapeng? Does her father not approve?"

Feier's jealousy of the mysterious, unnamed woman sharpened her voice. It sounded detached, almost rasping. Angwan laughed.

"*He* doesn't know... and neither does she!"

"You shouldn't play games like this. Uncle Li told me Xiaopeng is to be your wife. It's been arranged. This other woman, she'd be no more than a concubine and village people don't have concubines!"

"He told you this, did he? Pah! He and my mother, they have no idea! Xiaopeng will make a good wife for a man wedded to his water buffalo. But me? No way! Why do you think I spent a month in a Buddhist monastery?"

"Why? So, well, perhaps you fear... I don't know... fear for your soul? After death? No path to follow, perhaps?"

"Nonsense! Like I said, her father doesn't know now but soon he will if Fate delivers him back to her. He's a Buddhist. So is she. At heart. There must be nothing about her that is unknown to me when I make my intentions clear. Already I've learned from the monks all I need to about her ways and beliefs."

"This sounds so wrong. Besides, Farmer Li is the only Buddhist in your village."

"Who said she comes from my village?"

Feier remained silent. Now she wished Xiaopeng would return, and this other woman, whoever she was, would disappear forever. If her friend and Angwan should marry, at least she'd have an excuse to continue to see him.

"Feier, I can't believe you don't know who this girl is! After what happened."

"That? Oh no! Please! It's nothing to do with me! I'll hear no more about this. Why, poor Uncle Li would be devastated to hear you speak of it! Not another word, I beg of you!"

"Feier! Every day when you awaken, you hear her. You hear the crane that should be set free. She speaks to you all the time in that pretty head of yours! Since I was twelve and she was six, I've not wished to even look at another girl. Every week she used to come to our village and brighten it up. After she'd left with her father for her own village on the other side of the lotus lake I would long for that day to happen again the next week. A week always seemed far too long to wait, but I learned to be patient."

Feier stood still, staring fixedly at the ground.

"You mock me!" she accused, but there was no anger in her voice; only a fear that none of what she'd heard was true.

"Mock? Why should I do that? You asked for me to speak plainly, so why do you berate me?"

Feier felt confused. The last thing on earth she wanted was to upset the man, but he'd already said enough to split apart her fragile life, alienate those she loved the most and, worst of all, have her beaten to death or banished forever from the province.

"What you say is impossible!" she said before hurriedly taking off again towards the hill that separated them from the Miao village rice fields. There was a determination in her step that belied her inner bewilderment. He called after her, the very words she wanted to hear:

"No path is impossible. You, a Buddhist, should know that!"

She worked hard for Farmer Li over the next two weeks. It seemed to her this might make amends for what the young priest had said. The farmer was amazed at the girl's dedication to duty and daily grind; the rice harvest was gathered at twice the speed his own daughter could achieve, and still the child had the energy to walk to the Han village and back six days a week where she produced exquisite flowing calligraphy with hands chaffed raw by toiling in the fields, cleaning, washing and cooking. Not once did the farmer's daughter complain, and not once did she let down her guard about her secret: that she loved the young priest with a fire fierce enough to consume the largest of celestial dragons. Like everyone else in the village, Farmer Li was bewitched by the girl's deer eyes and gentle smile.

But the girl and the priest shared another secret, one too terrible for either to mention, not even in the privacy of the open road between the two villages.

∼

Jinjin slipped down from the back of the cart after the trader had tethered the old nag to a spreading ginkgo tree at the edge of the Miao village. He crawled on hands and knees and hid behind the tree's broad trunk from where he peered cautiously as Chen Jiabiao dismounted and handed the trader a string of coppers. The trader headed towards the village whilst Chen went to the rear of the cart and removed several sack-cloths, one of which, moments earlier, had been Jinjin's only protection. A voice called out from a pig-shed beside the nearest house. The trader halted. Three guards wearing imperial yellow and purple emerged from the shed and ran to the trader. Strings of coins changed hands, the trader rejoined Chen Jiabiao beside the cart whilst two guards ran back to the pig-shed and the third ran on into the village. The squeals issuing from the shed were definitely not porcine. Soon, each guard appeared with a kicking, struggling bundle draped over his shoulder and ran with it to the cart. Chen Jiabiao wasted no time. He smothered both girls in sackcloths, thus rendering their fraught cries inaudible to anyone further than a few paces away. The guards helped Chen and the trader push the girls into the cart, covering them with more sackcloths. The trader climbed in after them, crouched down and whispered something to the writhing double-humped mound. What he said must have terrified the girls for they immediately went quiet.

There was an agonised shout from the village. The trader looked up. Moments later, the third guard reappeared from beyond the first clutch of village buildings. In one hand he gripped a red-stained sword, a girl's head held firm under his other arm as he dragged her along, backwards. The trader leapt from the cart, ran to meet the guard and covered the struggling child with another sackcloth before roughly tossing her into the cart to join her village sisters. The girl's captor cleaned his sword on the sackcloth, the smeared blood of possibly a father or brother her last link with the Miao village and the only world she and her two friends had ever known.

Chen Jiabiao clambered into the back of the cart as the trader turned the old nag around and coaxed her along the track towards the Chang'an road. After binding the sobbing girls together with rope, he crawled up front to sit beside the trader. Meanwhile, the three imperial guards mounted horses tethered to fencing behind the pig-pen, kicked them into action and sped on past the ginkgo tree and the trader's cart in the direction of the imperial city. Shrieks from the village informed Jinjin the body of a slaughtered village man must have been discovered. The trader whipped the old nag into a laboured trot and Jinjin followed, slinking unseen from tree to tree, more determined than ever to see his plan through. His desire for female beauty aroused, nothing would prevent Fate from delivering to him a girl far more lovely than those pretty Miao villagers.

Out on the road to Chang'an, keeping up with the cart was easy, for the horse soon slowed to a pace befitting her age. The boy's main concern was about being spotted and suspected. He'd already witnessed evidence of these men's brutality. Fortunately, Chen Jiabiao and the trader were too engrossed in conversation to turn round and check on their precious booty, for on stretches of open road he would surely have been seen. They passed through several villages unchallenged. Perhaps, Jinjn wondered, the men were known. Had the White Tiger League already claimed territory on the way to Chang'an? The boy neither cared nor fretted about the distance involved as long as he learned where they were taking the Miao girls. His reward: the right to wed the most beautiful girl in his province – and maybe the whole of China. The emperor would ensure the teacher offered no objection. With the courage of a tiger he could do anything.

The first evening the boy slept in the street. Chen Jiabiao and the trader had entered the courtyard of a small monastery at the edge of town. The boy remembered the teacher's suggestion about certain monks being in collusion with the abductors of Miao girls and wondered whether the place was a safe haven where the captive girls could be fed, bathed and groomed for an uncertain future. Jinjin soon found another street urchin to prick for information. Tempting the lad with a bun stolen from Wong Wenling's kitchen, he fabricated a story about being in the pay of imperial officials to spy on two brigands who had entered the monastery with a cart-load of illegal produce. The boy, a stocky lad named Kong [14], was made to swear he would keep watch on the monastery and awaken Jinjin should they show any sign of wishing to leave town.

---

[14] empty space

Jinjin found a dark, narrow alley within sight of the monastery, where he scoffed Wenling's remaining buns and drank cold tea, checking on the tools he would need: a knife, ink and cloth 'borrowed' from the room where innkeeper Wong would puzzle over his accounts.

~

Feng opened his eyes. He blinked a few times as he tried to make out what it was he was looking at. When last conscious, having just dismounted, he'd been asking a distressed young man at the roadside what the problem was. He tried to raise his head to get a better view then cried out in pain. It seemed as if the back of his head and neck were held fast in the jaws of a tiger, the beast's teeth piercing holes the size of copper coins. He flopped back and felt for Minsheng's money strings. Gone! The magistrate's sword too! How naïve and stupid he'd been!

The light was dim. He fixed on a grey patch above him. Slowly it came into focus, together with the dark object in its centre: a spider clinging to its web, inches from his face. Disturbed by the teacher's attempt to raise his head, the spider crawled to one side and now descended on an invisible thread, legs outstretched, to the floor. Feng twisted his neck as far as the tiger jaw grip would allow, enough to see the little creature hurry off into the darkness.

A spider descending on silk surely signified good fortune sent from Heaven. He was alive. Good fortune enough, until his memory kicked reality into the frame. Feier was back at the Miao village. The unwritten deal with Yueloong had been amicable, but things could change so easily. Should he fail to return with Xiaopeng, his own daughter might become Miao property to be played with and debased, forcing her into a fate worse than anything the mean-minded marriage maker had in store for the girl.

Clutching the back of his aching head, Feng rolled sideways so as to preserve the spider's silken home and found that he was staring down from a straw-strewn stone bed at a filthy stone floor. Where he was, and how he'd got there, was a mystery, but lying on his side he became aware of a new pain, something tearing at his belly.

As his eyes grew accustomed to the low light, he noticed he was wearing a monk's robe.

For a brief period, he wondered whether he'd died, returned to Earth and had already lived half a life as a monk before recalling his former existence, but all became clear after he lowered his legs to the ground, crying in pain. His hands didn't seem to know whether they should reach up to the back of his aching head or journey down to the searing agony across his belly.

An elderly monk appeared at the open doorway of the cell, alarmed by the noise.

"Teacher Feng? At long last! Several times we gave you up for dead, but my brothers and I turned the prayer wheel eight times a day for luck, and I see from your samsara time for rebirth hasn't yet arrived."

"How...?" began Feng, before emitting an anguished howl as the pain from his belly ratcheted up several notches when he attempted to stand. "Aaargh!"

"Wait, friend!" warned the monk. "Not too hasty. Lie back. We must tend to your wounds!"

Feng eased himself back onto the bed of straw. The belly pain reminded him of Merchant Chang impaled with a bamboo stake. It was how the whole thing had started, with young Feier rushing into the school room, alerting him of the gruesome crime. Had *he* also been skewered by a pole? Would 'tending' his wounds mean trying to keep his guts from spilling out?

The monk returned with two others, younger than himself. One held a burning lamp that threw grotesque, moving monk shadows onto stark walls. His companion carried a bowl, with a folded cloth draped over his forearm.

"We must keep it clean, Teacher Feng. You can bite on your robe as we wash the wound."

The senior monk lifted Feng's robe, exposing his belly. The teacher's head jerked back when the man tried to stuff the rough robe cloth into his mouth.

"Just tell me why I'm here," he demanded after spitting out the taste of the cloth.

"Why? I told you. Your destiny gives you another chance! Your attackers must have assumed you were dead."

"Where am I?"

"Xiangjisi Temple."

"Xiangjisi? Near Chang'an?"

"Do I have to say everything twice?"

"But... Ouch!"

The monk, stooped over Feng's bared belly, dabbed away with a wet cloth.

"How... what...?"

"Your name? Easy! We were expecting you."

"But..."

"Your new magistrate, Minsheng, sent word to me as the *sun wu kong*. He should have given you a sword as well as a horse."

"He did... but... Ow!"

"The characters *bai hu*[15]. On your belly. That's why it's so sore. Carved with the sharpened bamboo we found beside you, probably. So many strokes, huh? Should have asked them to carve '*nu*' instead. Only three strokes!"

"White Tiger? I remember stopping to help that young beggar man... But do you mean he...?"

"I mean nothing. Only it's a miracle you're alive. The White Tiger League always carve *bai hu* characters on victims' bellies. As a warning to others - and to annoy the imperial officials."

"But I was many *li* from Chang'an when I stopped. Xiangjisi is less than an hour from the city, right?"

"They've taken to leaving the bodies outside the temples. And we know why."

"Why?"

"Isn't it obvious?"

Feng screwed up his eyes from pain when the monk playfully patted the smarting cuts decorating his belly before pulling the robe back down.

"They reward you teachers too well, huh? Hope you pay your dues to the local monastery!"

"So that's it. The White Tiger League has infiltrated the monasteries. They try to frighten you."

"Try, but don't succeed. You're the first body that's come back from the dead, though. Can you stand?"

---

[15] white tiger

Feng eased himself forwards then stepped down from his bed. Holding on to the younger two men, he took a few stiff steps.

"Brilliant! The *gui* holds on to his corpse! Hungry?"

"Yes. Thirsty too."

"We eat in the refectory. Then you can tell me why the White Tigers wanted you dead."

"Stop!" Feng spotted the murder weapon leaning against the wall. "The bamboo pole... " he began.

"Your attackers' calligraphy brush."

"And the pole they used to kill my friend. I was taking it to Chang'an. To warn the emperor. Why leave it with me and take everything else? And it's all to do with the missing Miao girls. I'm certain."

"Missing Miao girls indeed? Come! No more of your nonsense."

Feng stayed silent as he was helped along a covered corridor lined by small cells then out into a wide courtyard in the centre of which wafted smoke from a stone incense burner before an expressionless, kneeling monk. The man looked up and stared at Feng. For a moment the teacher felt like a pig being dragged half-dead to a slaughter house, the gazing monk trying to work out whether his karma would return him as pig again or human.

"Over there," said the *sun wu kong*. "The refectory. Our food is simple but wholesome."

With great gentleness, the younger monks led him up a short flight of steps, through a wide doorway into a bright, spacious hall packed with shaven-headed monks seated around circular tables. Several lowered their chopsticks and gazed as Feng was eased onto a drum stool. The elderly monk positioned himself beside the teacher whilst one of the other men fetched a bowl and chopsticks for their guest. In the centre was a deep platter of thick, wide noodles, another of vegetables and a wooden board heaped with mantou buns.

"Afraid you'll miss your rice here, I see?" remarked the monk. "And your pork!"

Feng had read about the diet of the north, the noodles and the buns. The smell of the food before him was almost too good to be true.

"What are you waiting for? Fill the teacher's bowl!" commanded the old man before one of his underlings hurriedly snatched the bowl from under Feng's nose and filled it with slippery noodles and a mound of steaming vegetables.

"When you've food in your scarred belly you might think up something better than 'disappearing Miao girls'. Seems there are others out looking for you. Like the young White Tiger who passed by yesterday. That's how we know who you are."

Feng was only half paying attention and more focused on his stomach crying out for noodles and vegetables. When his bowl was empty, he reached for a Mantou bun, but the monk grabbed his wrist with strength surprising for one so old.

"'Has he not passed by?' asked the boy," the monk said. "'An overfed teacher called Feng? Carries a murderous bamboo pole. Full of crazy stories about missing Miao girls.' I saved your life by keeping you hidden, but he just wouldn't take 'no' for an answer. Talked non-stop, too. Accompanied by a silent rough-looking youth with murder in his eyes. We had to forcibly evict them when the one who talked at a gallop refused to tell me what his true purpose was. So, come now, teacher! Your life has been preserved once. We need to know what's going on."

Feng withdrew his hand. So Jinjin had betrayed him! He thought about Merchant Chang ending up dead after paying a visit to the local Buddhist Temple – assuming he *had* gone there – and of Magistrate Minsheng playing mole in the monastery – if that *had been* his true purpose for pretending to be a monk. He pictured the bodies of White Tiger League victims placed gruesomely on display outside Chang'an temples, his included. Never before had he felt so utterly detached from what he'd always regarded as his karma on the path to enlightenment: simply to bring knowledge to the poor and the humble, girls included, who made up the real China. Why not admit defeat and concoct some elaborate story like the poets of old, beg for a horse to take him back to Houzicheng and the Miao village and to Feier?

He knew why. Until recently, his chief purpose in life had been to find a worthy match for his daughter. Now this could only be achieved by solving the accursed business of the disappearing Miao girls and gaining favour with the emperor.

～

The thing she'd so dreaded happened.

The brightening sky in the east heralded the approach of dawn as she stood early one morning at the door of the farmer's home, aglow with anticipation of another daily walk to the Han village and back with Angwan. All was well with her life. She enjoyed both teaching and working in the fields for farmer Li; the villagers were gracious towards her, respectful of her learning for one so young… and she was in love. Angwan, too, it seemed.

He'd almost told her as much. So why was it not *him* leading the troupe of gabbling boys that emerged from beyond the bamboo grove that day? The sound of their excited voices growing from the silence always gave her a curious thrill, a reassurance, for it reminded her of their burgeoning love. Ugly maybe to others, the children's shrill voices had seemed like music serenading the twelve *li* dawdle to the Han village side by side with Angwan. When she saw it wasn't Angwan who led the boys that morning, but Old Xiang, Xiaopeng's crabby uncle who'd not yet learnt how to smile during his long and miserable life, her heart dropped like a falling temple bell. By way of explanation, he merely grunted at her in Miao.

No further words were exchanged as they trailed behind the unruly caterpillar of chattering children, past the rice fields, over the humpy hill and beyond the lotus lake and the monastery to Feier's village. Old Xiang left her and the children in the schoolroom of her father's house, and Feier struggled to concentrate during the lessons. The children, Han and Miao, sensed this and took advantage, with a whispering that crescendoed to shouting and giggling. They started to throw things about. A mix of relief and trepidation gripped the girl when Old Xiang returned with village elder, Hu.

Hu took her to one side whilst Old Xiang instilled fear into the children. The grumpy uncle told them he'd been listening to their racket in the courtyard and several would feel the full force of his bamboo rod on their backs when they got home. Tears of shame trickled from Feier's pretty eyes even before Hu explained the reason for his presence.

This had nothing to do with her lack of control during class. She learned that the mean-faced marriage maker had found a match for her and she was to pin up her hair. In her father's absence, he, the most senior village elder, had the authority to see her married off. Unless the teacher returned within three moons, she would be wedded to Zhang Tsiense, a miserable old cripple whose wife, it was rumoured, died from overwork and beatings. The man wanted to produce a son before joining his ancestors.

When they got back to the Miao village the girl knew that Angwan's absence, Old Xiang's presence and the arranged shock-betrothal to the cripple were linked: retribution for failing to hide her passion for the young Miao priest. How could her beloved father ever forgive her?

~

The sun had already risen when Kong returned the following morning with a bundle of food and a jug of water. The water was not for drinking but for something Jinjin had planned, although he'd have preferred a sharper knife than the blunt implement 'borrowed' from Wenling. Sitting cross-legged on the ground, his tools – knife, shallow dish and ink block – spread out on a cloth in front of him, he carved out a wedge of ink and worked it into a paste with dribbles of water. The other boy, transfixed, stared as Jinjin began painstakingly to cut an image onto the back of his right hand, working the ink paste into the red lines. Being left-handed gave him an advantage. First the head with its open jaws, the teeth, the eyes, then the curves of the crouched body and those powerful limbs preparing for the death leap. Finally, the curled-up tail, that instrument of balance and of warning.

"A tiger?" Kong sounded puzzled.

"Not just a tiger. A *white* tiger!" Jinjin announced, proudly taking in the beauty and power of his creation. With his keen memory, he knew every detail to be exact. The copy was perfect.

"But why?"

"Why? Have you no pretty young girls in your town here? Has your jade stem never once been stirred?"

"Yeah, all the time," replied Kong. "But a girl for me… an orphaned urchin? Any that get thrown into the street are snapped up more quickly than a snake could strike a rat. Best I can ever hope for will be some worn out old hag. Keep my eyes closed then, I shall, and imagine what she might have looked like in another life."

Jinjin grinned.

"Well, this tiger will get me the most beautiful girl in our province. No! I'll be bold. In the whole of China. Her father's a teacher."

"Wow! Can I have one too? Er… one of those tiger things, I mean."

Jinjin looked the lad up and down. At long last someone who respected him. Kong had large hands, seemed strongly built and eager to please.

"Could be a death warrant," Jinjin replied.

"A girl? Can you die having sex?"

Jinjin chuckled. What a great and tragic poem that would make, his life drained from him with his jade stem thrust deep inside Teacher Feng's legendary daughter!

"I think not. You can only get a greater *qi* force by being with a girl," he answered. "See, there are those who might wish to see all White Tigers dead as there are others who would kow-tow to us. If you join me you could die - or you might gain riches way beyond a night with a pretty little street girl."

The other boy's eyes betrayed uncertainty as he pulled up his sleeve and offered Jinjin the back of his right hand.

"Of course, there's a third possibility," Jinjin teased whilst carefully fashioning an identical tiger on the back of Kong's hand. Kong, wincing, looked up anxiously. "The White Tigers might kill you."

"But…?"

"A fox disguised as a chicken invading a farmer's yard is one thing, but two chickens disguised as foxes creeping into their den…?"

"I don't understand."

"You don't have to. The less you know the better. Just bundle our provisions and wait outside the monastery gate. Let me know when two men and a cart set off."

"What's in the cart?"

"Petals."

"Petals?"

"Yeah! Petals! Now go!"

Kong left. When he returned he was carrying a pole loaded with provisions across his shoulders.

"They just came out. Heading in the direction of Chang'an," he announced excitedly.

Jinjin and his newly acquired 'servant' soon caught up with the cart. They followed from a safe distance, though the trader and Chen Jiabiao were far too engrossed in animated conversation to notice a pair of urchins trailing them. A cover in the back of the cart rose up like a *gui* as one of the 'petals' struggled to find a more comfortable position, and Jinjin explained his plan to Kong: they would masquerade as White Tigers after arriving at their destination, find out where the girl Xiaopeng was being held, make their way to Chang'an and seek out Teacher Feng.

It seemed so easy. The boys followed the cart for several days, scrounging water, begging for or stealing food, finding shelter wherever they could. Jinjin treated his servant as would any mandarin, bossing, teasing and criticising.

"Shhhh!" he warned when they emerged from a dense wood to behold a vast camp of tents spread out on the plain below.

His wonder was tainted with fear, for it was a terrifyingly magnificent sight. Rows of grey tents of varying sizes striped the lush green meadows to the blue hills beyond. There were paddocks of horses, beautiful creatures that bore little resemblance to the old nag that pulled the cart full of 'petals' now winding its way down the path that descended towards the plain. Clutches of spears stood proud, like bristling stems of death, and all over the camp were scattered groups of warriors, tens of thousands of them, talking, resting, walking about or testing their weapons.

The rebel army!

~

Feng withdrew his hand. The temptation of a mantou bun would have to wait.

"I'm a man of words. And of poetry and arts. Like our Emperor," he said, watching carefully for some sort of a response on the other man's face. There was none. The monk's visage could have been carved from wood.

"Indeed! A man of great learning," the *sun wu kong* finally agreed.

"Not everyone sees it that way, but..." Feng paused, looking for a change in the wooden face.

"So you think those villains, the White Tigers, are up to something?" asked the monk.

"The monasteries… like this one. You know…"

"I know nothing!" interrupted the old monk. "But I'm all ears. Monks from other monasteries where some seem to have strayed from The Way tell me things. About comings and goings. Disappearances."

"The White Tiger League?"

"I was hoping you'd give *me* the answer!"

"Look, the only thing I'm certain of is that people are stealing Miao girls. Who they are I mean to find out."

The face of stone transformed. Wrinkles appeared, the lips, the eyes, everything changed. The monk was smiling. He broke out into a series of staccato guffaws, a curious noise akin to a pig being slaughtered, as he slapped his knees in mirth.

"Stealing Miao girls? Now why would anyone want to do that, huh? Chickens, maybe, oxen, yes… but *Miao* girls? Teacher Feng, you amuse me." His expression changed, the stony visage returned. "And you annoy me," he added. "*You* know why that young White Tiger monkey was looking for you, why you were left for dead. And I believe you're aware of the curse that's spreading through our temples. We're dangerously close to the imperial court here. Next thing, the court guards will sweep through our monastery like a swarm of farmers with scythes cutting a field of corn. They'll show no mercy if they suspect us monks of being involved with the White Tigers. Give me the truth, teacher. Tell me what's happening!"

Feng stared at the bowl of Mantou buns with disinterest, his appetite gone.

"I thank you for saving my life. The boy you mention - the one with the verbal flux - he… he seemed..." The teacher paused. How could he have been so wrong about Jinjin? He'd not even noticed the white tiger tattoo on his hand, but in truth he hadn't looked and with the state he'd been in that evening he could easily have missed it; or perhaps the boy had kept the tattoo hidden under layers of dirt. As for innkeeper Wong and his bubbly wife, were they also in on the intrigue and using the urchin as a fact-finder? But why had Wenling been so reluctant for him to go to Chang'an? Why was the innkeeper's wife so overly concerned for his safety as to advise him against visiting the capital of the heaven-sent-guardian of the central kingdom on Earth? Nothing made sense.

"From your description he has to be the young boy I met in Houzi-cheng. Can't have been much older than my own daughter who ... "

"Yes, your daughter. He mentioned her. Said he was seeking you out for her sake. To give her a better life. And he said ... " The smile returned. "Said she's the most beautiful girl in China."

Feng frowned. Jinjin had never met Feier.

"He's little more than eighteen, at a guess, but seems to think he's old-er. *Much* older!"

"And with the tongue of a brigand twice that age!" interjected the monk. The teacher nodded.

"I thought he might help me. It was he who suggested the White Tiger League had been planning something. Said he knew about the disappear-ing Miao girls. So why? Also said he'd followed a trader with a tattoo on his hand. So why come after me... unless ... "

"We do know *something* about them! Traders working for the empress and her nephew in the west. Government spies, perhaps?"

"The boy, a government spy? Jinjin, as he calls himself, said he'd spied on this man who paid an imperial guard to capture a girl in a Miao village. On the Chang'an road. Only he might not have been a true guard of the emperor, Jinjin thought. And my murdered friend, a certain Merchant Chang... "

"Merchant Chang?" The monk's surprise betrayed recognition.

"You know him? Travels widely. I mean *travelled*. Impaled with a bam-boo pole. The one in my cell. Did you realise he was... ?"

"Never met him!" interrupted the monk, avoiding eye contact. Feng could tell he was lying, but was beginning to understand the man's strange behaviour. Why should he believe anything from a stranger left for dead by the White Tiger League at the monastery gate?

"You see, it was the first time I'd heard about the White Tigers," Feng continued, "when I told my story to that little dog of a street boy and mentioned my dead friend's tattoo. But what he said - and what we dis-cussed - all made sense. Elements in the League... not my late friend, of course, but others who have connections through trade with the west... they might be involved in a plot to overthrow the emperor."

"You're a dangerous man indeed!"

"Not at all! Just caught up in this mess because of my karma. To honour my dead friend and my live Miao friend whose daughter's gone missing. Just thirteen. Small breasts. A lovely child, if a bit simple. You see, by telling Chang about the missing girls, asking him in good faith to help the Miao people, I've caused one death and a fate worse than death for a widowed father."

"Wait a minute. A White Tiger trader gets murdered by one his own then … "

"No, Chang was *not* in on this! I'm sure of it. Most merchants are hardworking, law-abiding. They bring wealth to our mother-land. But I begged him to inform Nobleman Chen and the *sun wu kong* at our monastery."

"The monastery near Houzicheng?"

"Yes. Suggested it because you monks seem to know everything!" Feng had regained the strength to give vent to his scorn.

"Everything? We only know what passes through our temples. And whatever truths you wretched outsiders tell us. Like you're finally trying to do."

"Well, whether it was the *sun wu kong* at the monastery near my village, or Chen, or both, I've no idea. My daughter discovered the merchant's body near the lotus lake, the poor girl. Thick with flies, it was. No-one in our village seemed to care. Guess they knew he was my friend, a man of the world too and, well, there are one or two problems back home with a marriage maker in league with a devil… because of disagreements over my views…"

"Your *views*?"

"On education. Treating girls as equals. Teaching them to read and write as well as any boy."

"I see our Buddhist ways have touched your heart, Feng. And that the master from Qu Fu hasn't completely warped your senses with his didactic aphorisms. Strange how even those who follow the way of the Dao seem to misinterpret *yin* and *yang*, don't you agree, wise man of education? Claim their *qi* force will only flow strongly when the *yin* is down there in the Earth with the darkness of ignorance and the *yang* up on top enlightened by closeness to Heaven. Are you a Buddhist, teacher Feng?"

Feng's mind filled with thoughts of Meili's swift and cruel death, Feier's distrust and fear of all religion, and of Minsheng's criticism of his failure to pay dues to the monastery.

"I was… once," he replied.

"Good, good! So *you* must be the teacher they all speak of. A little village school open to both girls and boys, right?"

"*All* speak of? No, that can't be. I run two small schools. A second one for Miao children. To learn the tongue and writing of the emperor must surely widen their prospects."

"And open up paths, teacher. Paths to follow! It's what we try to teach the ignorant peasants but so few understand!"

"But you do understand what I'm saying? I have to warn the emperor. If these men are murderers there's no telling what'll happen to our beloved mother country should this…" He narrowed his eyes at the monk who knew so much more than he'd let on. "Look, the empress's nephew, I've heard it said… is in with a power-hungry Governor in the far west. And the disappearing Miao girls are either a distraction or…"

He paused.

"Or what?"

"An idea I had. The tree of a thousand petals in the imperial palace. Each Miao girl - and they say only the pretty ones are stolen - each would be like the petal of a gigantic imperial flower. Combined with his *yang*, their *yin* could produce an overwhelming *qi*. *And* a future emperor's ready-made nest of beautiful concubines! Maybe he reckons few Han folk would worry about vanishing Miao girls. Certainly seemed true in our village. No-one but me and Feier seem to care back home."

"Hmm! I see you've the imagination of a poet, Teacher Feng. That boy - Jinjin, as you call him - he, too, claims to be a poet. Read me a poem about your daughter."

Feng sprang to his feet, stung by anger, fists clenched.

"That little ruffian knows *nothing* about my daughter!" he shouted. Rows of shaven heads turned and stared like interrupted grazing cattle. "I wouldn't let him within a hundred *li* of my child! She… she's being looked after by my Miao farmer friend. The one who lost his daughter to White Tiger thieves. She's keeping the school going. And helping him with the rice harvest… looking after his house… cooking…"

Poor girl! How could she ever learn to cook without a mother to teach her.

"A slave, huh?"

"I *will* keep my side of the deal and find the man's daughter. But only

101

the emperor can help me now. As for you monks, I thank you again for sending that that little upstart on his way and saving my life, but I really must leave!"

"And I must help you! Sit down teacher! Let's think things out. To-morrow will find you in Chang'an, maybe in the imperial palace. One false step and you'll lose your head. Even our peaceful emperor who loves art and poetry has heads stuck on poles. But as you say, if his first wife's nephew succeeds in overthrowing him, anything might happen!"

The teacher, uneasy, sat down again.

"Eat up! Feed that belly of yours!"

The old monk pushed the bowl of mantou buns towards Feng. The teacher took one and hungrily bit into it.

"I had a horse when I was attacked," he said through a mouthful of mantou.

"A horse no-can-do, but food and money, no problem. Anything to save our dear emperor. But beware, my teacher friend. Why should that boy have deceived you if he wanted you dead? I assume *he* was the one who set you up. Arranged for those thugs to jump you. Who else knew you'd be on the Chang'an road?"

"Could be," agreed Feng reluctantly. "On the other hand, might've been a farmer who put me up the first night. I told him the whole story. Maybe he sent word ahead. He seemed convinced I was wealthy. Kept moaning on and on about the hard lives of farmers."

"Don't I know it! We get nothing from farmers here. But they also hate whoever's on the dragon throne. I can't see one risking everything to back the emperor's nephew. No, it'll be that White Tiger rascal. Came to check on your body perhaps, make sure you'd been marked? Maybe this was planned… for you to be the corpse closest to the imperial palace. The first White Tiger victim dumped near the South Gate of Chang'an! Doesn't that make you feel good?"

He grinned mock humour at the teacher.

"Whoever attacked me, I've no time to lose. And in Chang'an, do you have any contacts? Buddhists who might…" He paused awhile as he recalled Feier's horrified face after finding Chang's mutilated body. "…who might have renounced *all* killing? Who would prefer an emperor more skilled with the calligraphy brush than the sword?"

"I was coming to that. Master Tsu. Two blocks from the palace. Teaches brush painting to mandarins' children and their women. Like you, he sees equality in *yin* and *yang* and is very much in favour at court. He was here yesterday. I told him about you - when you stopped being a corpse - and I told him I'd send you his way if my suspicions are confirmed." The teacher again searched the *sun wu kong's* unreadable face for explanation but saw nothing. The man enlightened him: "That you're up to your neck in something way beyond anything you could hope to understand."

That night, Feng ate and slept well in more comfortable quarters. The confinement of the cell had merely been a precaution before they'd sized him up and his precise purpose and place in the cosmic way of things was uncovered. Now, the teacher and the most senior monk were not only friends but allies. Apart from Feier and Li Yueloong, others, like the magistrate and innkeeper Wong, were either unknown quantities or treacherous enemies such as Jinjin. Here, in a monastery on the outskirts of Chang'an where he knew no-one, he no longer felt alone, and the old *sun wu kong* appeared to understand him almost better than he understood himself.

8.

A Flower, a Petal and a Fool

Feier hadn't the courage to ask about Angwan. Besides, there seemed little point in finding out what had happened for her fate had been sealed. Obviously Farmer Li assumed neither the teacher nor his own beloved daughter would be seen again, and she, a Han girl in a Miao community, had become a liability; perhaps more so since he claimed to embrace that great religion from beyond the mountains to the west. Other villagers, particularly Uncle's grouchy old brother Xiang might see the girl, who was also supposed to be a Buddhist, as a threat.

She disliked Xiang almost as much as she'd hated Chang. Although there was none of the predatory ogling or unwanted touches she'd suffered from the merchant, Xiaopeng's uncle was forever looking at her through cold, questioning eyes. He must have known of her love, and this surely had something to do with both Angwan's disappearance and the marriage maker's decision.

Of Uncle Li's own feelings, Feier was uncertain. As with religion, his loyalties seemed divided. They no longer spoke together of the past, of her father and Xiaopeng; instead, for much of their time spent together he sat and watched as she cooked and washed for him and they always ate in silence. But she felt sorry for a man forced to grieve so inwardly.

"Feel proud that the teacher tried, Feier," Li said on one occasion. So he still had respect for her father.

But there were times when his eyes told her things that caused her to fear for her innocence. She recognised a fire similar to the flames that flickered in the lecherous eyes of the merchant before they got extinguished by that bamboo pole, flames that had threatened to lay waste to her childhood. The Miao farmer's fire would fix on her and she would blush and look away, busying herself with things that needed no attention. She would nervously wait for the man to retreat outside to the pig pen, and under the straw on her stone bed was hidden a knife. One night, after he was gone, she'd sharpened it to a point so keen it could have cut through the hide of a dragon. Confused, frightened and very much in love, she vowed she would use it against any man who wished to take the only thing she had left to give to Angwan: her virtue. And she'd lie awake thinking in what ways she might give pleasure to the young priest, mentally yielding every fibre of her body and soul to those hands whilst they caressed her milk-soft skin and traced the goddess curves that of late contoured her body like magical hills rising mysteriously from a freshly sown landscape. She could almost feel his strong fingers stroking that body, and in her dreams it would happen...

$\sim$

The cart approached the plain below, the two men up front unaware of four young eyes trained on them and their covered cargo from atop the grassy mound. At the edge of the camp, Chen Jiabiao and the trader were met by a group of soldiers in imperial uniform and, after a brief exchange, leapt from the cart as three guards lifted kicking bundles from the back and ran with them to one of the tents. Dozens of other similar carts were scattered about the camp which hummed with activity. Standing away from all the action was a lone, broad, squat figure wearing elaborate armour and an absurdly high, plumed helmet.

"Kicking petals, huh?" chuckled Kong.

Jinjin grinned as his mind peeled off the covers, and more, from the captured girls.

"Lively, yeah! Hope the empress's nephew appreciates jumping petals. But just look at all those carts. If the teacher's correct we've not much time left," said the other boy. "Three girls to each cart - can't be far short of a thousand by now!"

"A thousand? What's he going to do with them all?"

Jinjin chuckled.

"Now there's a good question! If only I had the experience to answer, but I've heard them say you can try out different positions. Maybe even a thousand… I don't know! You see, the teacher - the one with the beautiful daughter - he seems to think a thousand Miao girls in the nephew's possession will be an excellent excuse for deposing the emperor. Like owning the imperial tree of a thousand petals and more, he reckons. Maybe he'll use some of the petals to pay off the generals who fight for him. Whatever, I'm going to get one little petal back to win a flower! The Miao girl's name's Xiaopeng, though chances are they'll have changed it in that place down there."

"What about me? Don't I get a girl for helping you?"

Jinjin gave his new friend a playful punch in the side.

"You can have Xiaopeng - after she's been entered a thousand times. Mind you, they go all wrinkly when they've been used that often."

"Don't believe you! How old is she?"

"Never asked. Hush… get down! That guard might spot us. Mistake you for a monkey, perhaps!"

The boys prostrated themselves then crawled backwards from the brow of the hill. The guard's attention was diverted and he disappeared into the nearest tent. "What we do is this," whispered Jinjin. "I go straight up to the fat guy with the funny helmet…"

"You're joking! Do you think he's a general?"

"Haven't a clue. Looks important, though. We'll do better going to the top fellow here. It's the underlings who'll give us a hard time. Use us for chopping practice! But watch your tongue!"

"Chopping practice?"

"Heads! Choppity-chop! Particularly empty ones like yours." Jinjin observed fear pale his companion's face. "Don't worry," he added. "Jinjin could talk his way out of a grave if he had to!"

"What are you going to say? Give me a girl called Xiaopeng, please?"

"You've no imagination, Kong! Stay close, watch me and don't say a word. Remember, you're mute! Got it? Or I really will cut out your tongue."

They scrambled down the slope, Jinjin in the lead, and were spotted by a guard who lowered his spear on their approach. Kong froze but Jinjin continued to stride boldly up to the warrior. Clasping his right hand over his left, ensuring the White Tiger tattoo was clearly visible, he gave the puzzled guard a short bow as he'd often observed others do at Wong's inn, low enough to show he recognised the man's authority, but shallow enough to indicate his own superior standing. He watched the man's eyes fix on his fist then falter. Jinjin's memory had never yet failed him, but for a few awful moments he wondered whether he'd got the tail of the tiger wrong. Should it have been more flicked up at the end? Could he have been that careless in detail? He gave a further bow, a little lower, shaking his cupped fist up and down to blur the image of the beast.

"I come with a warning for the leader of the forces of the intended emperor," he announced. 'Intended' seemed the correct word.

As he stood waiting, his eager, bright eyes settled upon the glazed face of the guard whilst an inner voice questioned why he'd ever got mixed up in something so outside his control, teasing him to turn and run back up the hill. But the point of the man's spear would have had no difficulty finding his heart through his back; also, the imagined face of the teacher's daughter – a face that haunted his every waking moment – was there on an imagined pillow of love, not a hand's breadth from his, her naked breasts soft against his bared chest.

"Will you take me to his general or should I arrange for your head to be displayed on that spear of yours?" cautioned Jinjin, spurred on by mental breasts to bravery beyond madness. Uncertainty displaced the glaze in the eyes of the warrior. He shifted his spear to the other hand.

"Your business, young fool?" he demanded.

"Now d'you think I'd be telling a dressed-up peasant?"

Jinjin, who could perfectly mimic the voice of an official, knew from the man's accent that's all he was.

"What about *him*?" the soldier asked, nodding at the other boy, statue-still, further up the hill.

"A mute! Carries my documents. Can't write, so no risk to us if the present emperor's pigs capture him, huh?"

A smile curled the soldier's lips as he lowered his weapon.

"Pigs! You're right there. The bastards killed my father when he refused to give up all the grain he had that year of the drought. The emperor's got no control over his pigs. Only cares about painting birds and flowers, some say. How can any man respect an emperor like that?"

Paint her! That's what I'll do. Paint my flower, breasts included, and keep the picture hidden till I see her for real!

"How, indeed?" agreed Jinjin. "And the pigs are still in Chang'an snuffling out so-called traitors, the very men who would save China from her real enemies. But perhaps the White Tiger League could do with a few pigs of its own, ay? Sniff out traitors of the intended emperor."

The soldier frowned and Jinjin grinned, realising the man now felt himself slipping dangerously close to his intellectual limit.

"You mean...?"

"Let's say I've information that should concern he who would next sit upon the dragon throne. Back there's your pig!"

The soldier gazed at the boy on the slope, failing to notice Jinjin's trembling hands and shaking knees.

"This way," he said at last.

Jinjin beckoned to Kong who followed at a distance as he was led to the high-helmeted man. His confidence gradually returned when he tried to imagine himself back at Wong's inn in Houzicheng and the general yet another of those passing officials wary of all men behind their backs. The boy's gift with words was his only weapon but to raise the spectre of doubt was a strategy he'd seen reap rewards on the verbal battlefield of Wong's place.

He bowed twice the depth he'd offered the guard, turning to ensure, with a nod, that Kong copied him. The other boy's head nearly touched his knees. The guard tried to explain the boys' unsolicited presence but a flick of a wrist from the general silenced him.

Although short, General Ma was an imposing man assisted in height by his tall helmet. His well-trimmed, short black beard and moustache seemed out of keeping with the girlish heaven-tickling plumage topping the helmet. Lurking behind unblinking, knife-cut slits, a pair of steel eyes studied Jinjin with the aloofness of a god who had little time to spare for mortal affairs. One hand rested on the hilt of a heavy sword hanging from his waist.

Instinct caused the boy to drop to his knees and elbows. Leaning forwards, he pressed his face onto the ground.

"Most esteemed general," he began, spluttering into the dirt. "I have..."

Speech abandoned him when the general erupted into a series of hoarse guffaws. He expected his head to be instantly detached from his body.

"Stop grovelling, you young monkey! Life's too short for formalities. Yours, anyway! Stand up if you've something to tell me. And make it snappy."

Jinjin stood and tried to remember the words he was about use before fear had wiped his mind clean.

"Wait a minute, you're little more than a child. Barely off your mother's breast - and yet a White Tiger Trader?"

Suspicion hovered from behind those eye slits.

"I… I was put to work at an inn in Houzicheng, most esteemed defender of our ancestors' glorious land. To find out things for the League of White Tigers. Which I did. At the command of Merchant Chang."

Lying was a novel experience for the boy and he rather enjoyed the way it gave freedom to his imagination.

"Chang? Never heard of him! Look I'll soon have a war to get on with. D'you know what that means? Pfff! You civilians! Find out things indeed! Money and Miao girls is all we need now - and the luck of the White Tiger of the West. They just brought in the last three girls so nothing can stand in our way. When the monks have done their bit…"

"Monks?" interrupted Jinjin. Pricked by curiosity, he needed to know how monks fitted into the story.

"Securing the monasteries for us. With the help of you lot. Warnings to their *sun wu kongs*. Hey… who is this Merchant Chang, anyway?"

The slit eyes seemed to focus on Jinjin's tattooed hand and the boy prayed his memory of the tiger had served him well.

"Murdered!" he replied quickly.

"Murdered? A *true* White Tiger trader? Not an imperial devil in disguise? And by whom?"

"That's what I intend to find out." The boy glanced back at Kong who was still lying face down. "My servant's mute and can't write so he's no danger to us but…" He cast a glance in the direction of the soldier standing rigid beside him.

The general seemed to waiver for a brief moment as he studied the bold young urchin, then burst into laughter.

"Leave us!" he commanded his underling. "If a child could kill the great General Ma, why, I'd no longer deserve to command our new emperor's forces! Ha ha ha!"

With a hand far too large for his short body, he brusquely pushed aside the guard before the man had a chance to take his leave and display the respect due to the man heading an army that spilled across the plain as far as the mountains that formed nature's barrier to the imperial city; an army easily capable of wiping out the emperor's forces.

Hills to the south and west and mountains to the north...

Jinjin made a mental note of the camp lay-out.

"The man who just arrived with those last three girls," he said quietly. "He's called Chen Jiabiao."

He observed the general's body language for the eye slits told him nothing. The man's hand opened and closed over the hilt of his sword. Jinjin knew something was wrong.

"What is this impudence? D'you think I don't know Nobleman Chen? Why, he provides us with girls by the village-full! If you're suggesting..."

"We trailed him. All the way from Houzicheng. My teacher at the inn there warned me. About Chang's murder... and Chen's part in it. The merchant was onto him, you see. Had to be eliminated, I suppose."

"Onto him? For what reason?"

Jinjin knew this man could not afford to put a foot wrong; he was listening.

"I think we should talk somewhere more private," was the boy's answer. He had to somehow alter the flow of words. *He* should be the listener, not the other way around. Nevertheless, lying was beginning to flow more freely. Perhaps he might turn the whole exercise into a game of chess as he'd seen men play at Wong's. He'd watched so much Chinese chess he considered himself an expert, although he'd never yet played his own hand. *What* he said would depend on the general's words; *how* he said it could influence the other man's words.

"Over there," indicated the general, nodding at the longest tent. "I've chosen the tent with the prettiest ones - not that I can make much use of my own jade stem." He squinted mischief at Jinjin through those narrowed eye slits. "If only, huh? Had a girl, yet, little monkey? Seem too much of a puppy to me!"

Jinjin said nothing as he walked with the general to his tent, Kong keeping a respectable distance behind them. It was painfully true. He knew *nothing* about girls, but his time would come, and with the most beautiful girl in China. Then the general and others – those ignorant drinking companions at Wong's inn – they'd no longer laugh at him. He, Jinjin would become Lord of the Jade Stem [16]. It's what this whole business was about, proving his worth to the teacher, allowing him no reason to give up the beautiful child to some worthless village idiot. The boy was beginning to see sense in the plan of the empress's nephew and to understand how dominion over the *yin* would set free the *qi* force of his *yang*. Having renounced all connection with his father, family name included, he would soon have the *qi* of a man of means and importance. Even General Ma would be forced to bow low to him.

As soon as they entered the long tent, the sweet, heady scent of virgins enveloped him. At Wong's place, the occasional presence of a young woman, usually a whore, would lighten his heart whilst her smell, as he served her, would excite that part of him that now stirred at the mere thought of the girl's name: 'Feier'. But here, in a tent full of girls, most untouched by men – forty, fifty, maybe more – his lungs could barely get enough of the air caressed by their virgin bodies. Why there should be such a strong fragrance about the Miao girls, he had no idea, nor did he care whether it was the oils and perfumes with which they adorned themselves, or whether, like flowers, they radiated some sort of intoxicating nectar to trap the unwary *yang*. He only wished to stand and allow its allure to play with his nostrils. The general sensed his confusion as his eyes flitted from one pretty face to another along a row of passive, reclining, silk-clad maidens.

"Now that is one thing you should never do, little monkey-come-tiger cub! Stare so! Either pass them by or take one for sport. But try that and the new emperor will feed you to the pigs! Mind you, that young one over there…"

He pointed to a particularly enchanting, shy girl whose timid, questioning, tear-stained eyes seemed to implore Jinjin to release her from torment.

"She comes from the other side of Houzicheng. Weeps for her *baba* every night. Why are these girls so stupid, huh? With a face like hers, she'll be one of the first to be entered by the new man, yet still she cries out for

---

[16] Jade Stem (*yu jing*) is a Daoist reference to the penis (also *yin jing* in pinyin).

the mean-minded, miserable peasant who just happened to sire her! I simply do not understand women! I *would* understand you, though, should you make a grab for her... but please don't try. For some strange reason I like you and would hate to be the one to remove your head! Ha ha! Not before you've told me the truth, anyway!"

"At least tell me her name. So I can say it in bed when I'm... erm... you know," implored Jinjin, feeling bolder. The general laid his broad hand on Jinjin's shoulder.

"What I really like about you, boy, is your total lack of fear. I can teach a soldier how to fight, but I can't tell his knees to stop trembling in battle. Remind me to test you with the sword, ay? We need men of courage!"

"What's her name? The one who cries for her father."

"That one? Oh, they all have new names. Flowers, of course. But," he chuckled, "I know *her* old name because she cries it out every night when she weeps for her *baba*. 'Your little Xiaopeng is here, *baba*! Please take me home. Please... *please!*' If I wasn't a soldier it might make me weep myself to hear her, but as it is... well, just makes me grow bigger where it matters, see?"

He stood legs astride and looked wistfully down at his crutch before again bursting into laughter. Jinjin, meanwhile, made a mental note of the unhappy girl's face. Pretty, for sure, but her eyes were dulled not only by fear but by stupidity. Placed beside the teacher's daughter she'd hold no more interest for him than would a young cow.

～

A cock crowed. Knowing how the crowing of the cock might ward off evil spirits, Feng kept his eyes firmly closed. To hear it once, his fortune might change; twice, and his head should remain on his shoulders long enough to see Feier again; thrice and she would be unharmed, but five times and luck would finally come his way. Because of his friend, the *sun wu kong*, this Master Tsu could arrange audience with the emperor. Chang's murderer and Xiaopeng's abductors would be brought to justice, the Dragon Throne saved and he, a humble village teacher, would be handsomely rewarded. Perhaps Feier might be wedded to a high-ranking court official and allowed to pursue her desire for learning with the emperor's own teachers.

The cock only crowed once. It was another sound, the sound of a measured breathing that caused the teacher to open his eyes. On the floor, at the open door, the old monk sat in lotus position, hands pressed together in prayer and drawing in deep breaths, each time allowing a long sibilant escape of air through those brown-stained teeth that sounded like the hiss of a dying snake. Then the chanting began, a low-pitched monotonous drone, and with it the still figure of the monk became a barrier between Feng and the outside world where things happened… a friend murdered, girls stolen and Feier held hostage, little Feier whose fate hung in a balance only he could tip.

The noise unnerved him, but interruption on his part seemed a violation. Ever since Feier had rushed into his schoolroom to tell him about the body near the lotus lake, the teacher had been driven only by anger, despair and guilt. Not even a near fatal blow to the back of his head, nor scarification of his belly, had deflected him from the urge to set right the wrongs of the past. Blinkered against the truth, he'd failed to question himself about the real purpose behind the insane path he'd chosen both for himself and Feier. Now, walled off from that world by a chanting monk, he felt anger leach from his mind like mud from the legs of a water buffalo in a fast flowing stream; not only anger, but also self-pity and guilt seemed cleansed by the sound. His body, soul and the very kernel of existence of all things hovered, suspended in that unearthly drone, but the strangest thing was a feeling of togetherness, not solitude. Out there beyond the monk he'd been alone, like a furious bee flitting from flower to flower to honey-pot, and searching, questioning, unable to trust in anyone or anything. Here, none of this seemed to matter. Heaven and Earth knew it all already, an inner voice told him, so why worry? But *what?* He wanted to ask, but even that question now seemed superfluous.

And in this blissful state of unknowing he felt even closer to Meili than when she'd last been in his arms and when he'd last entered her in that other life. She was now inside him, but not in body or spirit, and it gradually dawned on Feng that the whole exercise had been about Meili. Dead or alive, she, not Feier, was a part of him, and this fateful journey was no more than an attempt to make amends with his inner Meili. He must never allow her to die.

~

Feier still saw her mother's face as clearly as on that day they'd been playing hide-and-seek only hours before both were stricken by the flux. She recalled the clawing fear she felt when unable to find her mother, followed by sheer ecstasy on hearing that oh-so-familiar laughter from behind the broad banyan in the courtyard - then came the joy of running round the huge trunk, finding the woman and being hugged. As for *baba*, she loved and respected him but in a way that had always been different. There could never have been such happiness on rediscovering *him* behind a banyan tree. In fact, when sharing time with Angwan she'd felt almost pleased he wasn't around for there was no pressure on her to justify the flushes that pinked her cheeks in the Miao man's presence.

Angwan had awakened a new Feier. As a child accompanying her *baba* to the Miao village, she'd often been aware of the boy's eyes seeking her out, staring, but dismissed this as idle curiosity. Being Han, and because of this different, she would try to think of herself as a strangely exotic bird and therefore worth looking at. When she and Xiaopeng had grown older and when they began to talk about boys, as if these suddenly mattered, those sneaked glances from the Miao priest's son would excite Feier in ways she was unable to comprehend. His gaze always made her feel wonderfully warm inside and no longer just a strange-looking bird. Sometimes she feared this warmth would not only cause her to blush but set her aglow, and still she didn't understand; not until Angwan the man had confessed *his* feelings did her own desire for him open like a ripe flower bud. But why had Xiaopeng hidden the truth from her: that *she* was intended for the young priest? The child's deception helped disperse Feier's guilt; likewise, the Miao girl's father's refusal to discuss the young man's disappearance, for she'd done nothing wrong.

Uncle Li deliberately turned his back on Feier when she asked why Angwan no longer accompanied her and the children to her home village. Without mentioning his daughter's betrothal, the farmer was making it perfectly clear he laid the blame for their bonding on Feier. His disgust for her was evident in his every expression, the way he stood back whenever she passed him and in every word he spoke:

"Teacher's daughter, your food tastes like pig shit!" and "Why do you work so slowly, huh? I give shelter and sustenance and you repay me with idleness. The sooner they marry you off to that old fossil in your village the better! Let's hope there's yet enough strength in his bones to beat you into shape. Three moons, I agreed. If your father's not back within three moons his daughter returns to her own village and her fate."

"I'll leave now if you'd prefer, Uncle."

Feier fought back the tears as she said this, her limbs aching from overwork in the fields. To return to the Han village now would have meant the start of a living death enslaved to Zhang Tsientse.

"No! I'm an honourable man. Three moons means three moons! Would you have me shame myself as well?"

The look he gave the girl told her something different; that he had other thoughts, ones that involved her youthful body, before sending her to Zhang.

During long nights when Feier lay in Xioapeng's bed, wearied and alone in that smoke-filled room, and when the farmer lay with the pigs, she would let the tears flow. She loved Angwan from every corner of her soul and she believed he loved her as a man should. So why had he vanished? Unlike the other villagers, he was open and honest. Was that the problem? Had the young priest spilt out his true feelings to Yueloong and been banished to another Miao village, maybe the one on the other side of Houzicheng on the road to Chang'an? If so, would he ever return to live the truth with her, not the lie being forced upon them? Or was he at that very moment seeking some secret place, perhaps a hidden cave in the mountains where they might live as man and wife?

But those tears were also for other reasons: she cried for Xiaopeng, whom she also loved, however deceitful the Miao girl had been, for they'd always shared so much for so long. If her friend were to return, might she have been damaged as Chang would have damaged her? For this, Feier wept, praying *she* would never be taken in that way by anyone other than Angwan; and she wept for her *baba*, for she now doubted she would ever see him again unless, as she'd always feared in her mother's case, he should return reincarnated as a stranger... a baby, even, to her woman?

∼

Jinjin mostly felt at ease with strangers. It's why he so loved working at Wong's inn. Strangers were like boxes waiting to be opened. As such, General

Ma was no different to any other box. What was the man's true background? Who was his father, if still alive? Was he married - and with sons? And the biggest question of all, why had he abandoned the emperor in favour of the empress's nephew? There were many questions spinning in his brain about the squat little man so full of self-importance, but the boy was streetwise enough to know how to arrive at the truth without conducting an inquisition.

The general pulled back a curtain, stepping aside for Jinjin and Kong to enter.

No fool, this man, thought the boy from Houzicheng. *No act of deference. Rather, self-preservation never to offer an unprotected back, even to a couple of urchins.* Jinjin knew he could also learn *from* this man as well as *about* him.

A table, a bed and two drum-shaped seats; on a rack behind the bed hung a fearsome array of weaponry, and on the table was a mug half-filled with cold tea, a half-eaten mantou bun and a dragon-handled dagger. Jinjin took everything in, not least the dagger. It reminded him of the general's eyes, hard and sharp. Added to his beard and moustache, these made the man's expressions difficult to read. Jinjin's quest for truths about people relied a lot on the expressions he read in faces.

"Sit down urchin!" commanded the general, indicating the smaller of a pair of drum seats before removing his plumed helmet and lowering himself onto the other one, back straight, legs apart. He sat rigid as a stone Buddha and Jinjin adopted a similar position on the smaller seat. His head was at the same level at the general's and Jinjin's lips curled a smile for having worked out why they were seated. Standing, and without that helmet, Ma was shorter than him.

"The mute should stay upright," Jinjin suggested, jerking a thumb at Kong who still bore a provision-laden pole across his shoulders.

"Just a dumb kitten, eh? But you a White Tiger? Tell me the truth, urchin!"

Jinjin decided to stick to the truth. This was a man who played the same game as him; a man who could distinguish lies from the truth.

"My father," said the boy, "it began with my father."

"Your father, huh?"

"They tell me China is like a family. The emperor the head of our family. My father was a fool. More arse than head. Instead of answering my questions he'd beat me with his rod. I soon discovered why. He had no answers. He was utterly ignorant. Stupid!"

The general picked up the half-eaten bun, and handed it to Jinjin. The boy quickly devoured the offering, all the time watching the knife-slit eyes. Ma picked up the dagger.

"What made you so confident I wasn't trying to poison you, ay? Or that I shan't slit that young throat of yours with this dagger and silence your mouth forever?"

"Trust!" replied Jinjin, eyeing the point of the dagger. "I... I only knew..."

The general burst into laughter and slapped his thigh.

"You only knew I too had a father like that, right? With pig shit for a brain! We share much, urchin, but most of all courage, huh? And you want to know how I became a general?"

"Killed a man?" guessed Jinjin.

"Several! With my bare hands. Didn't even need one of these." He waved the dagger at Jinjin who was still unsure where this was leading, or where the tip of the dagger might end up. "A conspiracy, you see. And I used my ears and my brain. I was a mere imperial guard at the time. Hated our weak poet of an emperor with his feeble, over-inflated eunuchs, his idiot ministers. But I realised I could do nothing as a humble guard."

"Nothing!" echoed Jinjin! "I see that."

"Yeah, well what you can't see is the detailed planning, the thinking it involved. Began with those careless officers talking when drunk..."

"And you don't drink?" questioned Jinjin.

The general shook his head and stared at the boy, as if wondering whether he'd been too careless with his open talk. Then, perhaps deciding Jinjin had no more malice than the bite of mantou he'd just swalloed, grinned self-satisfaction. The man probably enjoyed little pleasure in this place other than the sight and scent of virgins.

"Too right I don't! Downfall of many an able man, the drink! So, you see, I knew what they were up to. Had two choices. Denounce them or join them. I was tempted, but knowing how thick-skulled their general was helped me to decide. He, the poor fool, was like our fathers. Stupid! In being so, he showed me the correct path to greatness!"

"So many stupid men in power," observed Jinjin. The knife slits fixed on him. *Playing with me?* Jinjin tried to focus on the eyes within the slits to better read the man. Nothing! But he knew this general was no fool. "Which is why I've chosen to come to you," he added.

"What they planned was doomed to failure," continued General Ma. "But I saw my chance. Over three moons I got to know everything about those dolts. Five of them worked for that donkey of a general. I watched every action they took, found out where they would meet up to drink themselves silly. Began to think like them. To destroy an idiot you have to do that! So, one night, when they were all legless, I approached as quiet as a leopard…"

"Not a tiger?" queried Jinjin.

"A tiger?" The general went quiet, his eye slits cutting into the boy. Jinjin squirmed. He thought he'd said the wrong thing. "A *white* tiger?" repeated the man before bursting into guffaws of mirth. "Tiger, oh no! A leopard. I hadn't the power of a tiger back then. Only the stealth of a leopard. Stealth and cunning were my weapons. And *these...*"

Ma raised up his thick-fingered hands into the boy's gaze. Jinjin thought how oddly large and out of proportion they were in comparison with the general's squat body and neckless head once bereft of that magnificent, plumed helmet.

"More deadly than all of these toys of war that my dozy soldiers play with!" With a sweep of one of those hands the man took in the fearsome weapons beside him.

"You strangled them?" asked Jinjin.

"Oh no! Far too noisy. All that gurgling and grunting. See… one hand so…" General Ma held his left hand cupped, palm up. "Like a woman, huh? The *yin*. The other, the *yang*, looks down at the vessel he wishes to enter. Right? You understand, little urchin who's never been with a girl?" The spade-like right hand hovered over the left. "Only there's a head in the way. A quick twist… and as silent as a leaping leopard…"

The lower hand flicked back at the wrist, the other downwards with eye-blink speed.

"Soundless! Dead… when the jerking stops! One, two, three, four and five. All five of them flipped over to the land of the restless *gui*."

Jinjin caught sight of Kong staring with curiosity, his own spade-like paws gripped tightly around the bending pole across his shoulders.

"But how did you...?" he began.

"In the planning," answered the general before the question could emerge. He tapped the side of his melon-shaped head. "Intercepted messages by winning their confidence. A fools' fool. Those poor bastards! Trusted me with anything because I said nothing. But *you*, young urchin, you speak too much!"

The boy squinted at the general, a habit he'd acquired at Wong's place whenever uncertain where to direct the conversation, which wasn't often. He remained silent.

"That very day I'd already informed the chief minister's special eunuch about their plot. A fellow who smelled like a woman and moved around the palace like a shadow. I promised to deliver the traitors' heads on a board and after I'd done that thing I became General Ma. From guard to general with only five twists of the hand. I tell you, when removed, those heads together weighed more than a stone Buddha. And two Buddhas later I added General Chin's!"

Jinjin wondered how much General Ma's detached head would weigh.

"So... at last I had access to court gossip. And the empress. That monkey of a husband she's married to is blind to the calligraphy of destiny written in the woman's eyes!"

Calligraphy of destiny? Have to remember that, thought Jinjin, annoyed a neckless general with animal hands could use words that invaded the sacrosanct territory of the poets. *I'll impress the teacher's daughter with the 'calligraphy of destiny'.*

"You know..." General Ma's head swivelled on his broad shoulders to check on Kong through those knife-slits then back again to study Jinjin. He curved his short straight spine towards the boy. Jinjin got the message and circled his hand at Kong who obediently turned to face the other way. He leaned up close to the general, close enough to hear whispered words:

"The empress can't stand her poet husband. Some say he hasn't entered her for years. Indeed, maybe never. Think of that! Nor his most beautiful concubines, either. What a waste of *yin*, ay? They also say his eunuchs are more than willing! This weakling head of the central kingdom - head of the family of China? A rabbit sits upon the Dragon Throne! A rabbit that enters eunuchs!"

The general sat back and guffawed. Jinjin copied him, although had no idea why he should find any of what he'd been told funny.

"So, urchin boy, the father must go. He's forfeited his right to serve his family." The eye slits then found their mark somewhere deep inside Jinjin. "So you left yours as well?"

"Had to," replied Jinjin, smarting. Mention of his father was like rubbing salt into a wound.

"Of course! No need to kill *him*, though. It's different with the emperor. Killing is the only way to prize him off that throne. The only way to make Heaven see sense. Listen, boy, the empress is a good woman. Her nephew has got to be better for China. And as for... you know..."

"The Miao girls?" suggested Jinjin, looking for a response in General Ma's slits. "*He* likes women, right?" The general stiffened, and what Jinjin saw in the narrow black lines between the man's eyelids was something closer to suspicion than to trust. Another series of guffaws from the man relaxed the tension. "A thousand petals? Gets strength from their *yin*? Am I right, your excellency?"

"As right as an urchin can ever be."

"But why Miao? Why not girls from Hangzhou?"

The teacher? Never asked whether the teacher's deceased wife came from Hangzhou. The most beautiful women have to come from Hangzhou.

If what was said about the teacher's daughter was true, he, Jinjin, would be furious if it turned out she had no ancestral ties with that celebrated city of the East. The girl's imagined face, perfect to the tiniest detail, had filled his mind most of the time since leaving Houzicheng. The nose, the chin and... oh, those eyes! They would be his. Yes, her ancestors would *have* to come from Hangzhou. He'd see to it they had no choice in the matter.

The general's expressionless face gave no answers.

"I mean, I know about the thousand petals. We all do. And Miao girls can be attractive. Skilful with the loom, too. But..."

Not a mere petal, but a complete flower, magnificent in her beauty. Hangzhou? But Chang'an is where he'd take her. Chang'an is where he'd show China his true worth. Meanwhile...

"But why not Han girls from Hangzhou?" repeated Jinjin.

"His mother was Miao. Died when the emperor-to-be was but a child. Fathers again, see? The empress hated her violent brother. So much so she had him, well, let's just say he got seriously ill. Rather quickly. She was a mere courtesan then. Had contacts, though. Sneaked her nephew out from under the chief minister's nose. Across to the mountains of the west. But you'll know all of this being a White Tiger, right?"

Jinjin squirmed. Kong was now staring as if to challenge him to get out of the fix. After a pause the innkeeper's urchin answered:

"It's not so much a question of what I know but what I understand. I mean, even one who's half Miao can surely still see how superior Han girls are to their Miao sisters."

The general drew in a deep breath and cupped heavy hands over his knees. It appeared he was about to stand, perhaps to remove a large sword from the armaments rack with which to detach Jinjin's head, or even do that flick of the wrists thing with those hands. Instead, he nodded, in agreement.

"The father… again," he said. "Blamed the man for his mother's death. Getting back at him by filling his own court with Miao girls, I imagine."

Then he stood and reached out for one of the larger swords on the rack, removed it and ran two fingers along the blade, testing its sharpness.

"Why am I telling you this? You White Tigers are supposed to be the emperor-to-be's brains and we soldiers only his fists."

Jinjin had never before felt as unsure in conversation as he did with General Ma. He would usually take the lead and direct the flow of words, but here was a man who played with him, provoking whilst pretending to put him at ease. But if nothing else, the boy was a fast learner, and it came to him in a flash. His mind was racing in several directions at once as he anxiously watched those thick fingers caress the cold steel of war, but just when he had almost decided to reconcile himself with the inevitability of death, he blurted out:

"Teacher Feng suspects Chen Jiabiao!" The general carefully replaced the sword and turned to face him, still listening. "I told him he could be wrong, but with one of our number murdered I had to be certain. After all, a flood has to begin with just one drop of water."

"And removing one drop of water won't prevent a flood," parried the general.

"But if that drop contains poison..." began Jinjin.

"Just tell me what you want," interrupted General Ma. Irritation had altered the tone of his voice, and irritation meant uncertainty.

"Time," answered the boy. "That's all. My ears and eyes will do the rest."

"Time? Do you think I'm a magician? Time's what no-one has! As soon as the emperor-to-be arrives from the west we attack. At first light the following day. You White Tigers have no idea how to conduct a war. We sweep down on the city from the mountains back there!"

A stubby thumb indicated the tent wall behind him, beyond which a wall of mountains separated the plain of their camp from the city of Chang'an.

"Could be tomorrow, the next day or even two moons away. So you see, I cannot promise you time. Huh! The fist is ready, but the brain, it wants only to sleep."

"All the more reason to check out what Teacher Feng told me!"

"Which is?"

A sneeze from one of the girls the other side of the curtain caused the general and both boys to turn heads. The sneeze was followed by a burst of girlish giggles. It was almost as if the girl sensed Jinjin's plight and was giving him thinking space, for he wasn't used to telling lies.

"It's hard, you know! All those virgins so near yet so far! So this teacher you mention has a beautiful daughter?" The general was still staring longingly at the limp curtain as he spoke. "Well?" Jinjin's anger swelled dangerously. "One for *this* side of that curtain, maybe?" questioned Ma.

The boy blocked the out words. The girl was his, whatever might happen.

"What if Chen Jiabiao isn't truly one of us?" he asked.

He had no idea what he talking about, but to introduce doubt into the general's brain, and give it an extra twist, seemed the best way to avoid immediate loss of his and Kong's heads.

"If Feng is wrong, I remove his head and the girl is mine," replied the general gazing at the curtain. "If right, you get a reward." *Reward? Only one thing I want, you worthless water buffalo!* "See how I have the power to decide your fate and his?" the general nodded at Kong. "And you can forget the teacher's daughter!"

Thus the general had sealed his fate in the mind of the urchin from Wong's inn. Until then it mattered little to Jinjin which path he and his 'servant' should follow, either that of the emperor or the emperor-to-be. Ma had made the choice for him and predetermined his own death.

"Chen Jiabiao's my cousin," announced Ma.

Jinjin held his breath. Not a single muscle in his body twitched whilst he absorbed the shock of the general's words. They cut through his brain like a knife, but he held fast. He thought again of the imagined face of the teacher's daughter, refusing it permission to abandon him. Words emerged from somewhere, perhaps the girl in his mind urging him on. Jinjin knew from what his ears had learned at Wong's that a man's greatest enemies are those closest to him, and had this not just been confirmed by the general: the emperor and the empress, the emperor-to-be and his father? If sensible, the general would have doubts about his cousin.

"That's why I came straight to you, general," lied Jinjin. "No-one else knows. And the mute... well he can't write, so what *he* knows no other person will ever know. I'll get proof, one way or the other. Just give me time."

General Ma sat down again and stared fixedly at the ground. He called for the guard who flicked aside the curtain and stood to attention.

"Take them away," grunted the general without looking up. The statue guard came to life, strode over to Jinjin and yanked him to his feet. He pushed Kong through the open flap, then approached Jinjin.

"Gives me no pleasure to kill a mere child," said the general to the boy's back. "Take them to Chen Jiabiao's tent. Tell him..." the stone-faced soldier halted, "tell him to take these boys with him to Chang'an as soon as the emperor-to-be arrives. If he asks why, just say it's the command of the General Ma."

So the seed of doubt took root in that head-without-a-neck. Although Jinjin left the general's presence with an unshakable determination to kill the man for daring to claim the teacher's daughter, he respected, even *liked* him. But Ma had sealed all their fates by underestimating 'the urchin' - including those of the poet seated upon the Dragon Throne and the nephew of his first wife, already travelling east from the land of the White Tiger.

~

The chanting ceased. The *sun wu kong* stood and stepped to one side.

"Please. We must eat before you set off," he announced. "But tell me first, are you still intent upon this crazy notion of yours? Are you truly ready for death and ready to leave your motherless daughter without a father?"

"More than ready," replied the teacher, sensing Meili's spirit.

Back in the refectory, Feng and the old monk talked openly about many things: the precarious state of China, the strengths and weaknesses of the present emperor, the inordinate power of the court eunuchs - and the empress.

"She's the one we must all watch," cautioned the *sun wu kong*.

"The empress?" Feng, with Meili refusing to leave his mind, was unable to conceive how any man could do other than dote on his wife.

"The emperor has no interest in war, no true interest in any live woman, only the brush stroke women - and who knows what *they* look like under their skirts!" The monk was beginning to sound like the traitors he risked his life to expose. "But he's a man who cares about his people. Those close to him should be helping him, the father of China! But enough of emperors and empresses. Let me tell you about Master Tsu. I've a map here."

Master Tsu? Feng left Meili behind as he prepared to meet a mental Master Tsu.

From under his orange robes the old man produced a yellowing folded page and spread it out on the table in front of Teacher Feng. He indicated the location of the South Gate through which the teacher would enter the Imperial city, a broad avenue leading up to the palace, the harlots' district and the narrow streets of the poets and the artisans' quarter. Feng took in every line, every curve and the untidy sweep of the calligraphy up and down the page; he saw not just a page but alleyways full of people, magnificent buildings, thoroughfares bustling with carts and wagons and vendors. He saw Houzicheng magnified to colossal proportions.

As the monk explained directions on how to find Master Tsu, without any explanation who the man truly was or why Feng should seek him out, an image formed in the teacher's mind, displacing Meili's beautiful features. The painter was a slimmed down Kong Fuzi, sporting a wispy grey beard, with dark folds underlining inscrutable eyes and a long flowing blue robe; the same colour he'd seen used for the sea in a scroll painting he'd once admired, although he had never actually seen the ocean. He recalled once suggesting to Meili, half-jokingly, that should he fail the civil service exams they could uproot and transfer to a small coastal village where he might learn to fish, teach on the side and show little Feier the waves from the vantage of a rocky headland; and how they'd both laughed when their little daughter asked whether waves were made by the dragon of the sea whenever he breathed out. But he knew neither would ever hear the sound of the waves in this life, or discover the true colour of the ocean. Instead, he'd have to make do with an imagined colour now cloaking the imagined painter.

Apart from learning the whereabouts of the artist's residence, close to the harlots' quarter, Feng found out that Master Tsu taught painting at the emperor's court and, like Magistrate Minsheng, had once been a monk. Both facts seemed of little use to him as he set off again in the direction of Chang'an carrying the bamboo murder weapon, a bamboo backpack of food, a water flask and the map.

Later that morning, he mingled easily with other travellers approaching the city gate.

~

Even the children tormented the girl.

Xiaopeng, both quiet and gentle, was eager to please and although a slow learner she'd always been much-loved by the other Miao children. Feier was almost a mother substitute for her little friend and as such had been unquestioningly accepted into the young Miao fold. With her knowledge and skills in calligraphy, all looked up to her, but this stopped abruptly the day Angwan disappeared, the awful day she learned of her betrothal to Zhang Tsientse. Not only had Old Xiang poisoned his *brother* against her, but also the other Miao villagers; to have the man's vicious venom spread amongst the children she taught and loved was more than Feier could bear.

A conspiracy of silence hung like a storm cloud over the village and the only fruit of her love for the young priest was hatred - hatred for her.

There was no-one she could turn to for help, neither here nor in the Han village. Her *baba* had been her sole carer. They had no relatives nearby. There was no shoulder for her cry on. The teacher and his daughter were outsiders even amongst their own people, only tolerated for as long as Feng could promise better lives for their sons and daughters through education. In their village, the younger Feier had been excluded from childish play perhaps because she'd been the teacher's daughter and also exceptionally bright. She'd always been 'different', but never before hated. What loneliness, to be so despised! It made darkness seem darker as she and Farmer Li sat together after eating, each evening and after she'd cleared up, tidied the little house, made ready his bed in the pig-pen and stoked the fire. That same fire gave her no warmth or comfort in that silence. Pig smells took over and filled her mind; the pig smells of a filthy farmer, reminding her she could return to this world as a pig.

But all of this was about to change.

~

Jinjin and Kong were taken to the far end of the camp where tents were more spaced apart, separated from the precision ranks of army tents. Outside one of the larger tents, a banner hung from a bamboo pole, limp in the still air. The guard disappeared behind the flap. Jinjin unfurled the banner and whispered the inscribed characters, Kong being 'deaf': *shui* [17] and *feng* [18].

"Teacher Feng, the 'wind' and his daughter the *shui*, fluid, like a girl should be? I've heard it said that when a man enters a woman she yields like water closing around the male. This has to be a sign, Servant Kong! And Jinjin means gold... wealth! Wealth, wind and water." Kong opened his mouth as if about to speak. "No, you fool!" exclaimed Jiinjin. "You're deaf and mute, remember? Besides, you have nothing worth saying. Your name means 'empty'."

The guard re-emerged from the tent.

"Inside! Quick!"

After the heady perfume of virgins, this tent smelt distinctly unpleasant. Straw mats were stacked againt one side of the tent; at the far end, in front of a curtain similar to the one that separated the general from Miao girls, two of these had been spread out, each bearing a dingy brown cover. There were no head pillows.

The guard left. Jinjin approached the mats.

---

[17] water

[18] wind

"You take the one closest to Nobleman Chen, servant. And if he does for you during the night, just make enough noise to wake me so I can get out of this stinking hole. Smells worse than Wong's inn when full of sweaty merchants and travellers. At least the harlots there give Wong's a whiff of *yin*, ay?"

But what did Jinjin care about this place without girls? Soon the most beautiful girl in China would be his by right. He'd have no further need to impress her or her father. He stretched back on the mat next to Kong's, already Lord of his imagined world. Kong dropped the provisions. He remained standing, gawping at his sturdy hands.

"Just remember you're a fool," commanded Jinjin, propping himself up on one elbow. "And forget your bloody hands. Difference between you and General Ma is that *he* is no fool! This is about survival, fool! Get that into your thick skull and you might survive."

He rolled onto his back and gazed at the grey cloth of the tent. "Maybe I'll reward the general with the little one who cries for her *baba* all night before I kill him. But whatever happens, never once question what I do! This tent belongs to wind and water. We go the way the wind blows and flow with the water. Never stop. Stop, and you become the target. Wong, he just could never understand. His place was a stagnant pool. Pfff! Jinjin will live up to his name. Gold. Gold for the..."

The guard returned.

"Stand, urchin!"

Jinjin sprang to his feet and stood beside Kong, but his and Kong's eyes told different stories. Kong's spelt fear, Jinjin's anger. Moments later a familiar gaunt figure strode into the tent. Chen Jiabiao went straight up to Jinjin, his right hand gripping the hilt of his sword. The urchin boy struggled to read the man's angular features, his sharp nose and fox eyes; if he'd been a woman and younger he might have been beautiful. From afar he'd appeared small beside the White Tiger trader, but close up he seemed large, at least a head taller than Jinjin. One question hovered in the boy's mind: did Chen Jiabiao recognise him? As the nobleman looked him up and down, he felt like a scroll painting being examined for forgery by an expert. He took the initiative:

"Nobleman Chen Jiabiao, your humble servants greet you," he began, before dropping to all fours. Anything to escape those piercing fox eyes! He felt for Kong's arm and pulled the other boy down beside him.

"Tell me what you know about Teacher Feng, young cur! *And* his daughter. Don't pretend you know nothing! My esteemed cousin has filled me in."

Jinjin angled his head, taking in the sword, the hand, the squared shoulders, the thin chin and those cold, grey fox eyes.

"I don't want to see your face, little dog. From where you are down there, tell me all you know."

9.

Duck, Duck and More Duck

Unnoticed, Feng took out the map, orientated himself and returned it to the bamboo backpack. He crossed the wide avenue and headed for a turn off to the right a short way from the South Gate. Beyond, at the entrance to the Imperial Compound, purple and yellow guards stood stiffly to attention. By contrast, the artisans' street was narrow, dim and dirty. Colourful rivulets of paint-tinged water curled out into the street from open doorways, trailing around the displayed paintings of mountains, waterfalls, bamboo plants and exotic birds. Silent in the shadows, the artists who had created these painted worlds ignored the giggles and shrieks of children who ran and skipped from shop to shop. Calligraphers demonstrated their skills on paving stones with giant camel-hair brushes whilst others worked with wood, with bamboo and with metal. An elderly Miao woman sat beside a jumble of vibrant, patterned cloths. She looked up as Feng passed by, their eyes momentarily linked. Her pocked, wrinkled face would doubtless protect her from the White Tiger League and from city pimps, but still those eyes spoke of misery, of torment and disillusionment. They also reminded the teacher of Feier, now in the hands of Farmer Li and the Miao villagers; reminded him of his purpose. He averted her gaze and above each door searched for the characters 'Master Tsu'.

The master's house was only five doors down from the old Miao woman. Nothing about the place indicated this was the home of the greatest living painter in China. The tiny house was a fraction the size of the teacher's humble village schoolhouse. The only thing that distinguished it was the absence of paintings in front of the door. Unbelieving, Feng re-read the words 'Master Tsu' several times before entering.

Still no paintings, only brushes and hints of colour on the floor. A half-open door led from the small room to a darker back room. Feng called out:

"Master Tsu? Are you at home? The *sun wu kong* of Xiangjisi temple sent me. Said you're the one person who..."

"Ah, Teacher Feng. Yes, I'm expecting you," answered the open door. "The man with the beautiful daughter - correct?"

Feng stepped backwards as a short, beardless young man holding a steaming cup of tea emerged from the dark. He couldn't have been more different from his imagined Master Tsu, shorter even than the teacher, and pig-bottom ugly. No wonder he kept himself hidden away, but to have a large face like that stuck on top of a ridiculously small body *and* become the greatest of all painters was, Feng considered, quite an achievement.

Tsu's eyes were lost somewhere behind puffy, drooping lids. His nose was a flattened two-holed button, his mouth a gash that tilted to the left, and rabbit teeth pressed dimples into his thin lower lip. A mole sprouting a tuft of black hairs decorated a receding chin. Nevertheless, thin and wiry, the painter appeared to be a man in good physical shape and his sleekly groomed hair and purple robe adorned with a white crane indicated a person of wealth. Feng could think of no earthly reason for someone of his means to live cheek-by-jowl with the struggling flotsam of Chang'an. Why did he not abide in a large house like that of Nobleman Chen?

"*Nǐ chīle ma?*" asked Tsu.

"No... I mean yes... I mean, the *sun wu kong*, he told me to..."

"Come, friend!" insisted Tsu, amused by the teacher's confusion. "There's a small restaurant just round the corner. Only frequented by artisans and musicians. Simple folk. Those who matter, like teachers and painters, huh?"

He chuckled and slapped a slender hand the Feng's shoulder. What a wonderfully fine hand for one with such a hideous face, thought the teacher.

"Yes," the painter continued, "the teacher with the beautiful daughter. The man whose enlightened ways also bring learning to the girls of our villages. Our emperor is less of a fool than certain people give him credit for. He knows all about you." The man took a few sips from his cup then placed it carefully beside a neatly arranged collection of brushes on a low table. "Your bundle and pole we can leave in my room here. No-one steals from Master Tsu, I can promise you. They all look out for me. But of course, you've little left - apart from that belly of yours. The White Tigers took everything, I'm told, but..." he tapped the side of that grotesque head with elegant fingers, "but you still have your secrets. In Chang'an they must remain secrets. At least 'til this business is over."

The teacher left his bundle on the floor by the door to the master's room, for in there, he felt sure, might be secrets that should be kept hidden from his own eyes. Whatever the painter's connection to the court, Feng's only desire was to lighten the burden of guilt by finding Chang's killer and returning Xiaopeng to her father. Besides, he was still unsure about the old monk in the monastery of Xiangjisi – indeed, all monks – and therefore about the master painter too.

He followed Master Tsu into the street. They crossed to the other side, stepping over heaps of waste food, donkey shit, and colourful splashes of vomit. A narrow lane led to a low building with a red lantern. A woman appeared wearing a food-stained, red robe, her hair curled into an unruly bun held in position with two black chopsticks. She bowed hastily and stepped back.

"Always, you come here to eat our food, Master Tsu. You do me a great honour," she said with a short bow. Her cheerful, rounded face seemed to be stretched even wider by a mischievous grin. "Why, I was just telling a new customer, Master Tsu graces our establishment every day. Sometimes *two* times a day."

She turned and spoke crossly to two young men seated together at a table, waving her hands like a clumsy fan dancer. Without a word, they shifted sideways to make room for Tsu and Feng.

"See!" continued the proprietress, her bright, darting eyes alighting on Feng. "Everyone makes way for Master Tsu. And who are you?"

"Just a teacher," Feng replied, glancing nervously at Master Tsu.

"*Just* a teacher?" she echoed cheerfully. "No-one in Chang'an is 'just' anything. I'll want to know everything there is to know about 'just a teacher!' When you've eaten, of course."

As they sat at the table, Feng felt dangerously like a painting on display for all to analyse and criticize, stupidity exposed for anyone to see!

Eight years after Meili's death he'd finally made it to the great capital, but why? To prove to her spirit that he could actually use the brain passed on to him by his ancestors, something he'd failed to do when she lost her hold on life? If only she could have survived until after his civil service exams, how proud she might then have been. But now, after causing the death of a good friend, unable to prevent the loss of another and, recently, a hair's breadth away from rendering their beloved daughter an orphan and condemning the child to a life of servitude… these two young men had reason to stare at him with such contempt.

Tsu turned to address them.

"This is my friend, Teacher Feng. Highly respected by our emperor," he explained. The rabbit teeth seemed to grow larger when the man spoke. "He humbly begs permission to eat from your table."

The scowls were replaced by blank expressions of assent.

"Of course, teacher. Please eat at out table."

Master Tsu coughed and the speaker understood. He offered Feng his seat then he and his companion took their bowls and searched the crowded restaurant for somewhere else to sit. The woman in red, still grinning, asked:

"Duck?"

"Xiuxia, how could I ever refuse your duck?" queried Master Tsu.

"And the teacher?"

"What?" Feng looked up.

"Duck?"

"Duck?"

"Yes, friend. Duck today," affirmed the painter. "Had it yesterday and the day before that and…"

"They say you haven't lived until you've tried our duck," explained Xiuxia.

"Duck," agreed Feng.

He should have known. The whole restaurant smelt of duck; duck and sweat and the sweet sauce that went with the duck. The floor was littered with duck bones, chewed duck skin and gristle. A partly gnawed duck's head stared up at him through a squashed dead eye, only two duckbills away from his right foot. The sightless gaze of death reminded him of his inability to help little Feier come to terms with her mother's death. Was this, after all, the one thing he'd been avoiding all these years? Rather than seeking still to prove himself to Meili, was his life now about shirking his responsibility as a parent?

"Master Tsu, today the duck is *special.*"

"Away with you, Xiuxia! Every day it's special. And can't you see my friend is starving?" The painter called out to Xiuxia as she left for the kitchen: "And bring something for the teacher's brain too. Pak choi, maybe. Teachers must feed their brains. We painters, we have no brains. Rely on our feelings!"

Without turning, the woman in red halted and replied:

"So *this* is the teacher they tell me about, then? The one who would change the lives of my sex? Have us all writing poems?"

Change lives? Or ruin lives - allow them to be stolen?

"Because of Teacher Feng a new wisdom will one day flow from the countryside to our capital here. But only if you feed the man's brain, Xiuxia."

"Chef Wei will do as you bid, Master Tsu. But I warn you, your friend's brain may grow so large you'll have to carry him home on a camel."

She chuckled as she ran off into the kitchen and Feng closed his eyes against the wave of laughter that rippled the restaurant in her wake. He already hated the red-dressed proprietress and wondered why he'd been brought here - and who this painter really was.

After quickly establishing there was now no-one within earshot, Master Tsu spoke quietly to Feng:

"So what happened to Merchant Chang?"

"You knew him?"

"We all did. He was our best contact for materials from the west. Got me my finest colours."

Feng's guilt carved harsh patterns across his mind.

"But the *sun wu kong...*" he began.

"A cautious man! Has to be to survive the unrest spreading through the monasteries. So, what happened?"

"My daughter found him. She..."

"The beautiful one? The girl they all talk of?"

Feng shrugged his shoulders. Before this he had no idea people in Chang'an had even heard about him, let alone Feier.

"She found a body covered with flies, half a face missing and that bamboo pole I brought sticking out of his belly."

"*Your* pole?"

"Well, not *mine* really. I took it as evidence. Anything that might lead me to my friend's killer is important. I knew it was him from the tattoo on his hand. And his big belly. But he'd never told me anything about the White Tiger League."

"Why should he? You approved of my handiwork, though, I hope!"

"The tiger? Yours?"

"Continue!"

"What more is there? He was a good friend. Always stayed with us whenever he passed through our village. Feier loved his donkey, Mimi. We used to joke, talk..."

"About?"

"Anything and everything! We had good times together."

"But not your daughter, huh?"

"I told you, she loved his donkey."

"Did you never wonder why his wife left him?"

"Wife?"

"You didn't know?"

Feng shook his head. It had never occurred to Feng the merchant might have been married. But Feier must have sensed it, about how his friend was when it came to women. Feng recalled that awful day he beat the child with a rod for diluting their wine. He'd never been able to forgive himself for that moment of drunken anger.

"Chang was cautious, like all the emperor's agents. He had to be. But his death makes no sense to me."

"Agents?"

"Exactly! But... wait a minute. He was a White Tiger working for the emperor..."

"Seems so!"

"This isn't easy. We all know about the empress and her nephew, but the emperor refuses to believe it. He showers her with gifts. And that story going around that he's failed to mount her... well, not the whole truth. *She* has the problem. Let's just say no-one can. She's still beautiful and he treats her like a goddess, dismisses all rumours about her nephew. But we agents..."

"*We* agents?"

"Me and seven others... eight for luck, until Chang... well, you know the rest. Then General Ma, agent two, disappears. Rode west with a large dispatch of troops to quell a revolt. Soon after we'd heard about Chang we got conflicting news. A messenger arrived at court to say Ma and his army were slaughtered to a man. The next day another man arrives with a report that General Ma never actually turned up. Simply vanished. With half our forces. Nor have we seen anything of Chen Jiabiao, the fourth agent. He should have been here days ago. I fear for him, too."

"And the other agents?"

"You know three of them."

"The *sun wu kong* at the monastery?"

"Of course."

"And?"

"At Houzicheng. The new magistrate."

"Minsheng?"

"Indeed."

Xiuxia arrived with a dish of steaming duck and a large bowl of rice, placing these on the table between the painter and his guest. Feng breathed in lungfuls of the aromatic fragrances before selecting the most tender pieces.

"Are you talking about me again?" the woman asked.

"Of course, agent Xiuxia," he replied. "Who else? But we're starting to die off."

"Well, feed this man then. Keep him alive and..." she bent forwards and whispered between their heads. "Watch out for the guard with a scar on his right cheek."

She straightened, gave Feng a cheeky smile, turned and left.

"Her?"

"The best. She's our ears. And there's one other. One without a name."

"That's seven, without Chang. He was the eighth?"

"And we must stay with eight. For luck. So now we've another. You!"

"Me?"

~

At night, after the little Miao farmhouse had been swallowed by darkness, Feier felt almost safe in her solitude. As the last flickering red and orange jewels died in the fire grate and the pigs, stirred into grumpy activity by Uncle Li, had ceased grunting, the only audible sound was the scrunch of straw as she turned over and her own breathing, and only then did she feel able to cry. She wept and prayed for dreams bad enough to make the nightmare of daily living more bearable. Her only hope, and a faint one, would be for *baba* to return with or without Xiaopeng. They wouldn't dare force her to marry that old demon if he were back.

She and Xiaopeng had never talked about what happened when a girl is taken by a man. It was a taboo subject, but the way they sneaked glances at Angwan and giggled made words unnecessary. Giggles of shame, not amusement, for each must have felt excitement in that secret alcove of her body, wondering... longing for the man who might transport her to another dimension. Ever since the younger girl started to lose blood each month, Feier played mother, explaining how this would make way for the baby that would one day come, but her longing for Angwan remained unspoken. Now that Angwan was gone, the fervour of desire set alight every female filament of her young body as she tossed and turned in the darkness.

This desire was always most intense for the days after her flow had ceased, and that particular night even more so. She'd been dry for two days. First his face appeared like a ghost in the darkness: his gentle, lively eyes, fine nose and those lips fashioned for pleasure. That night she willed the ghost to take human form in a dream, to caress her with his searching hands, press his thighs between hers and possess her with his soul. Once possessed, she could never belong to that filthy old dog in the Han village.

But there was no dream. Nothing... until...

Feier tried to scream but all that emerged from her throat was a stifled rattle. A heavy hand clamped over her mouth, and her night robe was up about her waist. A weight she'd never before experienced was pressing down on her and her splayed legs were as useless as if they no longer belonged to her. Her hands cupping her virgin breasts were flattened by the man lying on top of her. She attempted to kick against the animal strength of the fiend as something hard pressed at those parts that wanted only the young priest. Her mouth moved under the hand in a futile effort to bite the strong fingers imprisoning it.

"Quiet," whispered a voice.

The girl went limp and passive. The hand over her face softened, relaxed and there was no scream. How had she not recognised the smell of the young man, so alluring and secretive? The farmer smelled only of sweat and pigs. The body covering Feier now reminded her of scents carried by the winds that cut through the bamboo groves on the way back to her home village, of the colours of the sky around the sun as it set over the hills they'd traversed side by side. And as he stroked and pressed against that oh-so-secret-place, she became a lotus flower opening for the sun on the lake near the temple.

～

"Why do you think Minsheng sent you to us?

"But... I never... I mean... this is absurd. I'm only a teacher."

"And the best. We're all of us 'only' something. What unites us is that each is the best of that something. And we find out in our own ways, in our own time. Better like that."

"An emperor's agent? This is madness!"

"Why are you here?"

"To set right the wrong done to Merchant Chang. To find my friend's daughter."

"By serving the emperor?"

"If necessary. But..."

"It's that simple. Protecting the father of our country. That's all we try to do. But getting back to Chang - though the man was a danger to women, he was no traitor. Besides, he was wealthy, doing well under our present father. And there was a thing with Chen Jiabiao's house, too."

"That palace in the country?" Feng suggested scornfully.

"Obviously he wasn't going to tell people 'til the deal was over. Like I said, a cautious man in all other respects."

"So?"

"Let's just say Chang was likely to get the house as a gift. Chen's moving to Chang'an. To become a mandarin when this is all over. His house near Houzicheng would be a marriage gift for your daughter."

Feng pushed back his seat, fists tightening. He'd already had enough of the painter's wild notions, but to think of his dead friend being betrothed to Feier was too much. He thumped the table then stood up. Silence fell like a curtain, Xiuxia appeared in the doorway, a knife in one hand and a plucked duck in the other.

"Hush, teacher! The last thing you want to do in Chang'an is call attention to yourself. Sit before word gets around!" Feng resumed his position at the table, his fists still tight as a concubine's bodice. "Excuse me if I said something wrong, but I'd assumed it was all arranged. From what Chang told me. So your daughter's hair is still unpinned, huh?"

"Still long," replied the teacher weakly, recalling the last time he'd seen that sleek black hair that reached down to the child's waist. "She was terrified of him. I should have known. She tried to tell me. I thought it was just the uncertainty of youth troubling her. But why would Chang go around telling such a lie?"

"Because Chen would need to justify to the emperor the gift of his house, perhaps? I'm sure Chang meant nothing by it. Sadly, it's no longer an issue."

Feng looked down at the disembodied duck head. It seemed to have taken a new significance, as if containing the spirit of Chang, now out of reach and mocking him. He wanted to stamp on the head and kick it out of the restaurant, but perhaps Tsu was right. He'd already been licked by the tongue of death. To raise awareness of who he was and why he was there could only help the teeth of death find their mark. He waited till faces had lost interest and the chattering had resumed.

"I need help," he said at last, unaware Xiuxia had just returned and was standing behind him, her smile replaced by an expression of concern.

"Teacher Feng is tired," explained Tsu.

Feng turned, his face level with the woman's breasts.

Quite suddenly, for the first time since Meili's death, he felt a yearning for female comfort, for the soft smoothness of a woman's body and most of all, her breasts. His gaze travelled upwards to take in the woman's face, a safer haven than her ample bosom. The face softened his anger. How he longed for a return to that other life in which just a glance from Meili would have dispelled all fear and frustration.

"You poor man! Must be exhausted! Don't be too hard on him, Master Tsu. Not yet. Wait for the duck to heal him."

"Heal? Yes, those White Tiger brigands who set upon him were so close to finishing the job the *sun wu kong* says they'd left our teacher friend for dead."

Xiuxia ruffled Feng's hair and his *yu jing* flicked into life, forcing him to cross his legs. The woman left.

"Take care," warned Tsu. "You've not see her husband, Chef Wei, yet. He's in the kitchen back there and he's big. Many a man's stem has fallen foul of his chopper." Feng looked down at his lap in alarm before the artist erupted into laughter. "A bit of humour, please. You need it to survive in Chang'an. *And* Xiuxia's sympathy - but only her sympathy, I warn you. Don't want the number of emperor's agents reduced further by a meat chopper. So, you need *my* help? Wrong! The emperor needs *your* help. Needs your brain to protect himself from his gentle ways. Now, why the missing Miao girls, ay?"

"A thousand," answered Feng. "Collecting them `til he has a thousand. A thousand petals like the imperial tree. He'll believe that the *yin* flowing from a thousand girl-petals will match the strength of his *yang*. Give him the *qi* force to defeat our emperor poet."

"A thousand? That's a lot of girls. Even for an emperor. And if you saw that tree you speak of in flower - well, for an artist like me not even *ten* thousand girls could come close to its beauty."

"It's the only thing that makes sense!"

"But where, teacher? Where is the nephew's army hidden? That's what we need to know. What we hoped Xiuxia's ears might uncover. What Chen was supposed to find out - and now his cousin the general's either vanished or been vanquished. Whatever, the man's gone missing. These are bad omens, teacher. I fear for you."

"The army will be where they've taken the Miao girls to."

"Which none of us knows! Tired or not, Feng, you should learn from my painting."

"Your painting?"

"I paint a rock. I make a flat thing solid. Nothing can change it. Not rain, sun, snow or earthquake. A brigand, a general, a court official and a beautiful girl like your daughter - each could sit beside my rock, yet still it remains unchanged. You understand?"

Feng was in no mood for riddles and was beginning to find the painter irritating.

"Be like my rock. Take strength from it. Your daughter's safe from the dead man, but you'll do her no favours by getting yourself killed."

"Was what you said about Chen Jiabiao's house true?"

The painter shrugged his shoulders.

"As thick as thieves, those two. But deeply loyal to the emperor."

"So it could have been one of the monks who killed him. Found out Chang wasn't a true White Tiger. And nothing to do with me telling him to find out more about the missing Miao girls after all? Pfff! One burden less, I suppose."

Feng picked up a duck leg and chewed on it, spitting skin and bits of bone onto the floor. It was more delicious than anything he'd eaten at Wong's. As for Feier's dismal attempts to cook duck, the girl's food was, at times, close to inedible.

"And Minsheng?" he asked through a mouthful of duck. "Is he to be trusted? The old magistrate had been a good friend."

"He's *our* rock, that man."

Not the word that came to Feng's mind, but he ate on. Xiuxia returned with a bowl of tofu, pak choi, a bright, cheery face and those incredible breasts.

"Chef Wei says if this doesn't make the teacher clever then he has no brains."

Her proximity was enough to lengthen Feng's jade stem. He didn't dare turn again to face that bosom for fear one of his hands might take on a life of its own. The woman's breasts brushed against his back. He focused his attention on the duck's head, only daring to move when the woman was gone. Perhaps the duck had been deliberately put there as an antidote for desire. Why this woman, at least his own age, had such an effect on him when all those exquisitely pretty charges in his schoolroom had none, he failed to understand.

"One day someone will cut out that woman's tongue, my friend. But 'til then we must suffer it. And remember she has a heart of gold."

But it wasn't her heart or her tongue that occupied Feng's pak choi fed brain as he filled his stomach with more of her husband's delicious food.

~

Feier had no questions to ask; questions would spoil everything. These could come later for she wished the kiss to go on forever, beyond the reach of time and death. Her small fingers touched her lover's hand stroking her breasts then travelled up to his face, his cheek, as if to keep the kiss there in her total possession. As her lips parted against his, they came together in flames more dangerous than any thunderbolt released from the Jade Emperor's firebird, and with a fire not even a Celestial Dragon could have extinguished. And when Angwan, her very own dragon, lay spent on top of her, her legs encircling his warm, lithe body, she laughed. She laughed with pure delight, happiness and relief, and if she were put to death for breaking some unspoken, ancient Miao rule, what did she care? She was Angwan's and could never be given to that old goat, Zhang Tsientse.

"Quiet," repeated the young priest in a low voice. "Even in his sleep Yueloong will know pigs don't laugh."

"So... let him come!" she giggled, tickling Angwan behind an ear. "I'm happy, so happy... and I want to tell the whole world."

With both hands, she took hold of the man's head, now nestled between the soft mounds of her young breasts, and lifted it enough to see his face, though it was too dark to see more than the merest outline.

"I want to see your eyes again. Come close. Let me see your eyes."

As he moved his body up over hers she felt a damp trail streak her belly. She giggled when his comforting eyes came into focus just a hand's breadth from her face.

"Now you're tickling me! With your magical brush," she announced. "Please write something on my belly. Write 'Angwan' there. No! Write 'This woman belongs to Angwan'. Then no-one else can touch me!"

And the priest, too, laughed.

~

That evening, his head afloat with rice wine, Feng lay awake on hard matting, a simple wooden block for a pillow, tracing the painful ridged characters of 'White Tiger' scarred across his belly by brigands. His head wound was healing but the belly scars would forever remind him of his stupidity and his guilt - not for causing Chang's death, clearly not his fault, but for abandoning Feier in his haste to set right his wrongs. Could he *really* trust Yueloong not to defile her? How deep was the man's professed Buddhism?

The night was spent fitfully trying to work out what, as the emperor's eighth agent, he should tell the great man. The father of China would not want to hear what he already knew yet did not believe. As Tsu had implied, China's destiny laid with the Miao girls and that place where the forces of the empress's nephew were amassed. The White Tigers were the key to everything. The following day he would scour the city for White Tigers. Better, perhaps return to the restaurant to question Xiuxia, the emperor's ears. Xiuxia and her bosom! Would there be a time of day when Chef Wei had to pay a visit to the market to buy his ducks and vegetables, for that would be the best time to question the proprietress? He finally drifted off to sleep against a backdrop of images of Xiuxia slowly releasing her bosom from the confine of her bright red dress.

～

Feier traced the curves of Angwan's eyebrows with her finger tips then touched his nose and lips before taking his hands in hers and placing them over her breasts.

"I want to go to Taishan [19]," she announced, "to the holiest mountain. Will you take me there? So we can climb to the very top with all those pilgrims and cry out to the whole world: 'Feier belongs to Angwan! Feier is no longer a child!' If the First Emperor climbed that mountain, why shouldn't we?"

Angwan's lips followed the curves of the girl's neck and shoulders sending shivers of excitement through her body.

"Not like the First Emperor, please," he whispered softly, "He died but not you, my.... my... my... oh... Feier!"

After they'd made love again it seemed her orgasm would never end, but sadly it did and, as if the other might disappear now it was over, the young man and girl-turned-woman clung together in fond embrace. Feier sobbed.

"I don't care now if I do die. Just let it happen with me in your arms, my love."

---

[19] The holiest of China's five holy mountains, in the province of Shandong.

"No, Feier, don't you see? We've made a *new* life together. To keep hidden inside you. And before they take you away to dress you in red and cart you off in a covered rickshaw we'll tell them. Then they can do nothing. They cannot kill a woman with child. So, we're banished together! We can go a long way away. Escape from our ancestors. I'm a priest. I can marry us myself." But the girl continued to cry, this time for her *baba*. Suddenly he seemed so important, for he was her only living ancestor. "You, my girl, can give lessons," Angwan continued, softly stroking her damp, secret place. "A girl as a teacher… in this new China of your father's. And me? I could do anything."

Her lover's words brought no comfort. She didn't want to think about the future, only an unending presence in his arms. She kissed him again to seal that future inside his lips, to prevent it from escaping and separating them forever, and they found Heaven together for a third time.

The dragon and the phoenix became one, a force from which would spring new life.

~

A week earlier, when Angwan had approached Li Yueloong with, what seemed to him, a perfectly legitimate suggestion, the farmer's response had taken the young man completely by surprise.

"The teacher hasn't returned," the young man had said. "This can only mean one thing. Xiaopeng cannot be found and his shame prevents him from coming back. Or he's dead. Feier must replace your daughter. Xiaopeng's future shall become Feier's. She works hard, she's trusted by our people and her children will be brought up as Miao."

Before Li spoke Angwan knew from the other man's eyes he'd said the wrong thing. It was a hot day. The farmer and his elderly brother were having a break whilst Feier remained in the field with the water buffalo, gathering rice grain.

"What are you trying to say, Angwan?"

"I'm saying I'll honour Xiaopeng's memory by marrying Feier. She'll be an asset to our village. Without a teacher of their own, the Han people will come to us for their children's learning. They'll pay us handsomely. With tools for our farms and homes, with bowls and plates and things the Han craft so well. I know our cloth can fetch a higher price in Houzicheng market than theirs, but..."

"I forbid it," roared Old Xiang who'd been lurking in the shadows. He stamped a foot into the dust.

For a while, Angwan had been wary of Xiang. He knew of his antagonism towards the girl and feared those darting eyes that bored into the souls of others. The man had never married, perhaps because he was too busy interfering with the lives of others. Angwan had no recollection of a smile having ever brightened up this drawn face, and he'd always looked old, even when the young priest was a boy. Yet the younger brother remained in awe of him. Perhaps something had once happened that ensured Yueloong was forever beholden to the miserable Xiang. Angwan wondered whether the farmer's Buddhism had something to do with it - or had that merely been the younger brother's last act of defiance? Whatever, the burst of fury took Angwan by surprise. He'd hoped for support from Yueloong, but the famer's eyes showed confusion.

"*You* forbid it? But..." began Angwan, approaching Xiang. He wanted to hit him, but that would have played right into the bitter old man's scheming hands.

"I forbid it absolutely. Your future lies with my brother's daughter. Her alone. And if she fails to come home, if those Han devils have destroyed her, you remain a bachelor. Like me. You can think about little Xiaopeng and the children you'll never beget. Oh, don't imagine I haven't been watching you and that girl. I've seen the way the teacher's child looks at you and I've warned Yueloong many a time. Send her back, I told him! Let her make eyes at some poor Han boy. But my niece's husband-to-be? Never!"

Yueloong appeared troubled, as if trying to understand. As the young priest had said, Feier was a good worker and he enjoyed her company. Also, she was pretty almost beyond belief. It appeared his heart was telling him one thing whilst his brain, controlled by his brother, was saying another. At first, his heart spoke:

"Brother, don't be too hard on the girl. She's tried her best here. Her cooking may be atrocious, her weaving skills non-existent, but... well, she brings cheer to my home. Angwan was only..."

"No! You know nothing, I see! The children tell me everything. About what happens when this son-in-law-to-be and that little vixen are together.

They hear things, too. Yes, our village children have ears, you know!"

Xiang turned to Angwan.

"You didn't think of that, so captivated by her snake-like charms! Yes, the things she says about Xiaopeng! Tell her father! And tell him why you've failed to denounce that whore!"

Angwan flushed, for there was some truth in what the old man said. He kept silent.

"He'll not say, brother. His guilt seals his lips. Well, I'll tell you! 'Stupid'! That's what the little witch calls your daughter. The girl who'd taken the Han child into her home and who'd taught her what little she knows about the things a woman *should* know, who treated her as a good friend. Stupid?"

"It wasn't like that. I... I... I mean *we*..."

Never before had Angwan felt so lost for words. Yes, Feier had once used the word 'stupid', and out of context it must have felt like a hammer blow for Yueloong in *his* loss, but it was what the mischievous children had left out in their reporting that defined the Han girl's true nature.

"Xiaopeng might appear stupid when it comes to poetry and the noble words of Kong Fuzi, but she has a strong heart, is able in the home and has good health. She'll make you a good wife, Angwan."

The boys who had hidden unseen close to the young lovers, only fed the word 'stupid' to Old Xiang. Roles had been reversed in their delivery of Angwan's proposal to their young teacher: they'd lied that Feier had asked the young priest to marry her.

Still Angwan said nothing.

"Stupid?" repeated Xiang to his brother. "Your daughter weaves the finest cloth for miles around. And another thing she said. 'Xiaopeng's only fit for a man with one water buffalo'. That's you, Yueloong. One man with his buffalo. As if you and your daughter are unworthy."

"No," protested Angwan in a desperate attempt to set things right. "*I* said that. Not she. In fact..."

"You? She? What difference does it make when you're poisoned by her?"

That's when doubt vanished from the farmer's face. Maybe it was too close to the truth for his heart to bear for, seen through another's eyes, his life of servitude to Sheng Nong, the Han god of farmers, was meaningless.

Truth is always more painful than lies. The farmer's face hardened like a carved temple Boddhitsava, and turned as bitter as the priest's medicinal plants. With a sound like a carcass being dragged over gravel, he trawled his throat for the anger welling from his soul and spat it out onto the ground at Angwan's feet.

"Leave at once or I'll kill you both! Why did I protect you, huh? Answer me! Even before my friend, your father, died, I helped pay for your education. With my hands and my sweat! It was I who persuaded your mother to give you time in the monastery. To learn the Buddhist and the Han ways. To help both our peoples. To understand them, for our trade. Make better cloth for their ancestors' miserable children... not fall prey to their demon daughters. And *I* was the one who hid your shame from others before Xiaopeng was taken. But you lied about that too, didn't you. 'Stupid'? My dearest little girl 'stupid', when *you* bring disgrace upon your own ancestors in such ways, huh?"

During the ensuing silence the three men were balanced in anger and hatred, the young priest standing stultified between the brothers.

"I don't blame the teacher," added Yueloong finally breaking that silence. "He's my friend. We had an agreement. I never break my word with a friend. I'll give him a full three moons, but you, Angwan, must vanish. Xiang can speak to the girl's village elders. Find an old Han goat for the child to wed."

Angwan attempted to stifle his anger and clear his head. He needed clarity to draw up another plan, one that he'd tell no-one. Not even Feier. Not yet.

"Tomorrow my brother will go to their village. He'll seek out the marriage maker her father so fears. *She*'ll find a goat for the girl, without a doubt."

The young priest, a volcano about to erupt, left. He saw the girl he loved bent low in Farmer Li's fields and halted. The farmer stood watching him from the doorway. He could do nothing, was unable to call out, explain... even say goodbye. Suppressing the urge to run to her and carry her like a bride over his shoulder, away from his village, he left for the only place where he might find refuge: the Buddhist monastery.

～

As he grovelled before the nobleman, Jinjin's attention was diverted by the man's shoes. Unlike the cousin's sturdy footware, these were not the shoes of a warrior. Indeed, they were more the shoes of a woman, silk with an embroidered trim. The soles were probably made from soft leather. His gaze travelled up to the sword and the hand resting on its hilt. Looking at these things released a resurgence of the confidence for which he was famed at Wong's inn and which had helped him find common territory with the general.

"The teacher is much respected, Nobleman Chen. All across China, some say. Even in the Imperial City. For bringing girls into his class. And communities together. Why, once a week..."

"Yes, yes! I know all of this. *And* about his friend, the Miao farmer who pretends to be a Buddhist. Do you take me for some sort of a fool?"

"No, excellency. Just that they say..."

"I don't want to hear what 'they say'. Only what *you* have to tell me - and why you're here, little scum!"

"Merchant Chang!" announced Jinjin. It was the only thing that came to mind.

"My friend Chang? Who was murdered by the teacher's daughter?"

It wasn't often that Jinjin felt himself thrown off balance. Whenever it happened, speech deserted him until jumbled thoughts ceased to dance around. They were still dancing when he peered up at Chen's face. He tried to focus on those eyes that resembled calligraphic streaks of ink drawn across fresh parchment. They were similar to those of the man's military cousin, but lights were visible in them and that made a difference. He could read them as he had with so many eyes at Wong's place. They were searching his face for a response that might give his game away. An expression of surprise, perhaps? That, too, Jinjin had mastered. Chen's casual reference to the teacher's daughter made no sense. The girl who had grown more real inside his head than anyone outside was incapable of such a brutal act. She was a mere gentle child who would soon yield to him in total obedience, and in that obedience would have nothing to fear from him. He would teach her respect, so there'd be no need for the beatings and harsh words as suffered by his mother. And when he'd secured himself a place at court, whichever emperor ended up sitting upon the Dragon Throne, he would display his wife, the most beautiful woman in China, dressed in robes of the finest embroidered silk, not the cheap garments of the Miao folk.

Chen Jiabiao was playing games. The boy's face remained impassive, but behind that face bubbled anger that this gaunt figure who called himself a nobleman should taunt him with such untrue words about his future wife.

"I assume that's why you're here, urchin. To get permission from me to kill the girl. Because you're uncertain about the new magistrate in Houzicheng, huh? Well, you'll not need to worry much longer about that uneducated, overinflated buffoon."

"I... er... had to be sure, excellency," answered Jinjin.

"Sure? Sure of what?"

"The girl. I mean she's very young. *And* beautiful. How can I just...?"

"Beautiful? Pah! *He* is beautiful!"

Chen turned slightly, enough to take in the frozen figure of the other boy. The shimmer of confusion on Kong's face gave everything away. He could hear! Jinjin would have killed him if there'd been an easy way.

"I... I had to be certain the girl had no good reason to kill the merchant."

"Stand up!" ordered Chen. "I'm fed up watching the fleas on your head practice their martial arts. You may - indeed you *shall* - execute the girl. Do not believe a word the teacher says. He'll only cover up for her. As for the new magistrate, just know this: the girl's father and the old magistrate were as thick as thieves. Why do you think he got off so lightly when he failed to turn up for the civil service examination? And that stupid notion of teaching girls... for what purpose? And only possible because of that magistrate."

This was a problem Jinjin would need to rectify. The girl's education might pose a threat to his hold over her as head of their family. She would need 'un-educating' or, more acceptably, 're-educating'.

"If you still need proof of the child's guilt just ask the *sun wu kong* at the monastery beyond Three Monkey Mountain. The one near the lotus lake where his body was found. He knows everything. Teacher Feng thought the murder would frighten us - a White Tiger merchant killed by a girl child. Symbolic! But *he's* the one who must suffer, when he sees the head of the girl he dotes on stuck on a pole outside that pathetic little village schoolhouse. You *will* do it. You *must*!"

Chen Jiabiao laughed at a mental image of the disembodied head of the most beautiful girl in China grinning down at her father one morning from its lofty resting place as if this was the funniest thing he'd ever thought up.

"But first we go to Chang'an when the emperor-to-be arrives," he said when his mirth finally subsided. "I have something to attend to there before the big day and you, little cur, will watch my back. Just as my cousin told you. Fail him, and *your* head ends up on a pole, like the girl's."

Jinjin observed how the nobleman's delicate fingers curled around the hilt of his sword like the tendrils of an exotic orchid. Such fingers could know nothing of swordmanship. They were fingers of decoration, not purpose.

"I've a better idea," the boy boldly suggested. "You wish the teacher to suffer. That sword of yours, is it sharp?"

Chen Jiabiao directed his reply at the trembling Kong:

"He wants me to slice off his head to prove my weapon's truly sharp, right?"

Kong gaped his bewilderment.

"You misunderstand, excellency. I wish that sword of yours to become famous," insisted Jinjin. "And *you* with it. See..." He paused to study those brush-stroke eyes. His words had drawn a veil of uncertainty across the man's face enough to alter those eyes, uncertainty spawned by greed and pride, about which Jinjin was an expert. Once he'd observed a hardened official at Wong's make a dangerous mistake when tempted by fame. Jinjin-turned-spider was weaving a silken web of words; a web from which the mandarin-to-be, joyfully unaware of what was happening, would not be able to disengage himself. "I've been thinking it over and really wanted to check first with you. It could go like this..." the boy suggested:

The general and his army will await the arrival of the emperor-to-be with his extra troops. The battle will be in their favour since they'll be able to descend on the city, at dawn, from the mountains with the opposition largely neutralised as a result of Chen Jiabiao's contacts within (a simple deduction of the reason for a prior visit by Chen), *and once the emperor-to-be is no longer 'to-be', but 'is', the teacher can get his prize. He and his daughter will be summoned to the new court* (Jinjin proposed to arrange this himself: *'the teacher trusts me ... which is why he promised me his daughter's hand'*). *Then, in a public square in the centre of Chang'an* ('Yes, I know the very place', agreed Chen) *filled with all the important people of the new China* ('and I know who they'll be'), *thinking he was to be rewarded for his educational services to rural China, the teacher would instead be ordered to behead the girl using Chen's sword. Afterwards, having listened to the crowd jeering and mocking the daughter's head grimacing from atop the bamboo pole with which she'd killed the merchant, Feng would be forced to submit to his own execution with the same sword at the hands of Mandarin Chen. All sensitivities would be addressed with the boy's plan.*

"The teacher and his daughter will be punished and the new emperor will have the satisfaction of seeing an end to Feng's ridiculous ways. They threaten to destroy the fabric of China. *And* male superiority! But most important of all, your excellency, you will receive public recognition for bringing the murderers to justice. Chief minister soon, perhaps?"

The boy waited, his gaze fixed upon those flower-tendril fingers which played absent-mindedly with the sword hilt.

"Stay here, in my tent," commanded the nobleman. "Take food only from me or one of my guards. Tell no-one else your plan. No other White Tigers. Understand? There are many we can't trust. Are there others, apart from my cousin and me and our guards, who know you're here?"

"None."

"My seal is needed in Chang'an. Certain documents, certain people. You will be rewarded, if things go according to plan." He glanced again at Kong then chuckled. "Mind you, you already have *him*!"

Chen and his guard gone, Jinjin peered through a gap in the tent flap to reassure himself there were no listening ears outside before returning to his bed. He again stretched himself out and grinned at Kong.

"Am I not brilliant, servant? Tell me the truth!"

Kong said nothing. Something was disturbing him, but Jinjin had no interest in what this might be. A yawning gulf separated them and he'd already decided to ditch the urchin boy at the earliest opportunity.

"I have the general wondering about his own cousin and Nobleman Chen now eating from my hand. Truly a reason to wed the most beautiful girl in China without the need for consent from the father."

Kong sat and stared at his hands, not taking in anything the other boy was telling him.

"How could anyone believe a girl child could kill a big, fat merchant? What a fool to think I might be fooled! Besides, the court will be bewitched by her beauty. That flower-fingered nobleman has no eyes for a woman, that's pretty clear. Seen men like him at Wong's. I'll talk to the emperor. Make him see sense. Oh, and another thing, Kong. Jinjin alone will determine the future of China. Think of it! An urchin turned out by his own miserable father. Listen..." Jinjin was so used to Kong faking deaf and dumb by now he doubted the boy could actually hear him. Like carved wood, he said and did nothing. "Before I heard those lies about the girl's hand in that murder I still wasn't sure which emperor to back, despite what Ma said. Now the fate of the empress's nephew is well and truly sealed. The empress too! No-one defiles the name of my chosen bride. And *nothing* gets in the way of Jinjin, the boy of gold!"

Kong, who hadn't seemed to be listening, turned his face to Jinjin, and for the first time his eyes showed terror beyond fear. A terror beyond words and which even Jinjin failed to understand.

~

When Feng opened his eyes there was only blackness. He remembered Xiuxia bringing rice wine, then more and more of the heady stuff... but he had no idea how he and the painter got home. The sun had long since set, so he must have slept the whole afternoon and much of the evening. His neck felt as if clamped in the jaws of a beast, his belly smarting from the White Tiger's claw marks. He called out to Master Tsu but the darkness yielded no response. As he eased himself up from his makeshift bed a sheet of parchment fell to the floor. He reached out for it, staggered to his feet and out in the street where there was sufficient illumination to read the beautiful flowing characters:

Nǐ chīle ma, friend? I believe not. Xiuxia has more than duck to give you. We meet there after you arise from drunken slumber.

Wary of another attempt on his life, Feng retrieved the bamboo pole and retraced his steps through the dim streets of Chang'an to the restaurant. Cheering yellow light flowed from the open doorway, picking out colours in the clothes of a group of men standing outside, talking. Inside, it was less crowded than before. Not seeing the painter, he sat by himself at a table in a far corner and rested his head on folded arms. Moments later he felt a gentle pressure on his back, then something lightly brushed his head.

"There's still blood here. Where those brigands struck you?" He recognised Xiuxia's Chang'an accent. "I told Master Tsu he should never have let you out his sight. The thieves in the city are far worse than country ones. They don't do half-measure. Kill without fail."

All the time she stroked his wounds. It had been so long since he'd last felt the touch of a woman he'd almost forgotten the joy of it. But guilt overrode the pleasure. He'd sworn celibacy after Meili's death. It would be dishonourable to her spirit to offer his manhood to another woman when he'd failed so miserably in his attempts to keep her alive. Even if his ancestors were to forgive him, *he* could never be so lenient… despite Heaven knowing how fickle the ways of women, with the exception of Meili and Feier, are. Another woman might use her sex to blind him and distort his reason, sending Feier along a path of ruin and destitution.

Self-enforced celibacy had seemed without question when he first saw that ochre-red mound of earth in the small field at the edge of his father's village in the adjacent prefecture. His ancestors would watch over Meili and he promised them they would never need to spy on her surviving husband. From then on it would be just Feier and himself, and that's how it had been for eight years - until he entered the little restaurant in the artisans' quarter of Chang'an.

Meili's parents had been killed in a flood that had laid waste huge swathes of land on either side of the *Chang Jiang* [20]. The girl, a mere six years of age, was found floating on an upturned table, shivering and terrified beyond tears. She had been taken in by a wealthy merchant who was without children, but whose wife feared the child's beauty. One day when the merchant was away, the *yin* and *yang* halves of their decorated circular table kept apart until his return, the woman took the child with whom she'd been entrusted to the local town to sell into servitude. Meili's ancestors must have intervened, for by some extraordinary coincidence Feng's father, a local town official, had also gone to market in the place of his sick wife to buy vegetables. Something about the girl's eyes entranced him. So taken was he that he kept walking up and down past the woman and child. Unable to hold back any longer, he approached the merchant's wife and later returned home with the child, but no vegetables.

---

[20] Yangtze River

The scolding he received from his sick wife must have been heard all over the village. Neverthless, the child remained with the official and his family. They grew to love her as their own, even the wife whose health quickly returned. A good omen, they believed.

Meili was lively and good-natured as well as beautiful, and the only girl child amongst a generation of five sons of whom Feng was the eldest. Together, Feng and his adopted sister journeyed from childhood to maturity, their relationship changing from one of playful friendship to a love rarely seen amongst the arranged marriages of China. When the girl reached the age of fifteen, no-one questioned the marriage arrangements.

The young couple moved into a modest house built by Feng's father, the house in which Feier was born, but when Feng's ability as a scholar became evident all agreed they should move closer to Chang'an, near the town of Houzicheng. The magistrate there had been one of the father's co-students. He was a man of culture and influence who, it was thought, might help pave the young academic's path to the imperial palace, either as a court teacher or an official of standing; but for reasons no deity or man of religion had been able to explain, the flux had destroyed that path.

"Wait here! Xiuxia will return with magical herbs that will heal all your wounds. Only then will she allow you to eat. Duck today, by the way. So popular yesterday Chef Wei went to market to buy more."

"Where's Master Tsu?" asked Feng tetchily, almost annoyed with her that a certain part of his body was again responding to her tender touch.

"Didn't he tell you?"

"Left a note. Said he'd meet me here."

"He saw them on his way over."

"Who?"

"Those guards. The other sort. One with a scar on his right cheek. Oh, why do men have to make things so complicated, you with your fancy words and poems and the master with his paintings? Why, some say each work has a thousand meanings. Far too complicated! Keep things simple, I tell him. But does he listen? He..."

"*What* other guards are you talking about?"

"The ones who aren't what they seem to be. Anyway, Tsu said to play Mama till he gets word to you and under no circumstances should you let on that you're the village teacher from near Houzicheng who... oh!" she clapped a hand to her mouth. "Just said it! Lucky the place is empty. Anyway, as I was saying, I'll tend to your injuries." She stroked the back of his head. "You still haven't told me what really happened."

"Robbers. That's all."

"No, before that."

"Before? Like you said. We men make things difficult for ourselves."

She left. He wanted to trust her, and if they were truly both agents of the emperor trust should be their common ground; but he'd already made too many mistakes. Back in Houzicheng, he thought that accursed urchin boy was to be trusted and how wrong he had been. Feng still wondered why the boy had played games with him before betraying him to the White Tigers. What could he have gained from such actions? Sexual attraction aside, Xiuxia seemed rather like the urchin with her unstoppable confidence and prying questions and this made the teacher wary.

Oh, the sexual thing! Feng crossed his legs as his mind removed the red robe from her bosom. He feared her imminent return with herbal concoctions, those warm soft hands and the smell of her. Should the swell of desire take over he had no idea where it might lead. By way of distraction, he gazed at each of Master Tsu's scroll paintings hanging on the walls, at the cascading characters of inspirational poetry describing each idyllic scene.

The paintings were mostly of the fabled mountains of the south where rock, trees, cloud and water blended into a whole of perfect balance. Like the calligraphy, streams flowed down from lofty cliffs, the movement held still in a moment of time like a restless soul trapped in the hand of destiny. In one picture, a tiny figure fished from a tiny boat. That he was only fishing in parchment, not water, seemed of no importance. In another, a solitary peasant with a wide-brimmed hat and a laden bamboo pole balanced across his shoulders, followed a filigree path beside a river, his worries lost somewhere in the whole. Looking from one scroll to the next, Feng realised how like these painted people he must appear. If only his guilt over Meili's death and his concern for little Feier could be brush-stroked into a picture! If only Master Tsu could transform him into one of those figures!

A voice disturbed his reverie. Feng turned. Two men stood in the doorway. One, tall and elegantly dressed, wore the high black hat of a court official and the other was built like a water buffalo. This fellow had on baggy trousers and sported a droopy moustache. He scanned the restaurant with darting flint-sharp eyes. The official beckoned to Feng. Feng turned, still hoping Xiuxia might reappear to play Mama with him in some dark corner.

"Quick! Before she returns," called the official, leaving with his companion.

Grabbing the bamboo pole, Feng pushed back his seat and hurried to the entrance. Already the men were a block away, walking fast, and Feng ran to catch up. Periodically, they would dive into an open doorway as if hiding from someone, and the teacher did likewise. Then, although dark, he saw the men were following two imperial guards in purple and yellow uniforms. They continued this stop-go journey through the unlit streets of Chang'an, with Feng close on their heels, until they reached a grand courtyard house beyond the artisans' district. The guards, followed by the water buffalo and the court official, disappeared into the courtyard. Feng approached the house with unease, fearing this is where he might make his final mistake and render his daughter fatherless, but he was unprepared for what awaited him in the courtyard.

10.

Hands of Death

Perhaps it would have turned out differently if they hadn't made love for a third time, but nothing could now part them. Their passion had been so energised it seemed the little farmhouse might take off into the sky, carrying them to a place where even the Jade Emperor would look on in astonishment at the strength of their *qi* force. When both were finally spent, Feier lay folded in Angwan's arms, completely happy for the first time since her mother left her behind. They drifted off to sleep, exhausted, and Angwan's plan was never allowed to take shape. Only after the cock had crowed four times did Angwan stir. A shaft of early morning light cut through the cool air. On one side of the shimmering strip lay a young Miao priest and a beautiful, de-flowered Han girl, still asleep, her breasts bared, and on the other side, the stark stone oven, the rickety table, the smell of pigs and the farmer seated like a temple demon awaiting the right moment to split the young lovers asunder with his sharpened *Dao* [21]. After the few moments it took for the priest to emerge from his torpor, reality hit him with arrow precision. He sat bolt upright. The farmer continued to stare in angered disbelief as Angwan quickly covered the girl's naked torso with a colourful rug tossed aside by passion. Yueloong sprang forwards, snatching away the rug.

"How dare you defile the cloth woven by the hands of my daughter!"

---

[21] sword

Feier opened her eyes and screamed. She flailed around until one hand made contact with her night robe, then pulled this up over her upper body to her chin. Angwan, scrambled from the bed to stand, without a stitch on, between Farmer Li and his girl.

"It's not what it appears to be," he protested. "She had nothing to do with this. It was my wish... my idea. I told you we should marry. This is the only way, Li Yueloong. I can marry us myself. I'm a priest. It's how it should be. Your brother has it wrong."

"My brother is proved right. The child is a sorceress. The only thing you can now do is to denounce her, when her enchantment has worn off. Take him away!" he shouted.

Half a dozen village men, who'd been waiting outside for this moment, crowded into the small room and began to drag the struggling priest from the building.

"Wait. Don't touch her! She's with child. *My* child. Touch her and you incite the wrath of your ancestors!"

"We shall see. She may no longer be with child when she hears what the elders have to say. Cover her parts that have bewitched our priest and stolen my child's future happiness. Take her to the cage!"

"No... Yueloong - you can't. Not the cage. She's but a child. Her hair's not yet pinned up," cried Angwan, trying in vain to kick and punch his captors.

"No longer a child, Angwan. You have just seen to that. As for being *with* child, time will inform us in due course. If she survives till her next monthly loss."

Angwan's shouts and cries dwindled to silence whilst the girl, shaking with fear, slipped into her robe and allowed one of the men to entrap her wrists in a narrow wooden frame with two small holes. A leather collar attached to a chain was fitted around her neck and, as if nothing more than a wild animal, she was led away from the farmhouse. Despite the early hour, all villagers, children as well, were gathered in Farmer Li's yard. They followed in silence, like curious cattle, as the Han girl was taken through the village to an open space at the far end of which stood a bamboo cage no larger than an oven. Two men pushed the cage to the centre, purposefully placing it over a mound of donkey faeces. Both chuckled as a third villager opened the sliding trap door of the cage and pushed the girl inside. She was forced to sit on the donkey shit with her knees pressed against her chin. The door slid shut and was secured with binds at the top and bottom.

Li Yueloong came up close and crouched beside the cage, looking away from the sobbing child.

"We will keep you alive until the wise men of the village have decided your fate - and until we know whether or not Angwan tells the truth about a child inside you. It's no longer of importance that your father keeps his side of our agreement."

Before dispersing, every villager showed his or her support for the farmer by spitting at the face of the girl in the cage.

～

Jinjin, the blethering urchin from Wong's inn, stood staring as if he'd seen a *gui*. In the shade of a tree lurked a sturdy black-clothed figure with folded arms. For what seemed an interminable period, though in truth only seconds, the teacher and the boy who'd deceived him eyed each other. Perhaps Feng was waiting for his mind to decide what fate to choose for the boy; unprepared, he felt bombarded by every emotion he'd yet experienced and more. Anger predominated, mostly about the poem concerning Feier whom the rascal had never met and never would. Holding the bamboo pole with both hands like a spear, the teacher ran at Jinjin.

～

So much is determined by chance it's a wonder anyone bothers to influence his or her destiny by trying to make decisions!

A few days earlier, the urchin from Houzicheng, enraged by Chen's ridiculous story about the teacher's daughter, vowed to kill the man in the most certain but quietest and safest (for him) way possible: at the hands of General Ma. Already he was amassing evidence of the treachery of the general's cousin against the cause of the empress's nephew.

The girl in his head a murderer? Sheer nonsense! Was Feng not risking his life? Would Feng really try to track down his merchant friend's killer if it was he who had arranged for the girl to kill Chang? Besides, he'd known nothing about the White Tiger League and more than anything else Jinjin prided himself in his ability to distinguish liars from those who spoke the truth. No, Chen *was* lying! Also, he was no more in with the White Tigers than he and Kong were. A few days, he reckoned, was all that would be required to expose his weaknesses and do the necessary.

But it took even less time and in a way that involved no effort on his part.

Chen liked alcohol, not women. What he used instead of women came to the fore whenever inebriated. His vitriol against the famed beauty of the teacher's daughter had no obvious foundation in fact other than his desire to destroy the power of *yin* that guides most hot-blooded men to better things. Every evening, the noblemen and his immediate guards would disappear, after eating in their tent, to drink themselves silly. Jinjin and Kong usually sat crouched in a corner until the men had departed. Liberated, they would mess around, laugh, tell jokes and have mock battles, for they knew they'd be safe until the early hours of the following day when Chen would re-enter the tent, belch, fart and stagger over to his curtained-off sleeping quarter before shaking the tent with snores. Jinjin always attributed the strange, glazed look on the nobleman's face to drunkenness. On the sixth night the true reason for this became clear. The boy had never seriously wondered what men without women actually did. That evening he found out.

An unsteady Chen returned, belched then farted, but instead of heading off for bed he stopped in front of the boys. His reddened eye slits fixed on Kong.

"Far more beautiful than any Hangzhou woman!" he announced grinning stupidly, his speech slurred. Jinjin noticed the hilt of the man's sword was partly covered by his tunic which hung in untidy folds from his waist. He was without a hat and long straggles of hair that had escaped the tight knot at the back of his head hung drunkenly to below his sloping shoulders. The stench of flatus merged with that of stale rice wine already filling the tent.

"Come with me, beautiful boy!"

As he leaned over Kong, saliva dribbled from the corner of his mouth. Like a frightened crab pressed against a rock, Kong tried to distance himself from the inebriated nobleman by scrambling backwards into a corner. Chen drew his sword and stepped forward.

"Beautiful boy, I promise only pleasure behind that curtain. Pleasure or death? Which is it to be?"

For a few moments it seemed the urchin would choose death, for he remained cowering on the ground before Chen. The sword glinted in the low light of the lamp and perhaps it was this that helped Kong to decide. He rose to his feet, standing over a head shorter than the nobleman. Chen gripped the boy's arm with his free hand, flicked aside the curtain with the point of his sword and dragged him backwards into his chamber. Jinjin caught the merest glimpse of a bed, clothes in neat piles and two bamboo baskets, before the curtain was pulled across, shutting out his fear of the unknown.

Was this enough to eliminate Chen? Jinjin wondered, both horrified and relieved he now knew why the nobleman had told lies about the teacher's beautiful daughter. By destroying the girl, possibly the prettiest in the whole of China, the man was defiling her sex. Surely this would be at variance with the ways of the empress's nephew, the man who would have a thousand girls to give him the strength to overthrow the current emperor. If he were caught attempting to enter a boy, would his cousin not behead him on the spot whichever emperor Chen would have on the throne?

Jinjin could not be certain. He hesitated as the sounds from behind the curtain informed his ears that most deviant things were happening there.

"Go away!" his dumb servant shouted, blowing their cover. Chen, perhaps too drunk, perhaps too desperate to expose an unwilling resting place for his jade stem to wonder how a dumb boy could suddenly speak, merely grunted. Jinjin had heard such grunts emerge from the upstairs rooms at Wong's inn whenever a whore had successfully persuaded a wine-filled merchant to part with a handful of coppers.

There was little time left. When the grunting was over, Chen would surely kill Kong then him. Jinjin crept towards the tent flap, hoping the guards would be as intoxicated as the man doing weird things to his servant. He'd only gone a few paces when the grunting ceased. An odd gulping sound caused Jinjin to freeze. A dead Kong could be of little use to him and Chen might turn the tables if he were to run and blame him for the other boy's death. However much Jinjin felt in tune with the general, the man was more likely to believe a nobleman's fables than an urchin's truth. Jinjin would lose his head and never gain his prize.

Without turning to look, the urchin became aware of movement just before the curtain behind him was pulled aside. He prayed it would be quick, for a long drawn out death whilst taunted by a tantalizing vision of the teacher's daughter would be the worst thing possible, like having his face rubbed in his own failure before his eyes were forced to close for the last time.

"Master?"

The voice was unmistakably Kong's. Jinjin looked over his shoulder. The other boy stood with his pants around his ankles, his broad hands stretched wide, palms forward.

"I think I'm going to be sick, master," he announced, avoiding eye contact with Jinjin and hurriedly retreating back beyond the curtain. Jinjin looked for something that might serve as a weapon. He picked up a bowl lying on the ground beside the tent flap, slowly approached the curtain and eased it open just enough to take in the scene.

Chen Jiabiao lay on one side, half-slumped across the bed. His tunic was ruffled up and he wore no trousers. From where Jinjin stood, the man's privates were hidden and the boy wanted to keep it that way. What drew his attention was the position of the man's head on his shoulders. It was bent back at an impossible angle; but far worse was the blank, sightless face seeming to peer over his shoulder as if the head had been detached and impaled backwards onto that slim neck.

Kong began to heave.

"Not here, not now," whispered Jinjin, but he was too late. Kong, leaning over the man who'd abused him, brought up strings of noodles, green vegetables and lumps of fatty pork onto that unseeing face. Again and again the boy vomited until Chen's head was covered by the evening's meal and more.

"Pull up your stupid pants and run!" commanded Jinjin. "You've done enough. His spirit's defiled for good. If we don't leave now our *gui* will soon join him."

Kong fumbled uselessly with his pants and Jinjin was obliged to assist before picking up Chen's discarded sword belt and sword from the floor and quickly stuffing anything of potential value into a bamboo basket. This he gave to Kong, together with a bamboo pole he spotted leaning against the tent frame. Moments later they were outside.

The darkness was almost complete, just enough light to inform him there was nobody close by. At the entrance, he carved into the ground the characters for *Nu Wa*, the first goddess, and hoped the general would understand the reason for this: no self-respecting goddess could allow such a mockery of her sex as had been played out by the effeminate Chen. He knew the next time they were to meet he'd have no opportunity to thank Ma for saving his life by showing the servant boy what his hands might achieve. There was something about the stocky warrior general Jinjin admired, and the urchin felt almost sorry he'd have to kill the man, but Ma's fate had now been decided. Nobleman Chen had made the decision for him.

After they'd left the camp, ascended the slope and travelled a few *li* along the track towards the main Houzicheng to Chang'an thoroughfare, they stopped running. No-one would imagine them stupid enough to take the long way round when fleeing for their lives to the capital. If the general thought fit to pursue them it would have been over the mountains, but the chances of Chen being found before dawn were small. By the time the corpse of the man with the broken neck who chose boys over women was discovered, Jinjin and his servant would be far away.

"You'll have to teach me how you did that," said Jinjin as they entered the first village.

"The general showed you," replied the other boy. "Weren't you listening?"

Jinjin looked at Kong's large hands then his own.

"Must be the size of the hands," he decided. "Now remember! You're still mute. Use those hands if and when you need to, otherwise play the dutiful servant. Got it?"

"One thing, master ... "

"Yes?"

"A girl. When will I get a girl? My need is now all the more urgent!"

"Patience, servant! Do as I say and you might just survive. Survive, and one day soon you'll have a girl!"

As they sought a place of refuge in the unlit village, Kong said nothing more and Jinjin didn't question him. Rarely was the urchin from Wong's inn at a loss for questions, but something had happened to Kong, something so weird and so wrong he didn't want to know any more. For the first time since running away from home his eagerness for knowledge abandoned him.

The boys slept overnight in a pigsty, scrounged food and drink from the villagers and left early the following morning. Conversation with Kong proved impossible, locked away as he was in a shell of bitterness, but Jinjin sensed anger fiercer than fire waiting to burst open that shell. He knew now what the boy was capable of and decided to avoid all unnecessary verbal communication until such a time when fanning the fire might yield rewards. In silence, they headed back to the Houzicheng to Chang'an road, then on towards the imperial city. Jinjin asked at every farmhouse whether a teacher by the name of Feng had passed through, and each gave the same reply: 'Yes, but two days earlier.' He was so desperate to catch up with Feng he made Kong walk on for part of the night, only stopping briefly for rests and sustenance, but always the teacher remained ahead. Before reaching the Xiangjisi Temple outside the southern city gate of Chang'an, two days had been reduced to one. Surely here the monks would know about Feng. Indeed, there was a chance he'd still be there trying to work out whom he should approach with his theory about the missing Miao girls; but without the masterful brain of Jinjin to help him, the man would be lost, his daughter forever out of reach.

"A teacher by the name of Feng? A name we never hear much in Changa'an, young man. Why the interest?"

Jinjin didn't believe the *sun wu kong*. Nor did he trust the man. From what Feng had told him, it seemed there might be a link between monasteries and the White Tigers. He made sure his tattooed hand was visible at all times and got Kong to pour water from a jug when they were invited to dine with the monks just to be sure the man could also see his servant's ink-engraved, knife-cut allegiance to the League, but he saw not a flicker of response from the bone-faced old monk. He talked all evening, and tried every gambit learned from the Wong's inn days to uncover the truth, but the man remained an unrolled scroll. Jinjin even explained how the teacher's daughter was the loveliest girl in the whole of China, and recited a poem he'd written to honour her beauty (as seen in his head), but still nothing! The following day he and Kong had entered the city.

Not in his most ambitious dreams had he ever pictured himself walking the streets of Chang'an with a personal servant. The wide avenues and houses were more magnificent than anything he'd heard spoken of at Wong's, the dress of the mandarins and courtly ladies beyond his wildest imagination. Elegant men and women sped past, borne aloft in bouncing sedan seats carried by sinewy men whose exposed calf muscles tightened like balls of steel with every running step. But only a few hundred *bu* [22] further on were the slums of the artisans' quarter and the squalor of the district of whores. Nothing in Houzicheng seemed so close to hell as this quarter of the city. Even early in the morning, painted ladies tried to entice the boys into dark places that reeked of sickly perfumes tinged with urine and sweat. Some sold stale cakes and rotting fruit from stalls in the street, and several times Kong stopped to stare at these ladies and Jinjin had to urge him on. Only one, a woman younger than the others, caught Jinjin's attention. Her face was almost pretty, but her body was deformed and her eyes showed pain. No pleasure could possibly come from sleeping with a woman like that.

"Not here," whispered Jinjin. Kong's eyes were changed, filled with inner hurt like the whore's, but no good would have come from Kong attempting to go with this woman. "These cheap whores are only for men who have lost all hope. Not the servant of one who seeks to impress the emperor and marry the most beautiful girl in China. Come, we've work to do! I'll get you a classy courtesan later."

Rounding the next corner, Jinjin spotted a tattered red lantern hanging outside an establishment he took to be an eating place since delicious aromas of food now teased his nostrils.

"Hungry?" he asked Kong. The other boy merely nodded. "Wait here. I'll see what I can do."

Jinjin left his servant standing alone with their bamboo basket to talk with a woman dressed in red, busily sweeping away debris from the floor around the tables and drum seats out onto the street. She looked up as he approached.

"No children allowed by themselves," she announced. "Come back with your *baba*."

Jinjin took an instant dislike to her. She was shapely, and would have served as an introduction to the mysteries of *yin* for Kong better than any of those whores, but her haughty expression and ridiculous hair, held up by what appeared to be two black chopsticks, irritated him. Besides, he owned a servant and had been entrusted with the confidence of a general.

"We're not here for your miserable food, woman. I have my own inn at Houzicheng," he lied. "I seek audience with the emperor. Just wondered

---

[22] Chinese pace

whether you'd seen a..."

"Away with you! Before I sweep you and your dumb friend into the privy hole at the back! Off! Shoo!"

Jinjin, disappointed, backed away. It was the first of many such establishments he would visit over the following few days, none of which gave him information about the teacher. Thanks to a market vendor, he received a good price for Nobleman Chen's sword and some of the man's finer clothes that he'd packed into the bamboo basket, together with a few small ornaments, so they had enough to rent a cheap room near the whores' quarter at the south end of the city.

No-one seemed to know of Teacher Feng. After covering his tattooed hand with a bandage torn from Kong's shabby tunic, and covering Kong's with street filth, he made discrete enquiries about the White Tigers, asking people at inns and eating places whether they knew about the League and what its purpose might be, but he found himself up against a wall of silence. It was Kong who provided the breakthrough in circumstances for which, once again, Jinjin felt obliged to thank General Ma. This time the boy-servant's anger over what Chen had tried to do, or might have done (Jinjin never knew which) played a role.

Rather than talk, Kong would sit for long periods gazing at his sizeable hands, apparently still unable to believe he'd actually used them to kill not only a man but a nobleman. He would repeatedly curl his thick fingers into fists, uncurl them, grip his hands together, hold them up into the air and play at martial arts against an imaginary foe. He was sitting with his back against a wall, killing Chens with his bare hands, when a dark-robed figure wearing a tall hat of officialdom stopped and watched him with curiosity. Jinjin was further along the narrow street, standing beside the vendor who'd bought the sword, talking to whoever stopped to examine the vendor's wares. It had seemed a mutually beneficial arrangement, for Jinjin's engaging personality and easy way of talking appeared to help attract more custom. On noticing the official gazing at Kong, and fearing the worst, Jinjin ran back to his 'servant' and, after bowing to the official, began to explain:

"My servant's not been well. He does this sometimes. Take no notice. He..."

"Servant?" interrupted the official. "Those are no servant's hands. They're the hands of a fighter! Can't you see? Besides, you're far too young and poorly dressed to think about having a servant. But I'll give you a good price for him." Kong let his hands drop and looked up at the man with the tall hat. "He's no fool either. I can tell that from what I see behind those eyes."

Both boys listened. Jinjin doubled the offer, the official halved the increase, the urchin reduced this by half, adding the figure to the official's proposed price. The official met him halfway and they agreed. Kong would be sold to the stranger 'to fight', and for the first time since leaving the White Tigers' camp the boy with big hands smiled. To fight with no risk of meeting another Chen was more than he could ever have hoped for. He stood up, a good head shorter than the man but as solid and unflinching as a bull.

"One condition," announced Kong. "You get me a girl. And soon!"

"Your hands, please. Let me see them again," insisted the man.

Kong held out his hands then turned them over. The official took the boy's right hand and rubbed at the back of it with the sleeve of his tunic. On spotting the white tiger tattoo he continued to rub until the whole image was revealed. He laughed.

"A good copy indeed," he said. "One that might have increased your value tenfold! Hard luck! Should have been more open with me," he added for Jinjin's benefit.

Jinjin, thinking he might also sell himself as a fighter since he'd had no luck tracing the whereabouts of Teacher Feng, checked the immediate vicinity for prying eyes and unravelled the bandage hiding his white tiger.

"An even better copy," praised the official, "but the hands of a poet, not a fighter. Look, follow me, the two of you. I believe we might be able to help each other. But first I want to see the boy in action."

Uncertain whether they were walking into a trap or on a path destined for glory, Jinjin followed the man, Kong close behind, his hands ready to take on anything and anyone. Heading towards the imperial palace, they stopped outside a large courtyard house.

"Stay here," advised the official. "Later, two imperial guards will enter my compound. Only they're not really imperial guards. One has a scar on his right cheek. They'll be armed. If the boy can dispose of them with his bare hands he's already one of ours. An emperor's special guard."

Jinjin and Kong stood together, Jinjin now wishing he'd not sold that sword, for relying totally on the hands of the urchin suddenly seemed not such a grand idea. The official soon re-emerged with a bruiser twice the size of Kong. The ruffian examined the boy's hands, then his eyes, his teeth and his legs. He nodded at the official who slipped two strings of coppers from his shoulder and took a further silver coin from a leather pouch attached to his belt. He gave the coins to Jinjin.

"This, in exchange for your servant! Jianjun, take the boy away! Test him, then bring him to my compound," he commanded the ruffian, "and you," addressing Jinjin, "the one with a tongue and too much of my money, follow me!"

Jinjin saw Kong again later, terrifyingly transformed, but for the time being he felt a tinge of envy, for he felt sure the boy's training would include using his jade stem with some pretty little maiden picked up from the street. He tried to persuade himself a brief period of pleasure with a poor street girl would count for nothing when compared with possession of the most beautiful girl in China.

"Have you seen her?" the official asked later when he and Jinjin sat talking over steaming bowls of rice and vegetables in one of the local restaurants. Already the boy had off-loaded his story and explained how he was helping Teacher Feng for the reward of his daughter.

"Don't need to," was the boy's reply. "Her beauty is fabled in our pre-fecture. Many merchants have testified there are none in China who can match her beauty and that's enough for me. She'll be mine. When I find the teacher again. When the emperor hears what I know."

"So what do you know about Chang? I already know that he was one of the emperor's eight special agents."

"Like you?"

The official nodded.

"Yes. Like me. The one without a name. But from what you tell me there's little time left. The empress's son could arrive from the west any time. And Ma's one of the best generals we've had since the death of the last emperor. If he has the advantage of a surprise attack from the moun-tains, if the empress already has power over some of our forces within, we might as well hand over our weapons and our heads now. Save our civilians from slaughter. Whatever they say about our present emperor and his paintings and poems, he does care about his people."

"So?" asked Jinjin, his heart sinking. He'd told the official everything and only the truth. "I'll lead your general to the camp. We could attack from the south. Ma would never expect that. Steal the girls away before the nephew arrives. Why wait?"

"Before today I might not have taken the gamble. Our emperor is so fixated with the empress he simply won't listen. And he's unpredictable. But I met with my fellow agent, Master Tsu, this morning. At Xiuxia's restaurant. The woman is also one of us and nothing much escapes her attention. Your teacher, Feng, was with him last night." Jinjin put down the bowl of rice and chopsticks, his mouth open and speechless. "He's an honest man, Tsu tells me. He has a daughter, as you say, and her looks are indeed legendary. The emperor himself has praised the man's achievement in rural education. I told Tsu to arrange audience with the emperor. He'll be at the palace this very minute, arguing his case with the eunuchs. But meeting you has changed everything now. Eat up quickly. I'll leave you at the courtyard of my house and go back for the teacher at Xiuxia's. Can't risk taking you with me. Once she finds out, the whole city knows and there are imperial guards around the city who aren't what they appear to be. Like those two traitors I'll feed to your ex-servant."

Jinjin raised his bowl and hurriedly transferred what food remained into his mouth. They returned to the official's courtyard home where Jinjin waited in the yard whilst the black-hatted man and the ruffian called Jianjun went back to Xiuxia's restaurant to collect the teacher. Kong's bamboo carrying pole and their basket were there, but there was no Kong to be seen.

It wasn't long before two imperial guards entered the compound. Each carried a sword and they headed straight for Jinjin. The trap he'd so feared. Panic-stricken, he looked around for Kong. What none of them had seen was the crouched black figure on the low roof of the compound, invisible in the evening light. When the guard with the scar and a grin as fearsome as his sword was almost upon Jinjin, the squat figure in black leapt from the roof, caught the guard by the head, snapping it back as if just a plaything. The man would have been dead before he hit the ground. His alarmed accomplice gripped his sword with both hands and swung it wildly at the darting shadow. His blade sliced through the air as a blackened limb struck out from nowhere, unbalancing him. As he fumbled for his dropped sword he felt his head gripped by hands of steel. That was the last thing he ever knew.

When the nameless official and that brute named Jianjun returned, accompanied by a third man, Jinjin was staring nervously at the two corpses whilst keeping a safe distance from a black-cloaked Kong who stood alone, arms folded, under the shade of a broad-leafed tree in the corner of the compound.

On hearing voices, Jinjin looked up. Even he was surprised by the relief and excitement he felt on seeing the teacher again, but what he saw standing there at the entrance was not just an overweight, ugly man, for superimposed on this abomination, in his mind, was the most beautiful girl in China.

11.

One Less than a Thousand Petals

How could she have slipped so easily from Heaven to Hell?

Feier had difficulty turning round due to the confines of the cage, but shifting her position was the only way she could the ease the pain in her legs and bottom caused by the relentless pressure of bamboo struts. To stay still was impossible and to move about barely possible. Her cries of pain and tears brought no sympathy, only laughter from her captors. Not once was she left alone, for always two or three men sat around the cage, comfortable in their seats, talking, joking, drinking tea and eating. Even if Angwan were free, which was unlikely, there'd be no opportunity for him to end her torment. If they were planning to kill her why not just do it? To die and return as a pig because of what she'd done would surely have been more bearable. Maybe her karma demanded she should suffer to an intolerable degree till her limit of endurance had been reached and then for things to get worse. Or did they wish to keep her alive for some special purpose? Their pleasure - or something even more sinister?

They fed her rice balls and leftovers through the spaces between the bamboo rods. Water was poured from above; most escaped her mouth, and the dung she was forced to sit on turned liquid. Most of all she dreaded the approach of Old Xiang for each time he would release his aging penis, dangle it to the amusement of others then urinate over her. She'd be forced to cover her face with both hands.

Even at night she was guarded. She prayed for sleep to carry her away and never return her to the land of the living since even the most terrifying of nightmares would have been a welcome release; but the pain of confinement prevented more than brief interludes of slumber. After her own excreta had been added to the donkey shit and Old Xiang's fluid offerings, the smell became so awful the men guarding the cage sat further and further away until they watched from a distance and only came close, after drawing lots, with food and water.

Every day the girl prayed for death to release her but, as when she used to pray for the return of her mother, death remained deaf to her pleas.

~

The teacher's reaction caught Jinjin off guard. He ran at the boy with the sharpened end of his bamboo pole. If Jinjin hadn't side-stepped at the very last moment he would have been skewered. He kicked Feng in the back of a leg and tried to grab hold of the bamboo, but the teacher was surprisingly quick for one so fat-bellied. He swung round and hit the boy across the shins with a blow that immobilized him, and was about to finish the job by cracking his skull open when the official, alarmed by the boy's cries, called from the building:

"Stop, you fools!" he yelled. Jianjun joined him, together with Kong. Soon they were pulling the teacher and urchin apart. Feng, still struggling to get at the urchin, spoke first:

"You little cur! You were in on this business all along! Making a fool of me! Pretending to know my daughter, then setting your dogs... no, your tigers onto me. I tell you, no-one gets away with defiling my daughter's name."

Jinjin remained speechless, for this wasn't how he'd planned their reunion.

"Teacher Feng, you're wrong about the boy," said the official. "Give him a chance. Let him speak. Then we must seek out Master Tsu in the palace. There's little time left. General Ma probably realised his cousin was one of the emperor's agents for he's no fool, but he'll still be wondering where this urchin boy fits into the picture."

"Tell me the truth, then!" said Feng. "But first my daughter. Why pretend you'd written a poem about her. You've never even seen her!"

"The night before I left Houzicheng, Wong told me everything about you and your wife. How she was found and sold before being brought up by your father. That maybe she'd come from Hangzhou because of her beauty, and that a girl born to a woman like that would surely be as beautiful, if not more lovely. The beauty of the *yin* must be written into your destiny, teacher. To balance... well, you know..."

The boy glanced at the teacher's belly. Feng looked down.

"Wasn't always fat. Besides, that's nothing to do with it."

"I knew the *sun wu kong* was holding something back. I can always tell. So I mentioned your daughter to show I had your confidence. That I was to be trusted."

"Confidence? Trusted? What are talking about?"

"Get on with it," urged the official. "Tell the teacher what happened and why. And show respect for a change."

Jinjin eyed the official sharply before giving Feng a reluctant bow.

"I saw that trader again," he began. "I was up early, wanting to impress you. Thought of following him, finding out more about the White Tigers, to help you trace the Miao girl. And with your knowledge, search for your friend's killer."

"By disappearing?"

"Hid in the cart. Learned the other man was Chen Jiabiao, the man you spoke of when you told me about the dead merchant. Jinjin remembers everything." He glanced at the official. "The emperor *will* reward me, won't he?"

"Ask Master Tsu. He's more important than me. Number one agent!"

"Chen Jiabiao a White Tiger?" questioned Feng.

"Not as simple as that," responded the official. "But let the boy speak first."

Jinjin held nothing back. He recounted the whole story, up to and including the killing of the nobleman by the other boy, Kong, and their onward journey to Chang'an, stopping off at the Xiangjisi Temple monastery.

"They were trying to protect me," answered Feng. "The *sun wu kong* told me a lot about the White Tigers. But your tattoo? I'm sure it wasn't..."

"I did it myself. To get into their camp. Met their general. A man called

Ma. The girl's in his tent. Your Miao friend's girl. Blubbering for her *baba* all the time."

"They accepted you?"

Admiration had now crept into the teacher's expression as he stared at the boy. Jinjin glowed with pride.

"The general, yes. I think he already suspected Chen."

"An agent of the emperor. Like Tsu and Xiuxia and your murdered friend," explained the official. "There are eight of us. There were, at least. Very few at court even know who we are."

"Yes, yes, I've been told. Chang too," Feng interjected. "So your friend..."

"Servant!" corrected Jinjin.

"Your *servant* killed the man who would save China from the imposter from the west! A fine mess!"

"Wait, Teacher Feng. *I* believe Chen was truly with the White Tigers all the time. Working the other way round. He'd have been the downfall of our emperor. As Ma told me, his visit to Chang'an would have given him all he needed to destroy the city from within." The boy pointed to the bamboo basket. "In that basket. Some scrolls I found in his tent. Coded as poems. I know enough characters to realise they weren't real poems. Anyway, Chen was no poet. These proved he was a traitor. So what my servant went through probably saved my life. Ma only wanted to be sure before killing me, and he knew I'd have had nothing on Chen!"

"I'm sorry, Jinjin. Forgive me. I looked for you that morning in Houzicheng. Wenling just said you're unreliable. But I should have known. She didn't want me to come to Chang'an. Maybe thought she was doing me a favour, afraid you'd be a bad influence. So you found the girl! I can't tell you what this means to me."

Jinjin was tempted to suggest the reward he had in mind but decided the better of it having witnessed the teacher's earlier reaction. He'd leave this to the very last minute after confirming the child was, in life, as she appeared to be in his head - or more.

"Follow me," instructed the official.

Instead of taking a direct route, the official led Feng and Jinjin, accompanied for protection by the swarthy ruffian Jianjun and Kong, through the city's lush residential quarters in the west, with its temples and pagodas, past the magnificent palaces of princes and princesses, explaining how White Tiger spies, masquerading as imperial guards, had infiltrated troops lining the main avenue leading to the palace gate. There was a smaller entrance at the side of the west palace wall with trusted guards, dressed in black. They passed through the gate, following the wall round to a vast inner courtyard from where wide steps took them up to the palace. On either side, spear-bearing guards in black stood like carved figures, unblinking in the strong sunlight. Another long-cloaked, black-hatted official emerged from the palace entrance and ran down the steps to meet them, his haste suggesting to Feng he'd been anxiously awaiting their arrival. He bowed to his colleague in government, looked askance at the ruffian and Kong then approached Feng.

"Teacher Feng?" he enquired.

"I am," replied the teacher. "Master Tsu has spoken with you? About my reason for seeking audience with the emperor?"

"Hurry, hurry!" the man insisted.

He was a small man with a high-pitched voice. Indeed, if a courtesan's dress had been substituted for the cloak, and the high hat of office replaced by the towering hair of a court lady, with all its fussy embellishments, he could have passed for a woman of pleasure leasable only to the wealthy. Feng no longer knew whom to trust or when he should show his scorn.

"I'm not going anywhere until I know who you are and what dealings you have with Master Tsu, the painter."

The female-voiced man glanced back at the palace.

"He's waiting. Up there. In an ante-room. Spent half the morning arguing in your favour. You've no idea what a stubborn man our emperor is. Still lives in a dream of his own. The empress is nowhere to be found. Must mean something, but he still refuses to believe us."

"He'll have to believe *me*."

The man turned to face the owner of the voice, an urchin whose tolerance for idiots had dropped to an unrecordable low.

"You? And who are *you*, urchin?"

"One who'll see you beaten to within an inch of your life if you don't stop this nonsense and take us straight to the emperor," replied Jinjin.

Feng and the two officials gaped like carp in a stagnant pool as Jinjin ran on up the steps two at a time. The man with the high voice drew his sword, but the official without a name grabbed his hand.

"Leave him. He may appear an uncouth peasant boy, but what he's found out could save China from the empress and her nephew. *He's* not our problem. Our soft-hearted emperor is. You, too, will be needed, Teacher Feng. Follow the boy."

All the time the ruffian grinned. He seemed particularly amused by the stiff guards in their black uniforms, unblinking as he made faces at them, danced about and waved his hands, stabbing his fingers to within a cockroach length from their eyes.

"You needn't worry about Jianjun," the official reassured Feng. "They're his men. Don't be fooled by that clowning. He's the best in Chang'an. Trained this lot in the martial arts. The elite guard. He's just testing them. We've been scouring the city together. Looking for new recruits because of the times. Go join the boy. Before he gets himself sliced in two, huh? He's clever but still has much to learn."

By the time Feng reached the top of the stairs, Jinjin was inside the palace. Luckily, Master Tsu was there, talking to three black guards. The guards seized Jinjin before pushing him to the ground. One unsheathed his sword.

"Wait!" exclaimed Master Tsu. "Have you forgotten everything Jianjun taught you?" The guards stepped back. "Why, if you fear a child what hope is there when the White Tigers enter the palace?" The painter helped the boy to his feet.

Feng arrived at the top of the steps, panting.

"Yours, I presume, Teacher Feng!"

"His nothing!" objected Jinjin, rubbing his bruises. "I'm here to see the emperor. Save China from the empress and her nephew. I know where their army's camped. They'll attack the city from over the mountains as soon as he arrives from the west. And... and Chen Jiabiao was a traitor. Was really working for *them*! It's why I had to have him executed."

Master Tsu chuckled.

"Where did you find this boy, Feng? He amuses me so! And how come he's survived?"

"At Wong's inn. Houzicheng. And he survived because he's a child of the people. The people I try to teach. The country people. The poor peasants, as your teachers would have you call them!"

But Jinjin scorned Feng's offered defence:

"Poor no more! My name means gold, and I shall be rewarded," he insisted.

"Come on, come on! This way," indicated Master Tsu. The two officials by then had reached the palace, together with the jocular Jianjun. "It's arranged with the Chief Minister. And listen, oh little peasant of gold. Stay bowed to the floor at all times, ask no questions and leave no questions unanswered. Do I make myself clear? The emperor may be a good man, but these are not good times."

The teacher and the urchin boy followed Master Tsu and both officials. Should they have changed their minds and attempted to run from the palace they'd have got no further than Jianjun. Feng wondered whether that smile ever left the ruffian, even when he was busy eliminating opponents.

They passed through a second ante-room and waited in front of two huge red-lacquered doors whilst these were slowly opened by a palace servant. A large silk screen decorated with a red phoenix and yellow dragon, white cranes and clouds, blocked further views of the imperial chamber. A eunuch in silks wearing a hat of high office appeared from beyond the screen and whispered to Tsu. Tsu turned and beckoned to Feng and Jinjin. All entered the chamber, each immediately prostrating himself, his face pressed to the ground. A squeaky voice commanded them to come forwards.

Feng looked up first. Seated on the throne upon a high dais, accompanied by two beautiful women holding embroidered fans, was the imposing figure of the emperor. Eunuchs stood on either side of the women and two lines of court officials flanked the approach to the dais. The man's beard and moustache were smaller than Feng had imagined, but the emperor's distinctive hat and red robe of government were unmistakable.

Feng arose, alone, took several paces forwards, halted when he felt he was close enough to be heard then dropped again to his knees.

"His imperial majesty requests you speak, teacher of girls!" advised the squeaky-voiced eunuch standing near the emperor. "And be brief!"

"Your most esteemed imperial majesty, I come with ill news. The one who would steal the Dragon Throne, but who would first create for himself a human flower of a thousand petals, may have completed that task. His flower plucked, one of your agents in the south murdered, another exposed as a traitor, his threat to your divine throne now seems certain. My..."

The teacher paused briefly and glanced back at Jinjin whose untidy shock of black hair brushed the imperial floor. He had no idea how he should describe the urchin.

"My prize pupil in the arts and in poetry has risked his life to track down the White Tigers and uncover their camp. His name is fortunate indeed, your imperial majesty. They call him Jinjin."

Jinjin looked up and the eunuch beckoned him forwards.

"Speak, Jinjin of the arts and poetry who would dare advise his imperial majesty!" squeaked the eunuch.

With his eyes fixed all the time upon the emperor, Jinjin told his story. He spoke of hiding in the cart, watching the capture of the Miao girls, following the trader and Chen Jiabiao, and acquiring a servant:

"One who could protect me and give service to his imperial majesty as a guard to be trained in martial arts, your majesty. One named Kong."

The black-hatted court official hastily acknowledged the veracity of Jinjin's statement:

"Your imperial majesty, the boy that Jinjin mentions is indeed to be trained as a special imperial guard by none other than Jianjun. His skill in the martial arts is amazing. We should listen if Jinjin tells the truth. And he makes no mention of the empress. Only the treachery of General Ma and Nobleman Chen."

"Your imperial majesty," continued Jinjin, "General Ma... "

The emperor raised his hand, a sure sign he'd heard enough, and Jinjin prostrated himself on the floor as he'd done in front of Chen. Neither he nor Feng had noticed the tall figure waiting in the darkness behind the throne. The figure stepped forward, down the steps and stopped beside Jinjin. He kicked the boy in the side, not severely but enough to make the boy cry out.

"General Ma? What about General Ma?" the figure questioned.

Jinjin glanced briefly up at the figure, resplendent in military regalia far more elaborate than the uniform Ma had worn in the White Tigers' camp; wedged under one arm was the large plumed helmet of a general.

"Answer General Gao!" demanded the imperial eunuch.

"Attack," the boy said. "He'll attack from over the mountains. Not from the road to the east. He told me."

"So you spoke to our little fat pig, huh? And that's what he told you. You believed him?"

Jinjin was slow to reply, uncertain whether or not he was supposed to have believed the other general. The delay earned him another kick, harder than the first.

"No... I mean yes... at that time. I..."

"So he let you live whilst he waited to see which side his puny cousin was on. That makes sense. That's how the pig thinks. And he plans to attack from the road to the east. He knew you'd believe him, so told you the opposite. Thank you, urchin poet."

The general placed a foot on Jinjin's head and pressed it down, squashing the boy's nose and lips into the ground.

"An easy head to remove, your imperial majesty, but if the boy is correct we'll save your throne. We have an element of surprise to our advantage, but the pig is a tough opponent. And we don't know what troops from the west the nephew will have amassed. As Master Tsu and I have been telling you, we must leave tonight. Big difference is we now know to travel south, not east as your scum of an agent, Chen, told us."

He reached down, grabbed Jinjin by his scruffy hair and pulled him upright. Thrusting a hand under his chin, he pushed the boy's head back.

"But if you're wrong...!"

The emperor stood from his throne walked towards Jinjin. General Gao let go of the urchin and stepped back a pace.

"The boy tells the truth, my general. It is I who has misjudged my followers. Tell me young boy, what would you have as reward?"

Jinjin looked up at the imperial face half-expecting to see a dragon lurking behind the moustache and beard. Instead what he saw, and mostly in the eyes, was very human; far more so than the faces he'd scanned for stories at Wong's and the faces he'd studied since leaving Houzicheng urged on by *her* imagined face that refused to leave his mind.

"My reward would be for your place on the Dragon Throne to remain secure, imperial majesty," replied Jinjin. Though sorely tempted to mention the teacher's daughter, what emerged was indeed the truth. He knew now why this man was 'father' to the whole of China, whatever his faults.

"And you, Teacher Feng? Would you too have a request? If General Gao does his job?"

The general bowed and remained that way.

"That the poor people in China - especially our young girls - are allowed to learn about her greatness through the benevolence of her emperor, your imperial majesty," answered Feng without looking up.

Troops loyal to the emperor were already amassed outside the city. Jinjin and Feng travelled together in one of the carts as the column, headed by Gao, set off for the mountains. Neither spoke as each thought about the same girl; for one her image true, the other imagined - and the true was by far the more beautiful - but neither really knew the girl behind those exquisite looks and those eyes of innocence.

~

A while later, peering from the cart, Feng's eyes traced the winding snake of soldiers, carts and missile catapults in the moonlight all the way down the mountain and across the plain far below to the distant dark city of Chang'an where the imperial forces emerged from the darkness like a ghost army sent by the Jade Emperor. The teacher marvelled at the serenity of the scene. A few farmers in wide-brimmed hats still worked at night with their water buffalo in fields flanking the mountain as if in a world separated from the passing troops. He wondered what difference it would make to those farmers if this vast army were to end up slaughtered by General Ma's men and the Dragon Throne were to kiss the backside of the nephew of the empress? They would still be interminably shackled to the same destiny, tending the same crops in the same fields. But perhaps their children, especially their daughters, might notice the difference. Feng had to believe this. Without such enlightenment amongst the young people of China there'd have been no purpose in anything he'd done since Meili was taken from him.

They'd been travelling all night and all day, apart from a short stop for food, and still Jinjin refused to speak. It wasn't until the sun had sunk below the hills to the west illuminating the peaks above with a soft pink glow that the boy finally appeared to rediscover his voice.

"What's it like?" he asked.

"Being hit on the head and left to die?" queried Feng. "Why, it's..."

"No! Going with a girl. Offering her yourself. What's it like? How does the girl... I mean, what does she do?"

182

The teacher chuckled.

"A street urchin who knows nothing of coupling? Let's say it's like..." Feng paused. He'd never actually tried to describe in words the bliss of being as one with Meili. Had any poet ever succeeded with such a task? How could characters on paper, however beautiful the calligraphy, represent happiness such as that? "Do you swim?" he asked.

Meili had come to them having been rescued from the water. If the Miao were right, and the elements and all things in nature have spirits, was she not the spirit of water who once became a woman on earth?

"No!" replied Jinjin.

"Then I can't help you. The closest I can come up with is swimming - yet you and the girl are both water and swimmer."

"Does the girl keep her eyes open? I've heard men at Wong's talk about their eyes closing when it happens, when ecstasy binds the girl to you."

Feng chuckled.

"Eyes open, eyes closed? What does it matter? Soon we may both be lying dead in this camp you speak of. Will it matter whether our eyes are open or closed?"

"With a girl, everything matters. Every detail."

The poor boy may never know that pleasure. How can any man face his ancestors without having known this? What purpose would his existence have served?

"The Miao girl – Xiaopeng – she calls for her father every night. Why her father? What hold does a father have over a daughter, teacher? And should a girl not choose for herself?"

Feng sensed the conversation encroaching upon dangerous territory.

"You asked me what it's like for a man and a woman to come together. I've answered and need say no more. I only know Farmer Li will be the happiest man in China if you're right about his daughter and wrong about Ma's attack. The one thing her father will want to know, but which you, young urchin, cannot tell, is whether she's been taken."

Jinjin shrugged his shoulders. Soon afterwards the covered cart came to a halt short of a pass between two peaks. General Gao dismounted from his horse, an enormous figure made even bigger with his plumed helmet. Alone, he approached their cart.

"We'll go together," he said, shifting his gaze away from Jinjin and the teacher towards the mountain pass. "We'll look down from up there. If the boy's correct, we spend the night here and attack before dawn. Wrong, and he ends his days up here, his bones to be picked over by vultures, his spirit never to find the peace of his home town. And you, teacher, will remain in the palace an unpaid slave to education, never again to see that fabled daughter of yours!"

Jinjin and Feng climbed down from the cart. The boy scrambled behind the general up the scree. Before reaching the pass, Jinjin held back. General Gao looked round, saw the boy's hesitation and drew his sword. Feng feared the worst, but the general then sank to his knees and crawled to a view point from where he could survey the plateau beyond unseen. Jinjin's mind had been elsewhere, formulating a plan, one that might ensure the teacher's respect. The boy took off again, half-running, and when Feng saw him join the general on all fours, and the general re-sheathe his sword, he knew Jinjin had been right and would live.

From the high mountain pass they had a perfect view of a broad plateau that spread to the rolling hills to the south and black night pastures daubed grey by orderly rows of tents. General Gao's keen eyes appeared to take in every detail - where the horses were positioned, the catapults and the weaponry.

"You're a lucky young man," he whispered to Jinjin. "See! Everything ready, there on the road to the south. Ma's so predictable! It's why he defected. Brave on the battlefield, takes risks... but he knew I can always out-manoeuvre him. So he changed his allegiance at the first opportunity. Which tent, urchin boy?" Jinjin grinned. *He* would out-manoeuvre both generals! "Oh what a fool he must be! I can see it. Far end of the camp. The long one! Right?"

"Correct, your excellency! Guarding the prettiest girls for the empress's nephew," Jinjin informed him, in defence of General Ma's intelligence.

"Miao girls? Pfff!"

As the imperial army assembled itself in the dark across the steep slopes below the pass, Jinjin and Feng ate mantou buns in silence in their covered cart. Feng soon fell asleep, and when the coughs, the whispers and the whinnying of horses had stopped and Feng was snoring, Jinjin slipped noiselessly down. Crawling on hands and knees from rock to rock, curving round the side of the mountain out of sight from scouts on the pass, he descended slowly towards the unlit tents of the plateau below. He could scarcely believe how easy it was for a shunned urchin to determine the destiny of the Middle Kingdom. General Ma was no fool, whatever Gao might say. There'd been an understanding, a trust even, between the boy and Ma. Both had felt it, of this Jinjin was sure. The teacher had failed to answer satisfactorily when questioned about the role of a father in determining the fate of his child. What guarantee did he have the man would agree to his demand? With Feng dead and Gao's troops destroyed in their sleep, Ma-the-father-figure would give him protection, maybe even a small unit of soldiers. He could hasten on to the Miao village beyond Houzicheng, claim the girl and return with her to the imperial city. He'd become one of the new emperor's mandarins and the girl could forget all that learning. And why *was* the teacher so keen to treat girls as boys? Was it because he had no sons? He, Jinjin, would beget sons who could glory in his name.

Jinjin smelled the wine before he reached the first line of tents. Empty flagons, interspersed with half-gnawed goats' bones, littered the outskirts of the camp. This meant one thing to the boy: the emperor-to-be had arrived, swelling the ranks of Ma's army, and there'd been a celebration to mark the occasion. All save Ma would be drunk.

He slunk from tent to tent without encountering a single conscious lookout. Those entrusted with the safety of their sleeping comrades were slumped sideways over their impotent weapons. Creeping up to within a hand's distance of the face of the guard outside the entrance to the general's tent caused no more than a flicker of an eyelid as the man shifted his position. The boy's memory being infallible, he knew exactly where to sneak in and by choosing that spot rather than the far end where General Ma would be lying asleep, he once again altered the course of Chinese history.

It was the stench of wine that did it. His father had always inflicted the worst beatings when filled with wine. He'd seen men lose chess games, forfeit wives, homes – *all* possessions – whilst gambling under the influence of spirit. Drunkenness could lay waste China as it had destroyed his family.

He abandoned his plan, the one that came to him when he hesitated before joining General Gao on the mountain pass. Jinjin entered the tent by lifting up the felt halfway along the length of one side, transferring himself from a wine-filled darkness that reminded him of his father to one laden with the perfume of girls. Knowing she, the one who refused to leave his mind, would possess a fragrance far, far better, he stopped and listened. Sure enough one girl was crying softly, as Ma said she did every night. Jinjin prayed she understood enough Mandarin not to scream out in alarm and, crawling with cat-like stealth between the languorous bodies of delicious young females and the sloping wall of the tent, he approached the sobs. When level with the girl, he imagined the teacher's daughter also crying at some point in the future because he was away on an important errand for the emperor. He whispered:

"Teacher Feng sent me. To return you to your father. Stay quiet. Not a word and do everything I tell you."

The sobbing stopped. There was movement in the darkness. Then a face appeared just two hand breadths from his. He could see now why she'd been placed in the general's tent with the prettiest girls. Her features were exquisite and the urge to climb into her bed was overwhelming, but the girl in his head was even prettier and his wish to stay alive remained strong. Taking her by the arm, he helped the child down into the gap between the tent and the bed, lifted the canvas edge and, using the same route, skirted around the tents towards the mountainside. Progress was slow. The poor girl was barefoot so, crouching behind a boulder, the boy removed his shoes and set to work strapping them on Xiaopeng's feet. Only rarely did Jinjin wear shoes, his most valuable possession, at Wong's, and he marvelled at how small the girl's feet were. As she gracefully balanced each foot on his lap, not one word was spoken. He tied the shoes as tightly as he dared without causing her to cry out. Absurdly large on her young legs, they resembled the large feet of a little wading bird. Her eyes were those of a frightened rabbit, but there was trust in them and this was the first time any girl had looked at him in such a way, with trust. He wondered whether those eyes knew things yet unrevealed, and such musing helped to tame his young man's carnal thoughts. For him the first time would have to be with a girl who was as pure as the female in his head.

His hardened soles, as tough as clothes beaters, felt nothing as they scrambled on up the steep slope. Once again, slinking from rock to rock, always invisible to the imperial lookout up on the pass, they reached the cart in which the teacher still slept amongst soldiers' food rations. Without taking her sad, wide eyes off him, Xiaopeng got lifted onto the cart and the cover pulled aside. Jinjin jumped up after her and shook Feng awake. The man raised himself onto an elbow, rubbed his eyes and peered at the boy's grinning face.

"What?" he asked irritably.

Jinjin reached back, took the girl's sleeve and pulled her into the teacher's field of vision. Grinning triumphantly, the boy watched Feng's face, expecting it to glow with admiration for what he'd achieved and to promise unimaginable wealth; then he, Jinjin, would magnanimously offer to relieve the teacher of that burden of worry about his daughter and the marriage maker.

"Little Xiaopeng? Is it really you?"

"Yes, teacher," said the Miao girl.

"Shhh!" Jinjin cupped his hand over her mouth. "Not a word `til after the attack. `Til I've explained you to General Gao. Otherwise soldiers out there will turn you into a fish!" The girl frowned her puzzlement. "The teacher will explain another time - if you don't already know. Over there! In the corner! Behind me and the teacher! It's the safest place."

As the girl clambered over boxes and sacks of food to the back of the cart, her tempting curves and young breasts barely concealed by a thin sleeping garment, Jinjin worked out in his mind, before falling asleep, how to protect the Miao girl from fifty thousand female-deprived men.

~

It was still dark when Jinjin awoke with a start to a gentle knocking on the side of the cart. Feng and the girl were already up, in whispered conversation.

"What are you talking about?" he asked suspiciously.

"My daughter," replied the teacher. "Xiaopeng wants to know how she's looking after her father. She worries the girl has spent too much time in the schoolroom and not enough over the cooking pan and vegetables. I told her she's right."

Without replying, Jinjin jumped from the cart.

"Keep her hidden. Wait `til I return."

Normally, Feng would not have suffered such a string of commands from an upstart little older than Feier, but these were not normal times, and Jinjin was no ordinary young man. He listened to the crunch of Jinjin's thick-soled unshod feet on the gravel outside as the boy walked off to seek out the general. He felt around in the dark for food to give the girl, found a mantou and offered this to her but she shook her head. Something informed him all was not well, that perhaps she had been taken, but he didn't know how to ask. The only job he'd known was to teach young people, boys and girls, and he always thought he understood children so perfectly; but he realised there was gaping gap between him and the girl. There was something else, too, perhaps more of a problem than their age difference. If this had been Feier squatting timidly before him, and recently prisoner to an army of tens of thousands of sex-starved fighting men, would he really want to know whether or how she'd been deflowered? This being the case, surely he had no right to learn the fate of the farmer's daughter. Nevertheless, if she'd been taken he would have failed Yueloong.

The footsteps returned, augmented by the leather shoe tread of a man heavier than Jinjin. The curtain was pulled apart. Xiaopeng kept her eyes lowered in the face of the man's gaze. Feng watched the general's changing expressions, from disbelief, to lust, to anger until, for the first time, a smile pulled at the corners of the man's thin mouth. He turned to Jinjin.

"So, you're telling me the man who would wish to become emperor is now one short of a thousand petals? I like it! I really do! And because of this girl, he won't have the *qi* force to save his army from obliteration?"

"The girl is Buddhist," added Feng, as if this might protect her from being ravished by Gao's troops.

Jinjin continued:

"Your excellency, because of Xiaopeng's rescue the nephew's karma is being rewritten. She's the one who has changed everything. Altered the destiny of the Middle Kingdom! If she's destroyed, Ma will get stronger. Balance of force. Don't you see?"

"All I see is a girl as pretty as any painting in the Imperial Palace."

"Down there are another nine hundred and ninety-nine. Would you risk the wrath of the emperor's ancestors by putting the whole of China at risk for a few moments of pleasure?"

General Gao laughed.

"Few moments? When did you last have a girl, little urchin? But you're right. Besides, we must attack before sunrise. Stay here with the girl, Teacher Feng. Jinjin, you come with me. Help me track down the traitor Ma."

～

When Jinjin and the general had disappeared over the pass, together with fifty thousand troops, horses and catapults, when the noise of an army on the move had dwindled to silence, for the mountain blocked the clamour of battle on the plain beyond, then the teacher asked. And he watched as the girl who was little more than a child fought the terror blanking her mind; he thought of *his* child alone at night in the Miao farmhouse and imagined her being defenceless against a mob of village men even though his friend was honourable. As with his daughter, he had to know this girl with him in the army cart was untouched.

"Did those soldiers do anything to you?"

Xiaopeng, without looking up, shook her head.

Whatever the outcome of the soundless battle now waging on that plain beyond the pass, Feng now swore he would protect the honour of the farmer's daughter with his life. If that was lost, his spirit would return to drive away any would-be ravishers. She would be returned pure to her father as Feier would be returned to him, untouched.

12.

Heaven and Hell

Jinjin had never imagined a battle could have been won so easily. When the catapults first launched their boulders and globes of fire from the slopes, thousands upon thousands of troops already encircled the entire camp, having stripped away the enemy's weaponries. Archers released locust swarms of arrows whilst terrified warriors emerged from tents, staggering blindly in the dark. Waves of soldiers loyal to the emperor swept in from the periphery, slicing paths through the enemy with mechanical efficiency. Meanwhile, Jinjin directed General Gao to the long tent then followed in the man's wake as the general slashed his way across the camp.

The tent still stood and was one of several that screamed with shrill, young female voices. The general, with bloodied sword in hand, approached.

"The girls, General Gao! Please don't harm them!"

"First rule of war, Jinjin. Women are not for killing. Think of them as a bonus for a job well done."

Sitting in his night garment on the ground at the back of the tent, holding an empty flagon of wine, General Ma looked up as Gao approached.

"Only one prisoner, Ma! We don't have enough food to feed the rest. But I see at last you've discovered the pleasure of wine, ay?"

Ma made no attempt to resist when the other general kicked the bottle from his hand and dragged him to his feet. Using a tie that had kept Ma's hair in a neat bun at the top, General Gao bound his rival's wrists behind his back whilst the man's tangled hair fell untidily across his broad, bearded face. Jinjin emerged from behind the safety of Gao's bulk and approached the prisoner.

"Blame our fathers if you wish," he said to Ma. "You see, the stink of the wine reminded me of my father and all those beatings."

"Pah! I should have known when the crying stopped. This was all about that stupid girl, wasn't it?"

"*And* respect for the *yin*," added Jinjin. "General Gao was lenient to the girl. He showed respect. Like Teacher Feng. She returns to her *baba*."

"Go, Jinjin," said General Gao. "This slaughter isn't for young boys. Go back to the teacher. Take the cart and the girl before my weary soldiers return with their spoils. That virgin you hide won't remain so for long if she's still there when they do. Take the trail off the mountain towards the rising sun then join the road back to your province. I promise you, the emperor will hear of your courage. Go!"

Jinjin stood for a few moments staring at General Ma's feet.

"He'll not need those, will he? In his next life? They look about the right size."

"Take them! Pigs don't wear shoes!"

Jinjin hurriedly relieved Ma of his shoes before scrambling back up the side of the mountain to rejoin the teacher and the Miao girl. The sun had already risen when they turned the cart around and urged its two docile horses on towards a downward trail to the east. They had enough provisions to last a thousand men several days, but General Gao must have reckoned there'd be more than enough to feed his troops in the nephew's camp. Whether the nephew of the empress had been slaughtered that night, or would end up losing his head in a public square in Chang'an alongside General Ma, Jinjin never found out. From that moment on it was as if he'd never existed, and the titles of 'empress' and the 'emperor's first wife' were passed on to another woman.

The Miao girl smelt as delicious now as when he first saw her in that tent.

"Does she speak fluent mandarin?" Jinjin asked Feng.

"Ask her! She should do. She and my daughter have been close friends for eight years and my girl speaks barely a word of her language. Thanks to our emperor, some day all our communities in China will be able to talk with one another."

"Thanks to *you*, Teacher Feng! Xiaopeng, tell me about your young friend the teacher speaks of. His daughter. What's she like? Is she obedient?"

Feng scowled. To scold the boy who'd rescued the farmer's daughter and was allowing him to return home alive seemed wrong, but the ancestors might forgive a scowl.

"Why do you ask?" she questioned.

"Gao's a man of honour. He'll see me rewarded by the emperor. What better reward than to see Teacher Feng's daughter married off to someone in power? Xiaopeng, tell me. What's she like? Pretty?"

Xiaopeng nodded.

"No temper?"

The Miao girl shook her head.

"I hear you're also Buddhist. Like the teacher. Does the girl say her prayers? Pay her dues to the monks?"

"Ask her father."

"Feng?"

"What is it to you? Or to anyone at court?"

"Do you want my help? Haven't I made it possible for you to forget the marriage maker?"

Feng recalled his daughter's fear of death, the monastery - even the Buddha. Perhaps he'd been too caught up trying to erase the lingering memory of Meili, covering up the past whilst failing to explain things beyond his comprehension to little Feier.

"I'm sure I told you. About the monasteries," Feng replied.

"Oh yes! The monasteries and their *sun wu kongs*."

Jinjin had yet to solve the business of the merchant's death and the monasteries. He knew Chen had been lying and that the murder involved the monastery near Feng's village. Solve that and the teacher could not refuse him!

∼

Angwan spent only one day and one night in the Miao village the other side of Houzicheng to where he'd been banished. No-one there liked Old Xiang, and when the story had been retold in his words not a single man in the village saw any objection to his having had his pleasure with the teacher's daughter. They were envious of course, for those deprived of bed companions longed for women, but the disappearances only made Angwan's action more acceptable. Besides, with Farmer Li a Buddhist and Angwan having spent time in the monastery, each had a foot in the Han world. Better Angwan marry a Han than compete for the few remaining Miao girls. Old Xiang and his brother should be pleased, they decided amongst themselves. But Angwan had said nothing about the arranged betrothal to Xiaopeng.

The following day, he left for the monastery near the lotus lake. The elders had suggested a cooling-off period before returning to his village. Time, they said, was the best healer of anger, and early reappearance would merely worsen the Han girl's punishment.

It was a hot day, and on the trail from the lotus lake he stopped at the oil press halfway up the hill, since he'd run out of water. He knew the operator, for during his brief period as a novice monk he used to visit him.

The press was one of several in the area, all owned by the monastery. No peasant could afford such expensive equipment, but they paid rent to the monks which is how Angwan became acquainted with Chou, a thin-faced man with prominent teeth and a limp, who worked from day-break 'til sundown producing sesame and other oils from seed, whatever the weather. The young Miao priest had been aware of a rift between Chou and the *sun wu kong*, and that it was to do with taxes levied on the oil. Somehow, the fat trader had been involved. The operator never told the full story and Angwan now wanted to uncover the truth, but Chou would always dry up like an abandoned sesame press, saying he was too busy and that a young man would never understand anyway.

"*Ni hao* [23], Angwan! Back for more of that gibberish nonsense up there on the top of the hill?" asked Chou.

"If only it was that easy!" responded Angwan. "I may stay a while, though. 'Til things have blown over. What news from the villages, friend Chou?"

"Nothing for *your* ears, Angwan."

"Did the children go past this morning? With Teacher Feng's daughter?"

---

[23] hello (literally 'you good')

"Now there's a thing! Monks tell me she got herself into some sort of trouble."

"Trouble?"

"Big! But as I said, not for your ears. And from what I heard the teacher's unlikely to come back. What a fool! Chasing your missing girls and hunting down the merchant's killer. Pah! There's many glad to see that man dead. Why go asking questions?"

"Has anyone else been asking you about Merchant Chang? Any of the magistrate's men?"

"That new guy? Who used to be a monk up there on the hill? No. I've not seen or spoken with anyone from Houzicheng. Suppose you're after water, then?"

Angwan nodded. Knowing he'd squeeze little more out of Chou, he helped himself using a ceramic cup on the floor beside a water-filled pot in the corner.

"Surprised the *sun wu kong* hasn't decided to tax the water too. Mind you, with Chang dead, the man's going to want to play safe."

Big trouble? Play safe?

Angwan had no clear idea how he'd get assistance from the monastery. Perhaps the Buddha might take pity on him and mollify the guilt that was driving him insane, although he'd have preferred a small army to secure the girl's release to a flock of useless, silent monks. But help or no help, there was one monk he had to seek out before Li Yueloong's next visit to the temple; one monk who might save Feier's life.

~

It was the women who finally took pity on the girl and demanded the men free her for short periods from that awful bamboo cage. They washed her, fed her and rubbed oils into the red stripes and the bruises where the struts had pressed into her tender, young skin. No-one questioned the need to punish the girl, and the elders still argued and discussed her fate, unable to agree on the severity of the sentence, but the women insisted Feier was no animal and not to be treated as one, even if her religion was likely to shortly return her to Earth as a pig. Also, Yueloong now insisted she be kept alive until at least three moons after her father's departure.

At first she would scream and struggle before being returned to the cage, but when Old Xiang threatened her with a beating she would go silent and limp, as if her spirit had already abandoned her and, to the disgust of all, Old Xiang continued to urinate over her when she was entrapped in that bamboo nightmare. Only fading memories of the night in Angwan's arms prevented her heart from giving up. She tried to imagine the pain of the bamboo yielding to the firm touch of his fingers and his thighs, and she held on to life whilst the village elders deliberated over her death.

~

They made good progress along the road to Houzicheng. Whether it was the presence of the girl or because of the boy's attempt to play 'little mandarin', Feng couldn't make out, but the non-stop banter of the urchin from Wong's inn had been replaced by long periods of silence for which the teacher was grateful. He was able to think. There'd been little chance to do that ever since leaving the Xiangjisi monastery and he needed this time to plan his daughter's future happiness.

He'd played a role in protecting the emperor's throne, albeit small compared with that of the boy who had finally stopped talking. There was the distinct possibility of a reward from the emperor. His choice: a post in the city. He and Feier could open a school together; fame of his new teaching methods might attract attention in the capital, and for sure Feier's beauty would not go unnoticed. He could see her as a court teacher, sought after by princes and sons of mandarins alike.

Trusting no-one, all three slept overnight in the cart. Jinjin and Feng took it in turns to stay awake and guard the girl. The only available weapon was the sharpened bamboo stake that had travelled with the teacher from the merchant's final resting place beside the lotus lake to Chang'an and now accompanied him on his return journey. It had become for the man a symbol of his determination, but for Jinjin, still eager to solve the death of the teacher's friend, it was something different: a puzzle.

Why kill a man with a bamboo pole? Because the murderer had no access to more efficient weaponry? Because he could never be traced since bamboo was used by anyone and everyone for anything and everything? Or because bamboo stems yield in the wind and the merchant had perhaps upset someone – a White Tiger, maybe – through intolerance, and therefore his fate would have to be determined with bamboo? Although Jinjin spoke little on the road to Houzicheng, the voice inside his head never stopped.

They were only half-a-day's ride from Houzicheng when a familiar sound caused Jinjin, who was driving, to rein the two horses to a halt. He turned and peered over the cover of the cart under which the teacher and the Miao girl rested following a meal. He'd heard the approach of galloping horses, and held the bamboo pole in both hands as a posse of imperial guards pulled up alongside them. The lead rider gave a short bow without dismounting.

"A message from the emperor's court," the man announced.

The drape covering the front of the cart was lifted. Feng's face blinked at Jinjin in the sunlight, whilst in the darkness behind him the girl cowered amongst boxes of stale rice cakes, buns and dried fruit.

"The emperor? A message?" questioned Feng.

"For me?" queried Jinjin holding firmly onto the pole. The rider cocked his head to one side.

"For the emperor's special agent," he informed the boy. "One of you will know who that is."

"But..." began Jinjin.

"Report to Magistrate Minsheng in Houzicheng. He awaits you."

"The new magistrate? You...?"

Jinjin never finished his sentence. The riders kicked their horses and with a noise of hooves on loose stones, galloped off in clouds of dust. He waited for the air to clear before urging the horses forward. There was a short argument over whether they should go first to Wong's to eat and let the girl wash and rest, or visit Minsheng as directed. Feng won. He was too eager to see the magistrate, find out what the emperor's reward might be, and to learn news of his daughter. Besides, *he* was that special agent.

Mimi was tied to a post in the courtyard of the magistrate's house. The teacher left Jinjin and Xiaopeng in the cart, realizing now the boy was to be trusted, whilst the manservant led him to the magistrate's hall. Minsheng stood on the familiar rug, facing the other way, his hands clasped behind his back. The manservant coughed to alert his attention and left.

"Welcome back, fellow agent of the emperor," announced the magistrate. "There on the table. Your Sung Po scroll. Take the thing. You'll need it. Mind you, I've never seen much point in poetry. Or the pretence that you can change the meaning of things by making pretty characters with a calligraphy brush." Feng picked up the scroll, uncertain how to ask. "Oh... and your reward from the emperor. Let's just say I'll forget the sword you lost, eh? Save you fifty blows."

The stolen sword was the last thing on Feng's mind. Until reminded, he'd forgotten all about it. Besides, he knew the magistrate was withholding something and by keeping his back turned he was sending the teacher a message.

"You have news from the villages?" asked the teacher. "We return with one of the girls. And the others, well, General Gao will decide."

"Yes, General Gao. We have him to thank, too."

"Do you have nothing to tell me? About my daughter?"

"I cannot interfere with Miao ways. As with the disappearing Miao girls, now with your daughter."

Feng felt panic claw at his throat; his voice became weak.

"What do you mean? Now *what* with my daughter?"

"I told you. You'll need the Sung Po scroll. It's worth a small fortune though, as I said, why is a mystery to me."

Feng hated the magistrate for playing games and for his annoying lack of directness. He'd now have to hurry back to the Miao village without stopping off at Wong's inn. Cupping his hands together, he bowed to the magistrate's broad shoulders and backed away.

"Aren't you curious to know the emperor's message?" asked Minsheng.

Feng stopped. Was this part of the ongoing game? He remembered their last encounter when he believed he was only a few Mimi lengths from death.

"Your excellency?"

"Friend, please. Despite what's happened, call me 'friend'. I do hope Master Tsu told you we agents expect no reward for serving our emperor."

"What's happened? In the village? My daughter? Have they harmed her?"

"You, teacher, *you* harmed her. She's been a woman for too long and you stubbornly refused to see it. All because of your battle with that mean old marriage maker."

The panic now took hold of every fibre in Feng's body. He started to tremble.

"Tell me ... " he began.

"I *told* you, I can't interfere. And still you don't ask the right question!"

"Question?"

"The emperor's message!"

Feng bowed again, as if this might help him to release some awful truth from the magistrate's back.

"Yes. I was told to see you about a message from the emperor."

"Which I can only tell to the boy. Send him in."

"Your excellency?"

"Don't think I'm ungrateful," Minsheng continued. "Thanks to you we shan't have to meet up again. There are changes, you see. The governor lost his head yesterday. It's on its way to Chang'an with several others, including that of the empress. To be displayed outside the Imperial Palace. Those of her nephew and General Ma, too. And me? Well, as governor I'll be able to raise an army. It's what I've always wanted. So, thank you! Now send me the boy, please. *You* were never meant to be one of the eight. That was only Master Tsu's idea - until the boy turned up."

Clutching the scroll, Feng had to steady himself against a pillar on his way back to the courtyard. He felt faint, but to collapse in the house of Magistrate Minsheng was not an option. Jinjin jumped from the cart and came over to him.

"He wants to see *you*. I'll leave with Xiaopeng," Feng said. "She can ride the donkey."

"Me? A reward?"

"Ask *him*," replied the teacher. "I think you two will get on rather well together."

The manservant appeared at the door to take Jinjin into the hall whilst Feng busied himself transferring Xiaopeng from the back of the cart to the donkey, taking with him the bamboo pole and some food and water. As he was untying Mimi, Jinjin reappeared, his face stretched into a broad grin. Feng glanced up briefly. For the first time he realised what it was about this urchin that troubled him. Before, he'd put it down to annoyance, but he now realised it was far more than that. The boy frightened him - worse even, *terrified* him.

"You have your reward, I see," he said, pulling Mimi forwards.

"Yes. I'm coming with you."

Feng's heart sank. More of Jinjin was very the last thing he wanted.

"Get back to Wong's. Boast to the world how you saved China single-handed."

"You'll understand soon enough, teacher. I wish to see that daughter of yours. You also, I'll wager."

No further words were necessary, and none spoken, during that final leg of the journey back to Xiaopeng's village. The Miao girl thought only of the little farmhouse, wondering how her *baba* could possibly have managed in her absence. Jinjin was already in a different world, on his way back to Chang'an where, if the Han girl were to match the image in his head, his brain promised him the life of a wealthy married mandarin with a magnificent courtyard home. *Heaven!* Teacher Feng feared the worst: that *hell* was the only reality he'd discover.

13.

A Scroll for a Life

Angwan was accepted back into the fold of the monastery. That he'd been given leave from his duties in the Miao village - the story he gave the *sun wu kong* - was not untrue, and thankfully the young monk he sought was still there. Side-by-side during prayer, Angwan whispered a suggested meeting place and time, and later that day, in a shaded bamboo grove, the two men talked.

As Angwan suspected, Chou had got it wrong. It was the *sun wu kong*, not Chang, nor even the monastery, who had benefited from excessive taxation of those who ran the mills and of the peasants who worked the extensive lands owned by the monastery. The merchant had been spying on the *sun wu kong*, pretending to work for him whilst passing on information to the new magistrate. Most monks knew their head man had been supplying the White Tiger League with funds, and now it was only a matter of time. Once the White Tigers had been crushed, the monasteries would get 'cleaned up'.

But Angwan hadn't returned to the monastery to find out who had been behind the diversion of public money to a traitorous bunch of traders, nor was he too concerned whether or not the dead merchant had been implicated, although he'd have preferred to hear the man listed as guilty. He wanted to know what this particular monk had seen on the seventh day of the seventh month. And whom he had told.

~

In the Miao villagers' eyes, Feier was the evil one for seducing the young priest and her fate lay in the hands of the village elders: almost certainly a beating in the village public space for all to witness. What had yet to be decided, when Feng discovered this, was whether it was to be a thick or a thin rod; thick, and she would die.

Yueloong saw no other way out. He'd admired Feier and enjoyed her company before his brother warned him about the effect she had on Angwan. Angered on learning this, he struggled briefly with the desire he felt for her blossoming body, but he was a man of honour, not one to be bewitched like the young priest by the spell of the teacher's daughter.

"Only kissing," she had claimed, blushing like a red phoenix, but Angwan had said she was now 'his' and that, since neither Feng nor Xiao-peng were likely ever to return, the young priest would be doing the farmer a favour by relieving him of the teacher's child.

The farmer ignored his friend of old on first seeing him standing beside the black donkey in front of the post to which his water buffalo was se-cured. It was as if the other man wasn't there. Xiaopeng ran from Mimi to her father and wept, and from the way she clung to him the man feared she'd been taken by the one who so nearly became emperor, and for this he also blamed the father of the Han slut. After he heard that his child was undamaged, having had Angwan stolen from her by Feier seemed all the more unbearable.

Feng, unaware of recent happenings in the Miao village, called out:

"I kept my promise, Yueloong! We brought her back. Unharmed! Thanks to my accomplice here. And he has to meet Feier. Is she in the schoolroom with the children? Turned them all into little scholars, no doubt?"

Yueloong disengaged himself from Xiaopeng's embrace and turned to face Feng. The teacher couldn't work out that look on his face: a mix of disgust, of anger and sorrow.

"Yueloong, we did what we could! Why, if hadn't been for Jinjin, she'd be in Chang'an with those other girls now, just another petal in our great emperor's harem. So why the death look, my friend? And where's Feier?"

"Where, you ask? Where's your daughter-the-whore? I'll tell you. She's where she should be! In the criminal cage until the elders can decide her fate!" Feng stared in silent disbelief. Could the man truly be referring to

Feier? "You planned this, didn't you? All that talk about the evil marriage maker in your village - trying to get my sympathy, eh? And your pretence about wanting to help us get our girls back... that business about your murdered friend... I see it all. Taking advantage of my loss. An excuse to get your daughter into our village, so she could get her claws into him... you... you..."

He turned, grabbed Xiaopeng's arm and pulled the girl into his house.

"*Baba*? What do you mean? What have you done to Feier?" the girl protested. Feng ran to the door.

"Yueloong, stop this nonsense! We're friends, you and I. Just tell me what's going on."

"Your grand ideas about fancy education for girls - see what's gone and happened! It's those poems that did it! Why, if little Xiaopeng had the chance to learn what you stuffed into the head of that little whore of yours... well..."

Something flipped when Feng heard the name of his daughter treated with disrespect. He strode up the farmer and, fist clenched, hit him full on the face. Yueloong staggered backwards, crashing into the stove, knocking a pan full of scalding water to the floor. Xiaopeng screamed:

"Stop, *baba*! Please stop!"

The two men, breathing like stags locked in battle, looked at the child.

"Take me to Feier! At once, *baba*!" demanded Xiaopeng.

Yueloong picked himself up and dusted down his tunic before reluctantly following his daughter and a friend-turned-enemy outside.

All the time, Jinjin stood by himself, silent, as if awaiting the right moment to enter the scene. Inside he seethed. Since first hearing about the girl, her gentleness and purity had become etched upon his mind as clearly as the White Tiger tattoo cut into the back of his hand. He'd waited for so long to see her with his eyes, not just hear about her loveliness through that lesser sense of the ears. Silent as a spring about to open, he followed the others to the village square, vowing vengeance on the man who had destroyed her purity; being both secret agent to the emperor and newly-appointed local magistrate, he had the power to mete out punishment.

Others in the street, recognising Feier's father, joined them, and soon a small crowd had gathered in the public space. Feng stared in horror at the solitary bamboo cage. So these monsters had kept his little daughter cooped up in an animal cage! He'd kill anyone who had so much as touched a hair upon her sweet head! He watched whilst Xiaopeng approached the cage, untied the binding and raised the flap.

At first nothing happened and Feng feared the girl had died. Then her face appeared and the teacher stared in horror. Feier emerged, crawling stiffly on all fours, her tangled hair half-covering her face. The child's spirit was gone, her body hunched and her feet bare, those small hands bleeding from beating in vain at the cruel bamboo poles that had held her trapped. Feng's fury was so strong it rendered him without speech or power of movement for a few moments. Xiaopeng hugged her friend, stroking the older girl's hair away from her tear-stained face.

Jinjin, seizing the opportunity, stepped forward. Together, he and Xiaopeng helped Feier to her feet. The boy seemed unable to take his eyes of Feng's daughter as if, even in her dishevelled state, her beauty far exceeded the near-legendary accounts he'd heard about her. Xiaopeng stood to one side as Jinjin took Feier to her father. Too ashamed to look up at her dear *baba*, her expression betrayed fear that accompanies unspeakable pain.

"Feier... tell me, is it true?"

Feier said nothing.

"Feier, I need to know... and what they've done to you, too... I..."

"I'll kill the fiend who did this to your daughter, Teacher Feng, if it's the last thing I do!" interrupted Jinjin.

"Feng!" bellowed Yueloong. The teacher turned and saw his old friend surrounded by a group of village elders.

"Feng, they've decided on leniency. Now that you've returned with Xiaopeng, they say to let your daughter go back with you to your village. In exchange for your scroll. We heard the thing's worth a small fortune. Got word about it from Houzicheng. It might go some way to buying back our other sisters lost to the Imperial Court. But we none of us want anything more to do with you or your whore of a daughter. If you or the girl set foot in our village again, you'll be returned home wrapped in shrouds."

Still Feier said nothing.

"Wait!" warned Jinjin. "I'll not stand by and listen to you address Teacher Feng like that! Do you know who I am? Can't you people show any respect?"

"Respect? He asks us to show respect after what's happened?" questioned one of the elders. "And who is this urchin boy?"

"Be careful what you say!" warned Feng. "This boy has been given the job of prefectural magistrate, and special agent to the emperor. We learned of his reward in Houzicheng. From Minsheng. Jinjin saved the emperor's life! He saved China. The favour he asked, that one less than a thousand petals should satisfy any emperor's appetite for pretty girls as well as weakening the enemy, has allowed us to return Xiaopeng to you. If you want to know how Xiaopeng got rescued ask the child! And whatever my daughter's done - or hasn't done - it could never deserve this!"

"Teacher," interrupted Jinjin, "no good can come of this. We must leave. I'll help your daughter onto the donkey."

He lifted Feier onto Mimi's back and led the donkey away. Half-turning, he called out:

"Where is he, the man who did this… who destroyed her purity?" And he glowered at the elders.

The villagers looked at one another. One spat and worked the gob into the dust with his foot, but all remained silent. Feng joined Jinjin, Feier and Mimi. They left the village, passing over the hills through the wood, past the lotus lake and the path leading up to the monastery. Feier uttered not a single word of explanation, and Jinjin remained uncharacteristically quiet. The boy kept glancing at the girl, and the teacher should have read the danger in his eyes. Instead, he mistook the look for one of disdain for the daughter who meant everything to him. If only he'd realised then how much the urchin-turned-government-official idolised the child who meant more to the teacher than life itself. He misread the signs and, like a donkey trekking a road that leads nowhere, his inaction forced all three along paths of uncertainty.

Everyone in the Han village knew about Feier and Angwan. The young men hated the girl for 'throwing herself' at the Miao man who pretended to be a priest. It didn't take much to persuade the women to side with the men, for jealousy comes easily to the *yin* when unbalanced by the *yang*, and the children... well, they had either forgotten how much they used to love the teacher's daughter or had been told to forget. Children ran from the pitiful group as Mimi dawdled through the village towards the school-house, shielding small noses with cupped hands against the dung and urine smells of the girl. No-one asked Feng about his long period of absence, or sought to enquire who Jinjin was, the urchin whose eyes were afire with anger. The teacher and the boy might well have been *gui*, visible to only a chosen few, as all stared at the girl with contempt.

Jinjin helped Feier to dismount. What young man would show such courtesy to a girl he despised? But even such a gesture of deference was misinterpreted by Feng as he led his daughter across the schoolhouse courtyard which looked exactly as he'd left it. The teacher felt Feier had been humiliated enough; Jinjin, only a few years older than the girl, was surely now mocking his beloved child and he wanted to be alone with her when she recovered her speech.

"You should leave now, Jinjin. Thank you, but I need no more help," he said without turning.

"But..." the boy began, about to suggest he take the girl back to Houzi-cheng after she'd been fed and bathed, to formalize their union immediately.

"Leave!" shouted Feng. "At once!"

If the man wasn't so blind in matters concerning Feier he'd have known everything the boy had done was with one aim in mind: to gain favour with the teacher and impress the man's daughter. If Jinjin had explained this there and then, nothing might have happened. But the young boy, his secret infatuation with the girl now a reality, was overcome with emotions he'd never before experienced: jealousy, inadequacy in the face of such beauty, and fury. Raw, un-quenchable fury. He stared from the doorway when Feng took the girl inside and sat her down on the bed.

"You don't have to tell me anything you don't want to, my child. Did they feed you in that... that cage... that animal prison?"

Feier nodded.

"What about other things? Could you sleep? You had no room even to lie down?"

A shake of the head.

"How could they be so cruel? Nothing my little girl might have done would deserve such treatment! And to think what I've been through to rescue that daughter of his! Why, you'd think it was his girl who'd been defiled! Curse them all!"

Feier broke down. She sobbed uncontrollably and Feng hugged her, stroking her tousled hair.

Jinjin, feeling excluded, turned and fetched Feng's bamboo pole from beside Mimi where the teacher had dropped it, and ran without stopping the ten *li* back to the Miao village. He asked a lone child in which house lived the man who had disgraced himself with the Han teacher's daughter. The boy led him there.

"Will you kill him as well as Feier?" the child asked Jinjin, but the latter didn't reply. "There! Angwan - the new priest."

The boy pointed to a larger house away from the main street. Jinjin went on alone, leaving the boy staring. It was surrounded by a yard littered with utensils and broken farming implements. Angwan's father had been a skilled repairer. To the side was a pig pen where three silent, grey pigs lay stretched out in the dust.

"Coward, show yourself!" he shouted.

Not even the pigs responded. He spied a bamboo fence behind the house, separating the yard from the rice field beyond. There was a gap in the fence where a pole was missing. Perhaps the dog was cowering on the other side. Clutching Feng's bamboo, Jinjin went to look. On approaching the fence he noticed the poles were roughly the same diameter as the one in his hand. There was something on the ground near the gap. Closer, he saw that it was an axe, and beside it were splinters of bamboo. When Jinjin picked up the axe and examined the blade, then he knew. The shape of the protuberance, opposite the pointed edge of the bamboo that had killed Feng's merchant friend, perfectly matched the half-moon-shaped chip out of the middle of the blade. It was all suddenly so clear. Angwan and Feier. His anger erupted like a volcano.

He checked behind the bamboo fence. Deserted! He ran back to the house, shouting the man's name. Inside, he flung utensils off shelves, upturned tables, smashed jars and tore up the Miao priest's scrolls. He struck at the walls with the axe. But the walls were blameless. And there was no need to do the deed himself. He had the evidence, and murder deserved public beheading whoever the victim had been. Punishment for the priest's crime against the girl would come later when the man's headless, restless ghost would beg to escape from torment at the hands of ancestors.

Jinjin left the axe embedded in a table and ran with Feng's pole from the Miao village, back through the woods, past the lotus lake. As he passed the monastery path, muttering curses, he was too distracted to notice a seated monk hunched to one side halfway up the hill. Hearing Jinjin, Angwan looked up. He sprang to his feet and followed the boy to the Han village and the street with the schoolhouse. There he stood and listened from behind the trunk of a magnolia tree.

"The murderer! I have proof!" the boy shouted.

Feng, exhausted, appeared in the schoolhouse doorway.

"On the bamboo pole! The cut end fits a notch in the blade of his axe. It was he who killed your merchant friend, teacher. The Miao priest who took Feier!"

"What are you talking about, Jinjin? I've grown sick and tired of your ramblings!"

"Work it out! I thought you had brains when we first met! This tongue here..." He pointed to the rounded protuberance at the cut end of the bamboo. "It fits perfectly into the chip on the edge of Angwan's axe-head like a... like..." He glanced at the girl standing beside Feng. "Ugh! *He's* the one who killed your friend. And why? He must have done a deal with the merchant! He got the merchant to arrange for Farmer Li's daughter to disappear so he wouldn't be forced to marry the poor girl! Then he killed Chang because he was the only witness. He would have known you'd feel guilty, teacher, and go off on a trail of madness to satisfy your conscience. And he knew you'd trust Yueloong to look after Feier. So he could sink his... his... his filthy..."

"It wasn't like that!"

Jinjin turned. Angwan, robed as a monk, stood but a few paces away. He was unarmed. Feier, who had followed her father to the schoolhouse entrance, looked up on hearing the Miao priest's voice. Having just bathed, washed and combed her hair, she now wore a clean blue dress, embroidered around the bodice with delicate yellow and pink flowers. More beautiful than a painted goddess, she caused both boy and man momentarily to forget their dispute and gaze at her. The girl stared at the young Miao man, not knowing what to say or do. Feng placed a cautioning hand on her shoulder.

"Angwan? Tell me, is this true?" asked Feng.

"She hated the merchant! But none of you would understand that, would you? Not one of you truly knows anything about the girl! If you..."

Maybe it was use of the words 'knows' and 'the girl' in the same sentence that gave Jinjin the courage to kill, or perhaps he was simply too young to comprehend, or too inexperienced to control his rage. Whatever the reason, there was no time for the priest to answer Feng. Jinjin ran at Angwan with the pointed bamboo before the other man could continue his verbal defence. Angwan, deflecting the blow, stumbled and fell backwards, banging his head on a large stone. Jinjin, a crazed animal, chose to play with his prey sprawled out, stunned, in the street. He held the bamboo high with both hands, for maximum thrust, its point directed at the belly of the man on the ground. He paused to savour the other man's fear.

"Is this how you did it, then?"

Angwan saw only a blur of the figure above him. He opened his mouth, but no words came. Jinjin raised the pole even higher and closed his eyes. Feier screamed, broke free from her father, rushed forwards and flung herself onto Angwan's body at the very moment when Jinjin struck down with the sharpened pole, driving the point into her body instead.

In different ways, all three men loved the girl who rolled in the dust, shrieking and writhing and clutching at the bamboo stake sticking out from her side. Horrified by what he'd done, Jinjin ran from the courtyard and from the village. Feng knelt and cradled his daughter's head on his lap whilst Angwan, dazed and splattered with the blood of the Han girl he so adored, rose to his knees, held her hands and wept like a child until her gasps ceased and the twitching stopped, until her body went still, all signs of life extinguished; then, after pulling the stake free from her limp body, he took her in his arms and cried out in grief whilst holding her against his chest.

Although Angwan knew much about Feng from Feier, the teacher had little knowledge of the man he'd only ever thought of as the young Miao-would-be-priest-part-Buddhist. It had never occurred to him that the Buddhism was for Feier's benefit, despite having seen the boy-turning-man hover outside the Miao village schoolroom whenever he and Feier had finished a class. Now, in shared grief, the two men took the body of the girl into the schoolroom, laid her gently on the floor and covered her with a silk sheet. Neither was able to formulate words, but there seemed no need for speech. They worked as one. Feng ran off for help whilst Angwan stayed kneeling beside Feier.

The girl remained in the schoolroom until a coffin was fashioned and either Feng or Angwan would guard her body. The young priest chanted for hours on end; to Feng the words made no sense but the haunting sound gave credence to the man's love for his daughter. Whether or not he had 'taken her' was of no importance. Her life and what they had done together whilst he and Jinjin were rescuing Xiaopeng now belonged to the past, lost somewhere in that tangled forest of the mind where memories merge like veils of morning mist and souls turn mad.

After Feier's funeral, Angwan could not leave the Han village. Treated with suspicion by other villagers, he lived with Feng and the two men would speak to each other although never about Feier. Then one cold winter's morning, several moons after the funeral, Angwan left without a word. That was the day Feng visited the temple for the first time since Meili's death. He'd hoped to find something there that might help him to understand - to forgive - but it proved to be a pointless visit.

He returned to the village, to the very schoolroom where they'd laid out Feier's body, took his scrolls from the shelf, and his ink and brushes, and squatted in front of the low teacher's table; he prepared for the following day's lesson, for he realised that's all he was able to do: teach. All he could ever do. Why had he ever thought otherwise? Being a husband, a father – the things that mattered – they had no part in his destiny.

14.
A Single Petal

Years later, Feng went back to the monastery near the lotus lake. What was left of his hair had turned grey. His once proud belly was shrunken and wrinkled and he walked slowly, with a stoop, as if he only had eyes for the ground at his feet since the horizon of his life had long since lost any meaning. He went back to that place because he'd heard there was a new *sun wu kong* and because he felt the closeness of death. Perhaps, at last, he might find comfort in prayer.

Even as he approached the temple gate, the sickly scent of incense stirred memories of the past; time had become a ladle in its hand and his mind a pot of congee in which swirled images of Meili, Feier, and a friend who'd died and a friend he once lost. Whilst kow-towing three times to the Buddha he heard the approach of footsteps. He remained kneeling forwards, his hands stretched out palms down on the ground. Someone came and stood beside him.

The teacher had turned recluse after losing his daughter. He only spoke to the children he taught, and since illness now prevented him from teaching, he spoke to no-one. If the stranger had been anyone other than the new *sun wu kong* he'd have got up and left the temple. He looked sideways from the corner of one eye and saw the sandals and yellow and brown robes of a monk. A helping hand reached down, easing him up onto one knee. Twisting round, he gazed at the monk's face, perhaps more rounded than he remembered but otherwise little changed. The wheel of time had ceased turning. The path of the Buddha had delivered the one person who might finally ease his agony.

"You?" asked the teacher as the other man helped him to his feet. "Angwan?"

"Me, yes, but Angwan no longer," replied the monk. "Now *sun wu kong* Niao. I was wondering when you'd get round to paying me a visit."

"I don't understand. You... the *sun wu kong*? And here, of all places?"

"See over there! There's a bench beside that banyan tree. Let's sit and talk, teacher. We should have done this years ago. And I should have come back to you. I suppose I too was waiting for the pain to go away. Now I know it never will. Pain is our shared destiny. That's why we must talk."

What is there to talk about? Feng followed the monk to the bench.

"You've come to learn the truth, then? After all this time?" The *sun wu kong* stared ahead as if trying to decipher an invisible scroll on which had been written a painful lesson that had to be read aloud. Feng knew this was one path he could not avoid, for he could evade truth no more than death.

"I'm dying, Angwan. For Feier's sake please let me call you that again. Yes, I must know the truth. Hold nothing back." Feng smoothed out the folds in his tunic as if it was important that his state of dress should be as close to perfection as had been his daughter's beauty. "I do know," he added. "Somehow I've always known from the moment she came running into the schoolroom that day, but never how. Or why."

Neither man looked at the other when *sun wu kong* Niao finally found the strength to read from that unwritten scroll.

"Yes, Feier killed your friend Merchant Chang. But I don't think it'll be as you imagined."

The *sun wu kong* drew a deep breath. Clearly, for him to speak the truth would be as painful as for the old teacher to hear his words.

"That day I had arranged to meet with Chang beside the lotus lake. He said he had information from one of the monks. About the *sun wu kong's* links with a plot to depose the emperor. It all seems so unimportant now, doesn't it, two emperors down the line? Chang had told me about the White Tiger League and how he'd offered his services to the emperor for fear the empress's son would have been bad news for trade links to the west. You see, the White Tigers were divided in their loyalties. It wasn't quite what everyone thought at the time of..."

He drew the back of his hand across his moistening eyes, perhaps in an attempt to wipe from his mind the characters for 'her death'. Feng gripped his tunic tightly with both hands.

"I brought that sharpened bamboo pole along in case Chang was followed. Those were terrible times, as you'll well remember. I heard screams as I came over the hill. It was her. Xiaopeng had told all the village children how your daughter had talked about those beautiful lotus flowers... for the seventh day of the seventh month. It meant nothing to our children, of course, but I knew Feier would be there. Meeting up with the merchant was just an excuse to see Feier on her own. I thought perhaps after Chang had gone I'd get a chance to speak with her alone. Ever since, I've blamed myself. But..." *Sun wu kong* Niao hesitated. Tears streamed his cheeks. "He was on top of her. Beside the lake. He was pulling at her skirt. He was about to..."

"Did he?" interrupted Feng. "Did Chang rape my daughter?"

The *sun wu kong* shook his head.

"I arrived in time. I'm sure of it. She was pure that night we were together. But he was going to. I ran down the hill waving my pole at him. He took no notice. The awful animal breathing... that twisted face... it was the face of a tiger at the kill. Mocking... invincible! I struck him but not hard enough. I should have killed him with one blow, but the fiend had a skull like a rock and the strength of a bull. Only dazed, he swung round, still astride your daughter. He hit me in the stomach and I dropped the pole. Then another blow to the jaw and that was it. I was out, on my back. Knew nothing till I came to. First thing I heard was Feier crying. I feared the worst, but when I saw the girl crouched by the water frantically washing her hands over and over, and a great brown mound of flesh that had been the merchant with my pole protruding from his belly, I realised the spirit of the water had entered the child and given her the strength to save herself... and me. He must have wanted to check I'd not disturb him before trying to rape her, and she saw her chance. She did no wrong - nothing that might have blocked her path to Nirvana. Caught him by surprise as he sat gloating over his double triumph. She told me he'd been taunting her when I lay unconscious. Telling her she was a fool, just like her father, only a beautiful fool."

"The blame has always been mine, Angwan. For trusting him. How many times had she tried to warn me? Naïvity is a greater crime even than conceit."

"She got her courage from you, Feng. And you'll never know how much she loved you. You were more than just her *baba*. You were the window to her world... and mirror to her soul."

"No. It was the other way around. If I'd been that, why didn't I realise her affection for you sooner? Why didn't I think about talking to your mother after your father died rather than fretting about our marriage maker?"

"We were different. Remember? Different peoples, different clothes, customs and gods. Why should you have?"

"Those things meant nothing to little Feier. She saw beyond them."

"I tried to comfort her after it happened. All she could think about was her punishment, her death. Rather than bringing her closer to her beloved mother, she saw death as something that would keep them apart for ever. Because, in her eyes, your wife had been good and she was bad."

"Never!" cried Feng. "Never bad! She was the sweetest child you can imagine. She was only... only defending what was hers!"

"I know, I know, but not all would see it that way. I had to protect her. I took away part of the man's ugly face to make it appear he'd been savaged by a wild animal. I smeared his donkey's shit over him to attract the flies and give the body a long-dead smell." The monk chuckled. "That bit I did enjoy! Then the worst thing possible! Standing at the far end of the lake was a monk the merchant was supposed to introduce to me. The one who knew what the corrupt *sun wu kong* was doing. He must have seen everything. He turned and ran when he spotted me. I told the girl to hurry home and get you. She was to say she'd just come across a body and that was all. The whole business about our disappearing girls and the merchant's connection with the White Tiger League, it all seemed too good to be true. There was no need for the truth to come out, but I prayed the young monk would remain silent."

"Yes, I think I knew deep down. And I played along with it. Feier too. Maybe it was the real reason I set off for Chang'an, to draw peoples' attention away from the awful truth. Ay, this thing has haunted me all these years."

"Not only you, Teacher Feng. Why do you think I've adopted a life of retreat? As for Jinjin, he too changed. Because of Feier. Never did become an idle wealthy mandarin, as you know, but a good hardworking provincial governor. And he learned to overcome a young man's impetuosity. As for the death of Chen Jiabiao, let's just say it saved your life. I discovered one more thing, going back to the monastery before Feier got killed. The monk had only told Chen Jiabiao… how Feier had been protecting herself and was therefore blameless. But he'd not have known who the nobleman really was, and would never have trusted the *sun wu kong* with the information. It would have been Chen who'd arranged for that attempt on your life."

"And that night… when Yueloong found you together…" began the teacher. He kicked at a stone and watched it streak a line in the dust. "Was Feier happy?" The *sun wu kong* remained silent. "Did she… I mean… oh, I don't know what I'm asking. I only ever thought of her as a child, but she was about the same age as Meili when *we* married. I want to know she was a woman just that once. Not a child being pleasured by a man."

"We knew Heaven together, that once," affirmed *sun wu kong* Niao.

"I think…" Feng stood up. He kicked the stone off the path into a shrub in the temple garden. "I think her ancestors will be proud of her, Angwan. The Buddha too. Most definitely. And no monk could dissuade me from that belief."

"No true monk would, Teacher Feng. Your daughter came closer to Nirvana in her short life than most of us could ever dream of. You may die with peace of mind."

"Peace of mind, ay? You monks are a strange lot. But please continue to turn the prayer wheel for Feier's spirit when I'm gone."

"For her benefit, teacher, or for yours?"

"Mine, Angwan. Mine. The blame was always mine."

As Feng walked slowly towards the temple gate, the *sun wu kong* called out:

"There's another path, teacher."

"And what's that?" enquired Feng halting.

"The one Feier took."

Feng threw both hands up in mock exasperation.

"Which is what? Like I said, you're a strange lot, Angwan!"

"The Path of Light, my friend. Light beyond pain and death. *She* always knew. It's why she feared death so much. But it was her karma and at the end I believe she accepted this."

Feng stopped at the lotus lake on the way back. He'd imagined the path from the temple to be that Path of Light, and the lake to be where his life would now end, as Meili's should have ended as a child in the great flood all those years ago. But within reach of the bank was a lotus flower, the most perfect he'd ever seen, and it had probably just opened as he'd not noticed it earlier when going up the hill to the temple.

He was about to reach out and pluck it in memory of Feier before leaving this world. Yet something prevented him. At first he couldn't work out what this might be as he sat awkwardly on his haunches, his hand held halfway towards the flower. Then he realised: it was the flower's absolute perfection, a perfection that showed the way not only to death and rebirth but to ultimate freedom from suffering, to Nirvana. The flower seemed to tell him that to end his life now in that lake would lead nowhere; the *flower* was the Path of Light, the path that would lead him. And within it was Feier's petal, a single petal in a flower of perfection.

A List of Characters

Feng	a village schoolteacher in central China, living ten days journey from the ancient capital Chang'an, the eastern end of the Silk Road.
Feier	Feng's 14 year old daughter.
Meili	Feng's deceased wife.
Li Yueloong	the good friend of Feng and a farmer in the nearby Miao village.
Li Xiaopeng	Yueloong's 13-year old daughter and a friend of Feier.
Chen Jiabiao	a wealthy local landowner.
Merchant Chang	an itinerant merchant and a friend of Feng.
Mimi	Chang's faithful donkey.
Rou	Feng's horse.
Wong Yungchin	an inn-keeper in Houzicheng.
Wong Wenling	Yungchin's wife, famed for her noodles.
Jinjin	an urchin youth, 18 years old, who ran away from home to escape his abusive father; he works, unpaid and intermittently, for Wong and his wife.
Angwan	a young Miao animist priest who spent time with Han Buddhist monks, then returned to the Miao village to help his mother with their farm after his father died.
Minsheng	an ex-monk, now the provincial magistrate for Houzicheng.
Old Xiang	Li Yueloong's miserable, elderly brother.
Zhang Tsientse	a widowed cripple in the Han village.

Master Tsu	a teacher of Chinese brush painting in the imperial city of Chang'an.
Kong	an urchin boy with large hands, befriended by Jinjin.
Xiuxia	a buxom restaurant proprietress in Chang'an; also an imperial agent.
Jianjuan	a martial arts instructor for the crack force of imperial guards.
General Ma	the commander of rebel forces.
General Gao	an imperial commander.

Bibliography

Daily Life in Traditional China, The Tang Dynasty: Charles Benn
  (Greenwood Press, 2002)

China, The Cambridge Illustrated History of: Patricia Buckley Ebrey
  (Cambridge University Press, 1996)

The Heart of the Dragon: Alasdair Clayre
  (William Collins Sons & Co, 1984)

China: Si Renzuo and Peng Wenlan
  (Flint River Press, 1994)

The First Emperor of China: R.W.L. Guisso, Catherine Pagani and David Miller
  (Sidgewick & Jackson, 1989)

China, Pocket Timeline of: Jessica Harrison-Hall
  (The British Museum Press, 2007)

Lightning Source UK Ltd.
Milton Keynes UK
UKOW030627011112

201515UK00004B/1/P